D1477493

MIGNON

MIGNON

JAMES M.
CAIN

THE DIAL PRESS
NEW YORK

DESIGNED BY WILLIAM R. MEINHARDT
MANUFACTURED IN THE UNITED STATES OF AMERICA

This story moves against the background of the Red River Expedition to Western Louisiana in the year 1864, toward the end of the Civil War, or the War Between the States, as the South prefers to call it. The military aspects of that campaign have been strictly adhered to and, to the extent that they actually figure, have been depicted as they happened. The characters, however, are imaginary. Though it is hoped they are typical of their times, and though the enterprises that engage them are typical of the fiasco they took part in, they do not represent real persons, directly or under a disguise.

J.M.C.

MIGNON

CHAPTER I

Iᴛ ᴡᴀs ᴍᴀʀᴅɪ ɢʀᴀs ɪɴ ɴᴇᴡ ᴏʀʟᴇᴀɴs, February 9 of this
year, 1864, but the extent to which I partook of the
merry fun was not visible to the naked eye. I was there, I
was lodged at a good hotel, I had cash in my jeans, but had
reason for taking it easy. For one thing there was my leg
with a sword-stab in it, my souvenir of Chancellorsville,
which had got me a discharge from the Army but compelled
me to walk with a stick and discouraged any jinks—high,
low, or medium. For another, there was my partner in the
business that had brought me to town, and the job he had
dumped on my head through a dumb miscalculation. He
was a naval lieutenant my own age, which was and is
twenty-eight, and had worked with me side by side in my
father's construction firm—Joseph Cresap & Co., at Annapolis, Maryland—he running the tug, I the piledriver. When
the war broke we both signed on, he in the Navy, I with

the Army, and for a time we kind of lost touch. But then, as I lay in Jarvis Hospital, Baltimore, recovering from my wound, I got a letter from him, written from his ship, the *Eastport*, which was stationed at Helena, Arkansas, all full of a grand idea for a construction firm of our own, based at New Orleans, that would use government stuff as gear, when it went on sale cheap as surplus at the end of the war. That hit me right because—in addition to the points he made—it tied in with a dream I'd had to be part of a big thing that was going to be done at the mouth of the Mississippi, something I'll get to all in due time. I'd been feeling pretty low, but this put new hope in me, so I asked for more details and we exchanged quite a few letters about it.

All my father saw in the scheme, though, was Sandy's habit of seeing things rosy, and he warned me to watch my step or I was going to regret it. But I was fed up with paternal control, and when my mother sided with me I took two thousand dollars that she slipped me, about the same amount of my own, mainly my back Army pay, and hopped a boat for New Orleans, where Sandy had gone on a fifteen-day leave and taken a suite for us both at the St. Charles Hotel. That's when the trouble started. Because, instead of the twenty-five hundred dollars he thought we would need, I soon saw it would take ten times that, regardless of government sales. In construction, there's your bond, your payroll, your materials, and your running expense; that must all be met in cash before you get a dime from your first investment. On top of which, the little money Sandy had he blew on a new uniform to dazzle the wardroom upriver. On top of which, to rejoin his ship at the end of his fifteen days he picked a steamer leaving on Mardi Gras, with an Indiana artillery outfit aboard, bound home for a rest. On top of which, Mardi Gras morning he vanished;

I had to pack him, he explaining when he got back that he'd been "detained at Lavadeau's, telling them all good-bye." Lavadeau's was the costume place that had made his uniform for him. On top of which, when I loaded him into a cab and took him to the boat, it was raining. And I had to take a Canal Street horsecar back. On top of which, a big fat Cleopatra beat a bass drum in my ear and a beautiful little fairy popped flour into my face.

So I wasn't exactly singing when I got back to the hotel in midafternoon and a session in the bathroom, sluicing flour out of my nose and still wondering where to get twenty-five thousand dollars, didn't help any. I was in a rage when a knock came on the door and answered just as I was, without even putting on a coat. A girl was in the hall with a man, she shaking drops off an umbrella, he edging away as though anxious to leave. "Mr. Cresap, please," she snapped when she saw me, as though addressing the help.

"I'm Mr. Cresap," I growled.

"Oh," she said, looking surprised—and no doubt a slouchy article in corduroy pants, blue flannel shirt, and no necktie did look more like someone fixing the steam pipes than a guest at a high-toned hotel. But she fixed up her face quick, and said: "Mr. Cresap, how do you do? I'm Mrs. Fournet, from Lavadeau's. I imagine Lieutenant Gregg has mentioned me."

"He never did, but please come in."

The man started jabbering in French, the town's second language, and, though I don't rightly understand it, I thought he was telling her that now he'd brought her here he couldn't wait to take her back. Then he was gone—and so was my sulk, at the smell that puffed in my face of warm perfume mixed with girl as she passed me to enter the sitting room. I followed her in, closed the door, and took her umbrella. I went with it to the bathroom, where I stood it in the tub. Then I ducked into the bedroom to fix myself up. I put on necktie, coat, and cologne, and had a lick at my hair with the brush. Even so, the hombre I saw in the pier glass looked rough, too tall and bony to handle a stick with grace, and colored wrong: brown corduroy, blue flannel, and yellow hair somehow didn't blend. But if I lacked beauty she made up for it plenty. When I went back to the sitting room she had draped her cape on a radiator and was marching around kind of nervous, so I could see what she had. She was medium in size, but so perfectly proportioned she seemed small, and in age she was younger than I was, I thought. It turned out she was twenty-four. Her face was pale, with shadows high on her cheeks as though she'd known trouble. Her hair was dark, her eyes big, black, and shiny. But her figure was what knocked you over, especially in the beat-out black dress she had on. It was limp from too much mending and washing and ironing, and clung to her in a way that brought up her curves. These were soft, round, and exciting, and said Louisiana French, the comeliest breed of woman I had seen in the U.S. so far.

I thought, from the direction my mind was running, I'd better get straightened out, and asked: "*Mrs.* Fournet —is that what you said? Then that was Mr. Fournet, your husband, out there in the hall?"

". . . Oh no!" she said, after looking kind of blank. "That was Mr. Lavadeau—he brought me from the shop. On Mardi Gras, no woman is safe alone. . . . My husband is dead, Mr. Cresap. He was killed at Fort St. Philip when the Union fleet came upriver."

"As a Reb, you mean?"

"Why, yes. The Rebs held the fort."

"And you're a Reb?"

"Well, I don't know . . . I try to obey the law, now the Union's running it. But in a way, I guess I'm a Reb. Yes, of course I'm a Reb. Why?"

"Just asking. Funny Sandy didn't speak of you."

"Oh—maybe he didn't want to. Maybe he thought I inveigled him—it was all so friendly, the night we were introduced, but then when I wouldn't go out with him after he came in the shop and had his uniform made, maybe he felt it was just a trick. And how can I say that it wasn't? In this war, when you've lost everything, and you still have to make a living, you do all kinds of things. Maybe I did lead him on."

"You sell for Lavadeau's, then?"

"On commission. Uniforms, mostly."

"You were why he went over the hill today?"

"We talked along quite some time, yes."

By then she had taken a chair and smoothed herself out very modest, especially the ruffle which ran across her chest with a startling deep dip in the middle. I wanted to smooth it for her, and also to string things out so I could hear her talk. She had a soft, low voice, with some Dixie drag, though not as much as I have. In the Chesapeake Bay country we pour it out so thick you can cut it with a knife, but in Louisiana, at least among well-born people, there's just a slight trace, kind of musical. I could have listened all day, but detected she was under a strain, and suddenly asked: "What do you want of me, Mrs. Fournet?"

"I'm in trouble, Mr. Cresap. I need help—and help from someone that's Union. Someone that's honest and decent and smart, as Sandy said you are."

"What kind of trouble, for instance?"

"My father's been arrested."

"For what?"

"That's it. I don't know."

"Well what do the police say?"

"It was not the police who took him. Soldiers came, this morning after I left, to the flat where he and I live, read a paper at him, and took him away. I knew nothing about it till an hour ago, when the couple we rent from were able to find a boy and sent him over to tell me. I don't even know where my father is held."

"Sounds to me like a job for a lawyer."

"No, Mr. Cresap, it's not."

She came over to where I was camped on the sofa, leaned close, and whispered: "We have a lawyer, of course. But my father's in cotton, and it's a horrible, cutthroat business, here now in the war. Could be our lawyer's the very one who's back of this arrest. Could be other people are, Union friends we have. Mr. Cresap, I'm not just a crazy woman, running around wild. I'm scared, because in New Orleans right now, you don't know who you can trust. That's why I come to you, a total stranger, and tell the truth, where to nobody else in this town do I dare open my mouth."

"What do you want of me?"

"First, find out where my father is held."

"That shouldn't be hard. What else?"

"Find out what he's charged with."

"That should be on the record. What else?"

"Well—if I knew that much, I'd kind of know where I'm at and be able to work things around, especially if I could talk to him, to try and get him out."

"You mean, you want me to get him out?"

"Oh, if you only would!"

By then my arm was around her, and she didn't seem to find it unpleasant. In fact, as I pulled the ribbons under her chin, unknotted them, and lifted off her hat, she cuddled to me just a little, staring up at my face as a cat stares at your face, to see if you're taking her in or putting her out in the cold. I patted her, said I was pretty busy on a job Sandy dumped on me, but that for someone as pretty as she was I might interrupt. She said: "I know what the job is. It's to raise twenty-five thousand dollars to buy machinery with, and put in a whole lot of piles down at the mouth of the river—and if you have to know, it's the reason I came to you. Because Sandy said you would raise that money, that you always finish what you start. And that's what I need now. You're going to start, aren't you? And finish? You're going to get him out?"

". . . For you?"

"Because it's right! He hasn't done anything!"

Suddenly a tear was there, and as she wiped it away she said: "I'm sorry, he's all I have—has been, ever since my mother got drowned, in the Flood of Forty-nine." I'd never heard of the Flood of '49, and my face must have showed it, as she added: "I mean, the Red River Flood of Forty-nine. We're from Alexandria."

"I see," I said, then repeated: "For *you?*"

"Well, of course for me. *Yes!*"

"What do I get out of it for being so nice?"

She looked kind of frightened, and started mumbling about money, saying she didn't have much, but that her father had some, made in cotton that winter, and "will pay you what's right." But before I could explain I wasn't talking about money, we were locked in each other's arms, and our mouths were mashed together. The kiss said she knew what I meant, but I wanted it on the line. I said: "You have to pay. Do you hear?"

"Well, maybe I wouldn't mind."

She whispered it, kind of shy, kind of flirty, and somehow a little bit holy, and of course it called for another kiss. Then I buried my nose in her dress, and inhaled the same smell I had caught as she entered the room. I asked: "What is this scent you use? It doesn't smell like perfume. It smells—*warm*."

She held her pocketbook up to my nose. "It's what they call Russian Leather," she said. "They steep it in oil of lavender, which makes it soft and gives it this smell— and then they tool it and stamp it. I have a prayer book to match, and a New Testament." Then, sniffing me: "You smell like corduroy drenched in cologne, but you have china-blue eyes like a dollbaby's, and hair that looks like taffy."

"My hair looks like wet hay."

"No, Willie! I want to lick it!"

". . . Where'd you get that name?"

"It's what your mother calls you."

"And you think you're going to?"

"It's sweet—matches your 'lasses-taffy hair."

"What did your mother call you?"

"My name, Mignon. *You* can, if you want to."

As our eyes met, as breath mingled with breath and smell mingled with smell, something unfolded between us, and then suddenly she jumped up, saying time was going by and we had to line out what we were going to do. On a piece of hotel stationery she wrote her father's name, Adolphe Landry, and said: "I must go back now to Lavadeau's, on account of their being so busy on the biggest day of their year, renting the Mardi Gras costumes. And if you find out anything, you come to me there—as quick as you can, Willie, before evening if it's possible. I must go to the Ball of Erato, and if I could know something before I do, if I could see my lamb just once——!" That's when we had our first quarrel. I said: "That's nice, I must say it is! Here I'm to go traipsing around in the wet, finding your father for you, while you trip the fantastic toe in some damned Mardi Gras ball."

"Willie, that's not how it is!"

"And Erato—who the hell is he?"

"He's a she—she wrote poetry, or something. She's just a name for one of these things we have. But will you listen to me? I have to go to this thing. In the first place, I'm going for Lavadeau, in a costume he's letting me have, to watch the rest of our costumes, and see that they don't get ruined when the people begin to get drunk. But that's not all. Willie, the one that's taking me *must* know about my father. He knows everything up at headquarters—and he has to know about this! Why hasn't he come to me? I told you, there's no one here in this town that I feel I can trust. I *must* go to the ball with him to listen to what he says, and, above everything else, keep him from suspicioning that I suspicion him. Now do you understand?"

"All right, now I've got it."

"Get my umbrella for me."

I got it, then got my oilskin and put it on, came out, and helped her into her cape. She already had on her hat. As I opened the door she put her arms around me again, whispered: "I'd much rather stay here with you—and pay." And I knew, as we went down the stairs hand in hand, more was between her and me than had ever been between me and a woman before.

CHAPTER 2

HEADQUARTERS WAS AT CARONDELET and Julia, one block
up and six blocks over, and I had the luck to get a cab. So
after one last kiss I set her down at Lavadeau's, which was
on St. Charles near the hotel, and kept right on. On Julia,
as soon as we turned the corner, the street was full of orderlies holding horses, so nobody could have missed it. It was
a three-story building with iron-lace balconies, and a four-
story annex in back that was soldered on wrong so the
floors didn't match up. I wanted to hold the cab, not knowing where my search might lead, but the driver wouldn't
wait on account of the Mardi Gras business he'd miss. I
paid him off, asked my way of the sentry, and went in. It
was the same old jumble of raw pine tables, camp chairs,
and chests painted circus-wagon blue every headquarters is,
with the same old military telegraph clacking somewhere,
so I wasted no time gaping but followed the sentry's di-

rection and went up to the second floor. I was looking for a captain I knew, Dan Dorsey, who came from Annapolis too and was now aide to the Commanding General. I'd already renewed acquantance when I bumped into him one night in Cassidy's Bar, so I could get down to cases at once without singing "Auld Lang Syne."

When I got up to the head of the stairs he was out in the hall, giving orders to a bunch of men I recognized as Northern news correspondents. They'd been kept waiting, apparently, and weren't any too pleased about standing around in a hallway. But Dan is a big beefy man who'd held a courthouse job back home and doesn't take any backtalk, so pretty soon he had order. Then, seeing me, he motioned me into his office, growling as he followed me in: "Actually, I'm on their side. They were told to come, for an announcement the General is making of an election we're going to hold on Washington's Birthday. But it's been one thing after another—especially some damned Indiana outfit that's on their way home but had to serenade the General on their way to the boat. So *he* had to make them a speech. So that called for asking their officers in and putting out booze for a toast. So it took an hour, and the election's still not announced. But what the hell? Everything's jumpy here, and at the least little thing we blow our pop. What's on your mind, Bill?"

"Man," I said. "Adolphe Landry. Ever hear of him?"

"Well—he's well known. He's held."

"Yes, but where?"

"Right here."

"In this headquarters?"

"Detention room down in the Annex."

"What's he charged with?"

"He's not charged, as yet—just held for investigation. I can tell you one thing, though: that lad is in trouble. He's been playing it sharp all winter, and now he's cut himself."

"In what way, sharp?"

"Working the godpappy sell."

"And what is the godpappy sell?"

"New one they figured out under this law that's just been passed, Confiscation Act of 1863, as amended. Reb, like we'll say Landry, buys cotton for peanuts out there in Secessia, loads it on a barge, and starts it down the bayou in the general direction of New Orleans. So lo and behold, we capture it as soon as it enters our lines. So we ship it here for storage, then go to court to condemn it, proceeds to apply to the cost of the war. But then, how did you guess it, who pops up but a Union trader, waving a paper around, a godpappy paper known as a bill of sale, a deed from his friend the Reb, conveying the paper to him? And that paper is good. The court must allow the claim—he's a loyal Union man, and loyal men make loyal cotton. So he gets the award, which includes free transportation here to market, as of course we can't book him for moving stock in our custody. So he and his Reb friend split—and that's the sell Landry's been working with a highbinder partner he has, a naturalized Irishman named Frank Burke."

"But the way you tell it, it's legal."

"Bill, it is, but he overreached himself. He began using the money he made to ship supplies upriver—to Taylor, the Reb commander."

"Ouch, that's not so good."

"He's playing a deep game, that's all."

"How deep, Dan?"

"He's squaring things up, we think, with the Rebs for the money he hopes to make on this Red River thing next month."

I'd never heard of the Red River thing, and Dan was quite shifty about it. But I managed to open him up, and he began whispering about "a campaign about to start to Western Louisiana—kind of an annual event. We had one last year, so now we do it again. Only this time we're after the cotton in storage out there—even Washington's stooping so low as to use the godpappy sell. They don't send us an order, but the word's been passed just the same; we're to take the traders along on our headquarters boat when we go, and nature will see to the rest. They'll buy off the Rebs, taking their godpappy deed; we'll transport the stock down here, the court will say hocus-pocus, and everybody'll be happy—especially the Northern mills, which'll get stock to run on, and even including the Rebs, who'll be paid some traders' tin and be won back to their allegiance, as we're told." He got up, peered out in the hall, closed the door, came back, and leaned close. "Bill," he whispered, very solemn, "you can win a war or lose it—with honor. You know what it's called when you try to buy it?"

"I bite," I said. "No."

"Treason. That cotton's already hooded."

But he called it *who did*. I asked: "Hoodooed?"

"That's what I said. It's hexed."

I almost wanted to laugh, but he was dead serious. "That cotton means nothing but trouble, as this whole damned headquarters knows—it's what makes this place so jumpy. It's what's thrown Landry—he's getting the sidewash already."

"He holds Red River cotton, Dan?"

"Hundreds of bales, at least so we hear."

"What supplies did he ship, by the way?"

"That I'm not free to say."

"Dan! I thought we were friends!"

"I hope so, Bill; at the same time, there's a limit. Frank Burke, the partner, the Irishman I mentioned just now— he was in, and I couldn't even tell *him*. If I had to turn him down, I can't justify telling you. Until authorized counsel shows up, we can't open that file to anyone."

"I *am* authorized counsel."

"You being funny, Bill, or what?"

I had heard my mouth say it, and was just as amazed as he was to hear myself stand by my bluff. "I'm not being funny," I said. "I'm his authorized counsel. What do you think I'm doing here?"

"You're not even a lawyer."

"He has a lawyer, but in a town under martial law, the family wants military counsel. I'm a discharged officer, I've sat on three or four courts, and I'm qualified to serve."

"He hasn't got any family—except for that daughter, the one that's been running around with Burke."

"Mrs. Fournet hired me on."

"Bill, quit playing games. You—"

"*Games? Goddam it, you're the one—*"

But even before I could finish, he cut me off with a wipe of his hand, jumped up, opened the door a crack, listened, and closed it again. "What do you mean," he whispered, "bellering like that, with those newspapermen in the hall? Do you want this thing advertised to the world?" Later on, when I remembered it, that scared look on his face was important, but right now I was bent on one thing and gave no thought to anything else. "All right,"

I said, "we keep it nice and quiet. But I have to see that file."

"It's in the Judge Advocate's office."

He slipped out, and in a minute was back with one of those stiff red envelopes tied up with tape. He undid it and took out papers, pushing them all at me, to give me a fair chance to read, but at the same time trying to help me. "Go through it," he said, "if you want to, but it doesn't mean anything—just a pile of rub-a-dub-dub, the covering blabber we write when papers move from one desk to the other. But here's the works, what he's up against, the anonymous note that came in by mail, in this envelope that's pinned on. The facts are being checked with the leads this thing has given us, so we're keeping our fingers crossed till we know what's what. Landry's mistake was he needed too much help—too many people knew. One of them turned informer—as bad a hex as there is."

He passed over the note, written on cheap tablet paper with a soft pencil:

FEBY 5, 1864

COMMANDING GENL SIR:

MR ADOLPHE LANDRY ESQU BEN SHIPING SHOES TO TALORS REB ARMY HE SHIP BY BOAT TO MORGANZA YOU DON BLEE ME GENL SIR ASK EMIL BOSWAY CLERK IN MIFFLINS JOBERS GENL I RITE YOU MORE SOON AS I KNOW.

LORL PATROT

That was a blow, and I decided to take myself off as soon as I checked on whether she'd be allowed to see her father. But before I could ask about it, a commotion came in the hall, and Dan had to duck out to attend the General while the General talked to the press and then ride with him to his house on Coliseum Square. I stuck around, but had to wait the better part of an hour. However, when he got back we resumed where we'd left off. He took a package from a shelf, a thing that looked like a Mardi Gras costume tied up in tissue paper, and walked downstairs with me to find out how things stood. He went back through the hall, up a little stairs to the Annex, and on to a door that he touched with his fingertips. You don't pound on a guardroom door on account of the men sleeping inside, and when the corporal appeared Dan whispered. Then he rejoined me, saying: "There's no special order against it, so visitors are all right until call to quarters at nine forty-five. So what the hell? Burke saw him, and if he could she can. Incidentally, Bill, if he's such a friend of Landry's, why didn't he tell her where her father is held?"

"I was wondering about it myself."

The orderlies had stabled Dan's horse, so we stepped out on foot in the rain and walked on down to St. Charles. There a funny thing happened. St. Charles, the heart of the theatrical district, was where the doings were lively and we fought our way along, through a wet mob of revelers, dancing and whooping and singing, to the light of red fire in the street. And pretty soon here came a witch, riding a broomstick she flogged with a whip. "Your Red River hex," I said, turning to him.

He wasn't there.

Later on, he swore he'd told me good night when he came to his rooming house and gone in to put on his costume. But I hadn't heard anything, and after what had been said, it gave me a peculiar feeling.

CHAPTER 3

LAVADEAU'S HAD TWO WINDOWS in front, one with a
wax admiral in it, the other a wax general, both very dignified, but inside it was a madhouse, with pirates, kings,
queens, Indians, Turks, jugglers, and harem girls pushing
each other around, fighting for space at the mirrors and
screaming to be fitted. I got bumped, but managed to hold
my feet while I looked around for the girl I'd last seen in a
draggled dress with a ruffle. When a vision came skipping
at me, a Columbine in black, with gauze skirt, silk tights,
and laced velvet bodice, a red rose in her hair, red shoes
on her feet, and red mask in one hand, I didn't even know
her. It wasn't until she grabbed me and asked what I'd
found out that I realized who she was, and even then she
looked strange, her cheeks rouged and her eyes touched up
with some kind of blue. But when I told her I'd found her
father and could take her to him, they opened wide and

were suddenly the eyes I knew. She darted to Lavadeau, jabbering at him in French, and though he was entirely surrounded, his mouth full of pins, he nodded and she ducked to the rear. Then she was back again, a red domino on, her umbrella in one hand, her cape in the other. Outside, Captain John Smith and Pocahontas were just climbing out of a cab. I grabbed it, loading her in. She snuggled close, saying "I knew you'd find him." She was so excited I reserved my detailed report, contenting myself with kisses.

At headquarters, the driver of course wanted his money, and while I was paying him off the sentry called the corporal, who took us inside at once and on back, up the little stairs to the Annex, where he knocked on a door. When it opened, he left us, saying: "Call to quarters is at nine forty-five." We went into a whitewashed room, a cold little cubicle with cot, chair, table, candle, and one barred window. Holding the door was Mr. Landry, who seemed surprised to see us, but took Mignon in his arms and began whispering to her in French. He was a stocky, heavy-set man of medium height, fifty or so, with pouter-pigeon chest, robin-redbreast throat, and round, thick neck, all signifying tremendous physical strength. He had black eyes like hers, a gray tuft on his chin and curled gray mustaches, with a handsome cut to his jib that showed where her looks came from. He wore gray pants, skirted coat, and plaid vest, all very dignified, as well as an overcoat and a scarf over his head. He shook hands when she introduced me and gave me his only chair, sitting with her in the cot. They resumed whispering in French, he looking drawn, she lovely in the candlelight as she patted his cheek and the domino kept falling open to show her beautiful legs. Once or twice

I caught the name Burke, or *Boorke* as they called it in French.

Then suddenly he turned to me, saying: "Mr. Cresap, I truly express my thanks for the help you've given my daughter, but feel I owe you an explanation. I'm held without charge in this place, as martial law permits, and assume I'm the victim of some kind of mix-up. I'm engaged in the cotton trade, which is legal and therefore open to me, but at the same time is disapproved in certain respects by the occupation authorities, which causes them to encourage with one hand and persecute with the other—a not unfamiliar inconsistency in official conduct. I assumed, therefore, that I'd be shortly released. That's why I asked my partner, Mr. Frank Burke—of whom you may have heard —not to alarm my daughter or spoil her Mardi Gras by informing her what happened. That's why she felt she must go to you."

"My pleasure in any event," I told him.

"And I was wrong, thank God," she said, staring at me, "suspicioning people for stabbing him in the back."

"Must be a relief to know that."

He went on some more about cotton, but time was going on, and I felt I had to make sure he had things straight. "Mr. Landry," I interrupted, "this has nothing to do with cotton. You're held for shipping shoes to Taylor."

". . . For *what* did you say, Mr. Cresap?"

"Shipping shoes—some informer has sent in a note, an unsigned note by mail, saying you sent them by boat, to Morganza I believe was the place, for the use of Taylor's Army."

"But that's ridiculous!"

"I'm telling you what's in the note."

His face, which had been handsomely solemn, went slack with consternation, and he said: "I did ship shoes upriver—I made a little in cotton, and felt I had to share, with men less fortunate than I was, Confederate boys, the ones paroled from Port Hudson, who reached home with not even rags on their feet. I sent them as Christmas presents, care of a friend, a Morganza storekeeper, and asked him to distribute for me. I've had no dealings with Taylor."

"He may have captured them, though."

"In that case, I couldn't have stopped it."

I felt he was telling the truth, but I also felt there was something about these shoes, not mentioned as yet, that completely took his nerve. And when Mignon started whispering again and I heard "Who else could have known all that?" I had a hunch what it was. He nudged her, and she switched at once to French, but I heard *Boorke* once more, this time pretty bitter, and deduced there *had* been a stab in the back, which of course could be pretty serious. Because shipping shoes was the kind of thing which might be (as he said) wholly innocent, but which, painted up by someone on the inside, could be made to look like a crime as black as the worst ever seen. However, he obviously wasn't discussing it, so I told myself shut up, as it was strictly none of my business. But that reminded me of myself, the peculiar status I had, which I hadn't even brought up, and I thought best to get it out in the open. I said: "Mr. Landry, there's something I ought to tell you. I've been acting so far as your counsel." I then told of the argument with Dan, and wound up: "Strictly speaking, I was telling the truth, as Mrs. Fournet had engaged me, which as next of kin she could do. And of course, I'm willing to continue doing whatever I can. But if I'm to act in an official capacity, I must have your direct authorization."

"Mr. Cresap, on that give me a moment."

"*But* Captain Dorsey's my only reference."

"Except one," Mignon chirped, very bright. "*Me!*" And then, to her father: "You don't need any moment! He's wonderful—look what he's done already! And he's not any carpetbag spellbinder!"

"I've now taken my moment."

He held out his hand and ground my knuckles to ball bearings. "Mr. Cresap," he said, "I'm a man of a hundred friends, right here in New Orleans—not one of whom could I trust. So it is when cotton is made semi-legal, and it begins coming between. And now you, whom I never saw till a half-hour ago, with my daughter, are my only reliance. I may say I count myself fortunate."

It was very moving, so much so that I thought I owed him to say: "There's just one thing: You'd better know this is partly a matter of principle, of seeing justice done, of clearing a man falsely accused—I hope I'm not indifferent to that. But it's also a matter of pleasing your daughter."

"That I had already guessed."

"I don't mind saying she takes my eye."

"Sir, I find her an eyeful myself."

"My intentions, Mr. Landry, are serious."

"This does not displease me."

She said: "*Doesn't* his hair look like taffy?"

"Daughter, to me it looks like hair."

He said it rather stiffly, winding that subject up. I said, after a moment: "There's one other thing, too. Whoever this informer may be, if I'm to pin it on him, prove this thing he's done, he must not have a suspicion that I'm on his trail. Is that understood?"

"It better be," he said. "Daughter?"

"I'd like to murder him," she answered.

"You'd wind up by murdering me."

"It's understood, of course."

On the way back we had to walk, I bundling her into her cape and wrapping my oilskin around her, she holding her umbrella over me. She took me by way of Carondelet, to avoid the hullabaloo, and pretty soon pulled me into a doorway out of the wet, to talk. She whispered: "You caught on, Willie, of course? He suspicions Frank Burke."

"Are you sleeping with him?"

"Am I——? Willie, how can you ask that?"

"I can ask it. I did ask it. Are you?"

"Of course not!"

"You've been running around with him, though?"

"I've gone out with him. Is that so terrible?"

"If for inveiglement, yes."

"Willie, when my father blew in last fall, with a whole lot of warehouse receipts covering cotton in Alexandria that had been signed over to him by people he'd helped in this war, he had a trunkload of worthless paper, as he thought—and as those people up there, who'd been living off him so long, thought but they wanted to give him something in return, to keep their self-respect. But I knew about this invasion next month that would turn his worthless paper to gold, if only we could find someone, a Union man, to act for us in court—to be our godpappy, as it's called. And Frank Burke had just got in from Mexico, where he'd been trading in Texas cotton. He was the biggest thing in sight, and knew the business too. So I worked things around to meet him. I got myself introduced. In the St. Charles Theatre lobby."

"And inveigled him?"

"I invited him home to meet my father!"

"But you started going with him?"

"Willie, Frank Burke goes through the motions—he kisses my hand, he sends me flowers, he passes oily compliments. But what he wants is the money."

"Then why would he turn on a partner?"

"My father figured that out, while you were there—it's what he was telling me in French. Willie, there's martial law in New Orleans, and do you know how they do in a case like this?"

"In Maryland, they'd confiscate."

"Yes, and here, to get confiscated, first you must plead."

"I don't follow you, Mignon."

"They'll suspend the prison term, *if* you make no defense and *if* you declare all the assets you have."

"Now I've got it. Go on."

"Well, he can declare the store, which would probably keep him out of prison. They could seize it as soon as they occupy Alexandria. But my father's biggest asset is his share of his partnership with Burke. You understand, Willie? The cotton has now been made over, all the warehouse receipts, to Burke as godpappy, and articles have been signed giving him half and my father half. If my father declares his share of course it's gone, so of course he can't declare. But if he doesn't declare, he can never claim in court—he can't sue Burke, even through an assignee. It's all gone."

"How much does this cotton amount to?"

"We have three hundred twenty-seven bales—worth a hundred twenty thousand dollars clear of charges."

"Quite a pot to be playing for."

"It's worth sixty thousand dollars to Frank to do my father in."

I'd got the point at last, but we were a long way from knowing what I could do about it. We both agreed, neither of us liking it much, that as he was supposed to take her, she must go to the ball with him as though nothing had happened at all. That left me and what she should tell him about me, which wasn't too easy, as almost any story was bound to leave him suspicious. At last I said: "Now I think I have it. You tell it just as it happened, your coming to me, since you hadn't heard from him, on account of Sandy Gregg's stories and all that. But now that you've got me in, you're getting cold feet. You don't like it a bit that first crack out of the box I named myself military counsel. And you think it very peculiar the way I'm talking money— a hundred dollars cash now, and a hundred fifty later, to be guaranteed by someone before I lift a finger. If you lay it on right, he'll not only not suspicion us, but he *will* suspicion me and feel that he must come to see me. Then he'll be leading to me, and I'll have something to go on."

"All right, Willie, two hundred and fifty. What else?"

I said I wanted a list of stationery stores ready for me when I called at Lavadeau's the next morning, places that might have sold a cheap tablet to an Irishman. "It's the kind of thing," I said, "that a clerk would be sure to remember. If I can find where he bought his paper, I'll have something resembling proof. But I should have a great deal more.

I wish I could line it up so I could demand a search by the Army of his home, to turn everything up—stationery, envelopes, memoranda, and so on. But I have to make sure the stuff is there. Where does he live?"

"The City Hotel, Willie."

"Ah-ha. Hotel rooms are easily entered."

"Maybe not his. He keeps a gippo, as he calls it—it's some kind of Irish word. What *is* a gippo?"

"I never heard of a gippo, Mignon."

"I think it's a man, but it *could* be a dog."

"Whatever it is, it can be dealt with."

"But when he's not there, *it* is."

"How do you know? From being in his rooms?"

"No, Willie! But he talks about it!"

It was just a second's flare-up, and left us pressing still closer. She said: "It must be going on for nine, and I have to get back. Willie, I've figured how I'll do, so as not to be taken home to an empty flat with somebody pushing in. Everything stops at twelve o'clock on Mardi Gras, so I'll ask to be taken back to the shop where my clothes are, and then, after I've changed, I'll spend the night with Veronique—Veronique Michaud, one of our dressmakers. Does that please you?"

"I've been worrying about it, plenty."

"Then kiss me. And say you love me a little."

"I love you so much it's more like being insane."

On St. Charles, Mignon pointed out the hall where the ball would be held; it was across the street from Lavadeau's, a few doors from the Pickwick Club. When we got to the shop, she pointed through the window past the wax admiral to a big, heavy man in Mexican costume talking with Lavadeau. "That's him," she whispered. I said: "I hate his guts already." She laughed, slipped out of my oilskin and gave it back, put a kiss on my mouth with her fingertips, and slipped inside. When I'd put the oilskin back on I started for the hotel, but on the way decided to take advantage of the cat being away. I kept on to Common, turned, walked down one block to Camp, and went into the City Hotel. It was a nice place, not quite in the St. Charles class, but a good hotel just the same, very gay just now, with quite a few people in costume. I registered: "William Crandall, Algiers, La." My baggage, I said, was delayed, but I'd pay two nights in advance. The clerk took my money, marked my room in the book, called a boy, and gave him the key. However, I took it, saying: "I'll go up later," and tipped.

Out on the street again, I walked up Common, checking a hardware store as I went. It was closed, but as I remembered it from passing once or twice, it had lettered on the window, in the lower left-hand corner:

LOCKSMITH
Serrurier

At the St. Charles, I had sandwiches and beer sent up and mumbled to myself as I munched: "What the hell have you got yourself into? You're supposed to have your mind on raising twenty-five thousand bucks."

CHAPTER 4

Burke SHOWED AT THE ST. CHARLES next morning, even sooner than I had hoped. I'd sent the corduroys out to be pressed, put on my dark suit, and stepped down the street to the locksmith's, to get him started on the skeleton I needed, made from a blank to correspond with my City Hotel key, for the rummage job I had in mind. I came back, had breakfast in the bar; when I went upstairs again Burke was in the hall, popping my door with his knuckles. In Scotch tweeds, cloth hat, and brown shoes, with a rain cape over one arm, he looked even bigger than he had in his red Mardi Gras costume, but I sang out loud and hearty: "Mr. Burke, I believe? Welcome to my humble abode—I'm flattered that you've come." His round, pink face broke into smiles and he held out his hand, expressing "the honest pleasure I feel at meeting our Good Samaritan." He spoke with an Irish brogue, but not a shanty-Irish brogue. I can say plenty against him, but—allowing for small things like *iv* for of, *he* for by, and *me* for my—he handled the English language in a most distinguished way; not saying he couldn't manhandle it, to the point of just plain filth, when his temper got the best of him.

But now he was graciousness itself, saying very respectfully: "Could I have a word with you, me boy? Poor Adolphe's me friend as well as me partner, and I think we should have a talk."

"Certainly," I said, unlocking. "Come in."

I hung his cape and hat in the armoire, and seated him; at once he began thanking me "for all you've done—not only for Adolphe, but the little one, too, Mrs. Fournet. She told me all about it."

"Then she got to the ball?" I asked.

"Aye—we were late but made a sensational entrance, she favoring the Black Tulip, I a Tipperary cardinal at his golden jubilee mass. I went as a *charro*, in a red velvet rig I once bought for a Mexican fandango. The hat has bells on't which I swear play 'La Paloma.' "

"You've been in Mexico, then?"

"In the cotton boom, early on in the war—at Matamoros and Bagdad. I didn't do badly. I made a bit."

"I've heard the sky was the limit."

"The sky? Me boy, it showed mirages, with minarets, date palms, and Moorish dancing girls nekkid as when they were born. Bagdad was not accidentally named."

"Just exactly where is it?"

"Mexican side, mouth of the Rio Grande."

"Must be quite a place."

"The stinkhole iv the Western World—built on pilings, iv slabs and adobe and canvas, populated be sailors, pimps, and *muchachas,* all drunk as fiddler's bitches, but paved, here and there, with gold."

"Gold made from cotton?"

"Aye."

He seemed quite fond of bragging, and as I measured him up, it came to me that the last thing I should be, if I meant to lull his suspicions, was a decent, honest man. So I encouraged him to run on, hanging on his tales, of the fortunes made in Mexico, racked up in just a few months, and the private armies that guarded them. He mentioned one Paddy Milmo, "me partner, who abused me confidence shamefully—though I came off with at least me share, a hundred thousand in gold, in spite of his damned *soldados,* looking for me all night, to clap me in the *picota* for the chinch bugs to eat out me neck." It occurred to me that partners "abusing me confidence" might be one of the mirages he saw all the time, kind of a chronic illusion. But after he'd told a few tall ones and I had made proper mirations, I did some bragging myself. I told of the thousand dollars I'd made at Chestertown one day, on a hurry-up job of dredging for some peach farmers on Chester River whose wharf had got silted up so the steamers couldn't get in to haul their crop to market. They were ruined unless something was done, "and so," I said, "as soon as the papers were drawn and the money put in escrow, I told them, 'Gentlemen, gauge. The agreement says seven feet, and I think you'll find you have it.' So, with the witnesses, they all piled into rowboats, with a red rag tied at seven feet on a bamboo fishing pole. And wherever they put down the pole the red rag went under, so they had no choice but to pay. Because what they didn't know was that while they were up at the bank signing papers with me, Sandy Gregg,

my tugboat skipper, was turning his screw at the wharf.
The screw churned up the silt and the tide floated it out.
We picked up a thousand neat for two hours' work by a
boat."

"But you saved the day for your friends?"

"Who were sore as a boil, however."

He burst out laughing and roared: "You're a man iv
me own kind—let the buggers pay, and if they don't like't,
lump't!"

"They paid, but because they had to."

". . . Aye, you mentioned escrow?"

"That's right. I like my money guaranteed."

He had a small, gray eye, kind of rheumy, and it
looked me over now, very close. In a moment, he said: "If
it's your fee you're talking about, for acting as counsel to
Adolphe, there'll be no trouble about it, *if* I accept your
ideas. Could I hear them, if you have any?"

It seemed to me that, starting out to be hostile, he had
now made a switch and would fall into my trap if I talked
the right way. So I decided to bring up the thing, going by
what she'd told me, that had to be the nub of his crooked
scheme. I said: "Well, Mr. Burke, I don't know what you'll
accept, but for my part, having read that informer's note,
having talked with Mr. Landry, and having had some experience with such things, I would say he's innocent, and
doesn't have a leg to stand on. I mean he may not have done
it, but how does he go about proving it? So the only idea I
have is: Plead, and get the thing over with."

The rheum in his eye took on a glitter. "Do you mean
it, lad?" he asked, very excited. "Are you serious in what
you say?"

"Why string it out, Mr. Burke?"

"I've been thinking the same thing meself!"

"They may confiscate—but they would anyway."

"And he'll not have to sit in prison!"

"That's the main thing, isn't it?"

"And another thing, me boy—what does he have to lose? The store in Alexandria, which they'll take when the Army arrives there. But these invaded towns have a way of being burned as the invaders leave—so what would he have, assuming he made a defense? A pile of ashes. 'Tis better to get it over with, so he's out! And another thing: He still will have his cotton, through his partnership with me. But 'twill be worth nothing at all unless we're on the spot to pick up our seizure receipt, the one the Army gives when the stuff is taken in. But how can he be there, me boy, and also be here awaiting trial? Perhaps I could swing it alone—after all, everything's in my name. But 'twould be a blight on the whole litigation to have a partner sitting in jail. Time is of the essence! And suppose he loses the store? What do they signify, a few bricks in Alexandria?"

It was all loyal and warm and moving, except there wasn't a word about the fix Mr. Landry would be in, not being able to sue, to claim his share of the partnership. So I said nothing about it, and went on: "All right, if we're agreed on the plan, the next question is: Which of us sells him on it? You? Or, as I'd assume you'd prefer, me?"

"If you would, me boy, 'twould help."

"Well. I should do something to earn my pay."

"And, in case he should resent it—?"

"Better you stand out from under."

"Aye! For the sake of me friendship with'm."

We fixed it up that he should talk with the Judge Advocate in charge of the case while I was seeing the prisoner,

and that then I'd report to him at the City Hotel. He took
out his *carte de visite* and wrote his room number, 346. My
heart gave a little flipflop; my room number down there
was 301, which meant on the same floor. He said: "Come
right up, without asking at the desk—the less they know of
me business, the better they'll sleep o' nights. But, me boy,
please don't be all day. I'm seeing the little one tonight,
and any good news I can give her, something to indicate
her father may soon be free, will cheer her up no end. Will
you bear that in mind?"

"I'll report by lunchtime, at latest."

"I'll be waiting, me boy."

"And I'll do my best to convince him."

"I'm sure of't. And now, the question iv payment."

He took out a wallet as thick as a book, slipped a hundred-dollar bill from inside, handed it over, and said: "I believe you mentioned to her one hundred cash in hand, with
one hundred fifty more guaranteed. Then would a small
escrow downstairs, in care of the hotel desk, take care of
the balance you want? If not, say what you want, and I'll
try to accommodate to it."

Now if plotting with him was called for, I would do
it as long as I had to, but I gagged at taking his money. I
stood snapping the bill in my fingers, and then not snapping
it, for fear it would come apart, as it had a small tear in one
end, a triangular jag half an inch deep. I said: "Mr. Burke,
escrow's according's according—you ask it if you need it.
With you, I figure I don't—so let's defer payment until I've
done what you want. And I'd rather you took this back."

"But me boy, you're welcome to keep it."

"I'd rather not."

"As you like, but if you change your mind———"

"I'll let you know."

And I handed the bill back, not dreaming it would become the bomb that would free Mr. Landry, and after that, almost blow me sky-high.

Plenty of cabs for charter today, so I took one by the hour, and reported first to Lavadeau's, where all the pirates, kings, queens, and harem girls were hanging on hooks, with her, Lavadeau, Veronique Michaud, and two or three others wrapping tissue paper on them, with mothballs sprinkled on. She took me back to a fitting room, a tiny screened-off place with a table in it and a chair, which she gave me, standing close so I could whisper. I told her what I'd done, explaining: "I'm pretending to go along, so he thinks he'll get what he wants, a plea that'll ring the curtain down quick. Your father, no doubt, will squawk like a stuck pig, but I have to gain time, and opposing Burke could ruin us. He must think he has things going his way." She listened, pulling my head to her, and got the point, but warned me: "Willie, don't be too long, don't take too much time. I'm going out with him again tonight, to pump him, but from what he said last night, another note's going in, perhaps has been already sent. And the more he spills in these notes, the worse it's going to be." I asked if she'd made up the list of the downtown stationery stores. She said she had and got it out of her purse. It was in her strange, French handwriting, with crossbars on the 7's, accent marks, and all kind of small touches I wasn't familiar with. Also, it smelled like Russian Leather. I kissed it, then buried my nose in her ruffle. She pushed her two big bulges to my cheeks, and for a moment, as my arm went around her, it was holy again, and close.

But her father was a man of ice when I lined things out for him. By then they'd given him a brazier, and he stood over it warming his hands as I brought him down to date, and suggested he "consider a plea." "I will not plead," he kept saying over and over. "I will not, *not*, NOT plead—and I'm astonished, Mr. Cresap, you would urge such a thing on me. Apart from general considerations, it involves a point of honor, the admission of an act I didn't commit, and therefore am not guilty of. I will not plead."

"Nobody's asking you to."

"I—I beg your pardon, sir?"

"I suggested that you consider it."

"That I consider it? . . . And then what?"

"Well, you've got nothing else to do, at least that I can see, but put charcoal on that fire. Can't you consider some more?"

". . . Consider? And then consider?"

"And—consider."

He looked at me quite a while, took some turns around the brazier, then fetched up facing me. "Mr. Cresap," he said, "you may consider me as considering."

"That's all I want to know."

So far, except for some stalling around, getting ready to start, I was strictly nowhere, but then, unexpectedly, I went ten leaps down the road. I went up to the Judge Advocate's office and was referred by the sergeant to a major named Jenkins. He was a tall, thin, pale man, with a black, spade-cut beard, who kept me standing beside his table and looked at papers as we talked. I led off, as soon as I'd given my name and reported myself as counsel, by asking what my client was charged with. "No charge as yet," he said. "He's being held for investigation—as I'd think you'd know by now, if you're serving as his counsel."

"What charge if I get him to plead?"

"Parole violation."

"He hasn't been given parole that I know of."

"All these people are technically under parole—if they don't like it that way, they can let us know and we'll fix it by putting them in the stockade."

"What's the penalty for parole violation?"

"Confiscation, of course. In return for a declaration of assets, we recommend to the court suspension of penal servitude."

"Isn't that pretty stiff?"

"Perhaps you'd prefer I sent his papers to the U.S. Attorney, who can ask indictment for treason?"

"Treason, Major? Are you serious?"

"Shipping shoes to the enemy's not treason?"

"No shoes were shipped to the enemy!"

He went into a perfect rage, saying the fact the shoes were shipped was prima facie proof of who got them, and winding up: "If you think it's stiff that a man who would do such a thing be let off with parole violation, then all I can say is you take a damned light view of this war."

"I was wounded in this war."

"Oh my! And that entitles you to what?"

"A seat, I would think."

He started a loud uproar, having orderlies bring me a chair, and then when I wouldn't take it got furious all over again. By then, I was furious at myself for doing so badly, but made myself shut up and stood there saying nothing. He said: "Cresap, if I may say so, you could learn from your client's partner, who was in a short while ago, and successfully made an appeal for the reduction of this charge to parole violation, the absolute minimum possible. He did it through courtesy."

"We could all use a little of that."

"Are you starting up again?"

How it might have turned out I don't know, but about that time the sergeant tiptoed over, bent down and whispered, and the major jumped up and brushed past me to a man in the hall who had a colored porter behind him, carrying what looked like a case of booze. The major blustered loudly that "those goods were to go to my billet." The man was nice as pie, saying the billet was where he was headed, but *first*—and he rubbed his fingers in the way that means money. The major took out a note, which the man held in his teeth while fishing into a weasel to make change. I was edging to the door and could see it was a hundred-dollar note, but paid no special attention until the man stuffed it into the weasel after handing the change to the major. And that's when I suddenly saw what "courtesy" meant. One end of the note was torn, a triangular jab about half an inch deep.

As the man went downstairs with his porter I followed, bellowing my thanks to the major for all his kindness to me. On the street I got the man's name, Lucan, and his business address on Baronne Street—after buying the bill off him for five twenties and a one. I told him: "I like a big bill in my poke; it impresses my friends." He was pleased as punch with his profit, and as I rolled down to the City Hotel, I knew I had something.

CHAPTER 5

I WAS SO EXCITED I told myself to forget the ransack job; I
had enough already, what with this hundred-dollar bill that
Jenkins must have got from Burke and the stationery as soon
as I traced it, to put up quite a fight. However, I picked up
my keys on the way, and when I went up to 301, which was
just a regular hotel room with bureau, chair, table, bed,
gaslight, and bath, tried both in the door. They both worked
perfectly, the skeleton even better than the other. Then I
went on to 346, around an angle in the hall, and knocked.
Letting me in was a human gorilla, a swarthy thing with
hair growing out of its nostrils, thick brows, and a fore-
head one inch high. It was squat and bandy-legged, and on
the back of one hand was an anchor. It had on a clawhammer suit, with patent paper collar of the kind European
servants wear, and called in kind of a croak: "M'sieu
Boorke!" Burke came out and shook hands, and called it

Pierre. "Me gippo," he said to me, and then: "Pierre, *c'est M'sieu Craysap*." The thing grunted, bowed kind of stiff, and flicked off one ear the salute that sailors give. Then he went out through a side door of the room.

"I didn't know you spoke French," I said.

" 'Tis one of me bonds with Adolphe," he told me. "Aye, I lived in Paris three years after Nicaragua—until Mexico beckoned, in fact." He shot me a glance as though to see if Nicaragua meant anything to me, and then when I didn't react, went on: "I joined the filibuster, and helped organize Accessory Transit—for Walker, early on. He abused me confidence no end, but I managed to sell out to one of Vanderbilt's men, at a bit iv a profit. That's when I went to Paris, to take me bearings a bit."

"Walker was something, wasn't he?"

"A homunculus, but a genius of his kind."

"He must have been—to steal a whole country, with just a handful of crazy boys he picked up in San Francisco, and then after he invaded, to start a railroad and make it pay. As Accessory Transit certainly would have, if Vanderbilt hadn't got in it, starting a feud."

"Aye. Aye. And Aye."

Pierre came back, in reefer and sailor hat with a red pompon on it of the kind worn in the French Navy, said something about *déjeuner*, and went out. Burke said: "The perfect retainer. I picked'm up in Matamoros, when his ship sailed without'm. He washes me clothes, minds the door, acts as me bodyguard, and in all ways is me factotum—or gippo, as we say in Limerick. He'd do anything, *anything* I tell'm, and it doesn't displease me he speaks not a word of English. One of us is always here, but you'll have to write your messages."

He waved at a desk, a big walnut thing with green baize top, drawers at both sides, and paper, inks, and pens in the middle, then said: "But sit down, me boy, and let's hear your news."

I sat, in a room like mine at the St. Charles, except that he'd made it his home, a little. It had the usual sofa, chairs, and footstools, but the big desk was extra, as was a big table with piles of newspapers on it—the New Orleans *Times*, and others in Spanish and French. The place smelled of tobacco, and he opened a drawer in the desk to take out a green pasteboard box of *cigarillos*, as he called them, and offered them. I said I didn't smoke, but noted the drawer was unlocked and full of all sorts of papers. He sat down, lit up, and blew smoke rings, tapping his cheeks. He said: "They're Cuban, these things, and not bad—I ran into them in Mexico. The wrappers are sweet to the taste—I think they're steeped in molasses. And the filler's perique—do you mark the thick, heavy white smoke, so tempting to pop into rings? Ah well, what's the good word, me boy?"

"*Not* so good, I'm afraid."

"But you saw Adolphe?"

"I did, and broached the subject of a plea. He rejected it point-blank. In fact he hit the ceiling."

"But 'twas to be expected. What then?"

"I reasoned with him, and he agreed to consider it."

"He'll open his mind to't?"

"That's as far as I could get with him."

"But he'll give in, I'm sure. With one of his kind, there must be face-saving preliminaries of a grand, dignified kind. The rest is but a question of time. Did he get the brazier I arranged for'm?"

"He practically glued himself to it."

"It'll warm'm. And remind'm the thing can go on."

"That's not all, Mr. Burke. I saw Major Jenkins."

He looked startled, and I said: "To get the thing lined up, what a plea is going to get us. I'm afraid I did badly up there. They're talking parole violation, and Major Jenkins seemed to resent me."

"He's a bit iv a churl, that lad."

"I left in the middle of it. Actually, I ran."

"I saw'm meself, earlier."

"So he said. He spoke most highly of you."

"He may have had reason, me boy."

He winked, then told how he'd called on Jenkins, and how Jenkins had scaled the charge down, "from the treason case he was dreaming of" to parole violation—all corresponding to what Jenkins had said and to the hundred-dollar bill in my pocket. I complimented him and, as I'd made a full "report," got up to go. So far, since I'd given up my original idea of searching this place for evidence, it was strictly shadow-chewing, chatter meaning nothing, except to go through the motions, keeping his suspicions lulled so I could go ahead with the small, exact case that I had. But then as I stood by his desk and he stared out the window, still talking, my eye fell on something that stood me right on my head, so I had to reverse my intention and get in this place somehow, no matter how I did it. Beside the desk, between it and the window, was a wicker wastebasket, and in its bottom a scatter of scraps, torn pieces of paper of the selfsame kind the informer had used for his note, each of them showing pencil marks. They had to be a trial draft or rough draft or spoiled draft or some kind of draft of the new informer note, the one she had talked about, that she was sure would be sent. They would nail my case down tight, and there could be no doubt at all that I had to get them.

He kept on talking and I edged to the door, out of sight of the basket, so my eyes wouldn't betray me. Then he got up, and we fixed it up I'd repeat tomorrow my visit to Mr. Landry, and then report to him here, "without further talks with Jenkins." I backed out, pretty respectful. He put his head out the door, asked if I'd changed my mind about payment. I said no, I wasn't in need of money, and better I put it off until I really had something to show.

I went downstairs, arguing with myself that I should forget this whole idea of burgling a suite in this place to get something to please a girl. I asked myself what Landry had done for me that I had to risk my life, perhaps, doing this for him. I reminded myself of Pierre and that strange remark, "he'd do anything, *anything*, I tell'm" to do. Coupled with the word *bodyguard* it meant armed thug, one I dared not disregard. I told myself to wake up and get back to the original problem, which was to raise twenty-five thousand bucks. I told myself all kinds of things and seemed to be making some progress, at least to the extent that I took out her list and began checking stores. At the first one I went to, Wagener's in Camp Street, just up the street from the City, I hit pay dirt. Yes, said the clerk, he remembered the Irish customer and thought it an odd kind of purchase for a person of such obvious elegance. I took his name, Bob Raney, and went up to the St. Charles, where I had some lunch in the bar. I told myself that did it: there was no need any more, now that I had the proof of who had bought the paper, to take any chance on a search. And yet all the time it gnawed at me that since rooms are done once a day, those scraps would probably stay there until the maid came in next morning, and with Burke dated up for the evening, Pierre was all there was between me and what I needed more than anything. And then, all of a sudden, unexpectedly and by accident, a way suggested itself whereby I could get rid of Pierre. Two men at the next table were having a growling match about a woman named Marie Tremaine for her greedy, grasping habits. One of them said: "All she wants is your money, and that ends it with me. I'll never go in her house again, from now to the end of my life. Do you hear me, fellow? I'm through."

It came to me I'd heard of that house before, sitting around this bar. As soon as I'd finished I went out and said to a hacker: "Have you heard of Marie Tremaine's?"

"Well, Mister, I hope so."

"Take me there."

CHAPTER 6

I<small>T WAS A HOUSE</small> on Bienville, in the Quarter, with two bay windows; a colored maid let me in. She started for a double door on the left of the hall. When I asked for Miss Tremaine she seemed surprised and opened the door on the right. I went into a red-plush parlor and sat down, first taking off my oilskin, which I folded beside my chair, putting my hat on top of it. I waited, and felt my stomach flutter when the door across the hall opened and a man came out with a girl, who whispered with him before he left. She was trim, neat, and shapely, and wore a red baize apron. What upset me was wondering what I would do if she came in where I was and sat in my lap, as I'd heard was the custom. She didn't, but went back through the door she had come out of and closed it. I was just drawing a breath of relief when a woman came in, stood in front of me, and looked me over. She was small, with blonde ringlets beside her face, and quite pretty. I took her to be in her thirties, and she had blue eyes and strawberry-and-cream complexion, but all she had on was a robe, a white satin thing that she wore, with a gold fillet on her hair and gold slippers on her feet, but nothing underneath—as she carelessly, maybe not so carelessly, let me see. I said: "Miss Tremaine? Crandall's my name"—giving the name I'd signed on the register of the City Hotel last night. I went on: "My *carte de visite*," and pressed a twenty-dollar bill in her hand.

She blinked, but I kept right on, determined to hit the thing on the nose, no matter how nervous I was. I said: "I've come on a matter of business, to ask some help that I need, for which I'm willing to pay."

"*Alors?* What help, please?"

She had a small voice, French accent, and cute way of talking. I asked: "Miss Tremaine, could you hire me a girl? For a little job tonight at the City Hotel? I kind of need a decoy, to entice someone out of his room——"

"La-la. La-la."

"Oh, I assure you there's nothing wrong. No—larceny, nothing like that. It's just—that a search has to be made—for something——"

I ran down, knowing nothing more to say, and damning myself for not rehearsing it better, because how could anyone, especially someone like her, who looked plenty smart, possibly fall for such a tale, one so thin I couldn't even finish it? However, she seemed more curious than annoyed and kept staring at me, as though to figure me out. Then a thought seemed to hit her as a smile crossed her face, which she hid with my sawbuck. Then she shifted her stare to my hat, which seemed to interest her somehow, though why I couldn't fathom. Then suddenly she said: "This *is* business indeed. This requires of thought."

I mumbled something, I guess, and then she said: "I should dress me. Shall we go to my apartment, perhaps?"

I was too rattled to argue, so picked up my gear and followed her out to the hall. She led up the carpeted stairs to the second floor, then down a hall to a door at the rear, which she opened for me. I went in. The room downstairs had been red plush; this one was ivory and gold. It had a white cotton rug on the floor, a white bearskin rug over it, white chairs with gold brocade upholstery, and a white grand piano with gold beading on it. At one end was a white bed with gold canopy, faced by white armoires. She said: "Please give me your things," and took them to an armoire, where she hung them up. Then she pulled a gold rope, and golden portieres closed after her, also cutting off the bed, on a white pole that ran across. I'd never been in such a place, and strolled around, to memorize what it was like. I had a quick flash at the prints on the wall, French by their style, all in gold frames and some downright saucy. Then I noticed the flower vases, of bright brass as I thought, some of them with the camellias which were just now coming in season. But then it occurred to me: Brass is not often used for vessels meant to hold water because moisture brings up the verdigris. Then I thought it odd that these vases showed no green cast, as all brass does, no matter how brightly shined. And then the truth hit me. I went over, picked up an empty vase, and snapped my finger on it. It clinked with the music made only by solid gold.

It clinked and she popped—out from behind the portieres, a blue flannel dress half on, silken froufrou showing. Her eyes were like blue glass. I said: "You've good ears, Miss Tremaine."

"*Alors? Qu'est-ce que c'est?*"

I went over, straightened her dress, put my arms around her, and gave her a little kiss, which she took on the cheek. I said: "I wasn't stealing your vase—just testing it."

"It is of gold, *non?*"

"There's no other such sound on this earth."

"I have six—from a *château* at Reze-le-Nantes."

"I compliment you. You like gold, I imagine?"

"I love gold."

"Turn around, I'll button you up."

She turned and I buttoned her, taking a seat and pulling her down in my lap. Then I dandled her and gave her another kiss. She took it this time on the mouth, and responded a little, but with an odd squint in her eye. She pulled my eyebrows, said: "*Doux,* as *coton.*"

"They're not cotton, they're hair."

"*Pourtant jolis,* as you are."

"If I'm pretty, so is a cigar-store Indian."

"*Et* sweet. *Et naïf.*"

"What's naïve about me?"

To tell the truth, I'd lost some of my fear, so I didn't feel so rattled, and was beginning to be a bit chesty—as though I was now experienced in matters of this kind and could almost act like myself. She kept on pulling my brows, and said: "Oh—you give me twenty dollars—you take kisses as *lagniappe*—is not this *naïf?* You think me madam —yet you remove the hat—is not this *naïf* indeed? Don't you know, *petit,* that with madam you keep the hat on? That this is the *insulte ancienne* a man pays to her who befriends?"

". . . If you're not a madam, what are you?"

"I am *joueuse,* of course."

To me it sounded like Jewess, and I snapped back,

pretty quick: "Well, I'm Episcopalian myself, but know only good of the Jews, especially Jewish women—"

"*Joueuse!*" she yelped. "I play! I operate gambling house! This is not such house as you think!"

"This? Is a gambling house? And you—?"

"Am *joueuse*, I have said! I am not madam!"

"Good God."

I dumped her off my lap, jumped up, and dived for my things, all at one jerk. I said: "I'm sorry—I apologize—I've been making a sap of myself and I-don't-know-what out of you, and I'm on my way, quick."

But she was right beside me, her hand on the armoire door, so I couldn't open it. She said: "Have I acted *désagréablement?* Have I expressed anger, perhaps? Have I desired that you go?" She yanked me away from the armoire, pushed me back into the chair, and camped in my lap again. She said: "Is *joueuse*, for example, *contaminée?* Might she not wish to help? Might she not have girls, *aussi?* Who deal stud, *vingt-et-un, et* faro? Cannot this matter be discussed?"

"Miss Tremaine, my ears are too hot for talk."

"They are red, very droll, *mais oui.* But the offense is not too extreme. After all, you hear of my place—"

"In a goddam bar is where."

"And you make some small mistake."

"Can I hide my face just a minute?"

She took a handkerchief from her sleeve, held it in front of my eyes, then wiped my nose and said: "Now! Enough! Even the girl may be possible, if I satisfy me she shall not be endangered, *surtout* with the law. This is of great importance, so please let us talk. You care for champagne, M'sieu Crandall?"

"If you do, I do."

By the door was a white china knob which she yanked, and a bell tinkled below. When the maid came, she ordered champagne in French. Having had a few seconds to think, I determined to spill what I was up to, at least enough to convince her I wasn't a thief. I gave no names, but spoke of a friend about to be railroaded by a rat turned informer "who lives at the City Hotel." I told of seeing the scraps, and showed her my skeleton key. I wound up: "I know he's going out tonight, but the trouble is his valet, who'll be on deck as a guard. If he can be lured out, I can slip in there quick, get those scraps, put other scraps in their place, and be out in five minutes—even the valet won't know I was there."

"Now I am convinced."

"But the girl should speak French—"

"She will. All my girls do."

The maid came, carrying the wine in a bucket of ice, followed by a child carrying a tray with two glasses and a silver dish with a slip of paper on it. When bucket, tray, and glasses had been set on a low table, the maid picked up the dish and offered me the slip. "*Non!*" screeched Miss Tremaine, and rattled off some French. The maid backed off, but I stepped over and took the slip. It was a billhead that said: "Champagne . . . $8." I fished up a ten-dollar bill, but Miss Tremaine snatched it from me and tucked it in my pocket. Then she tore up the billhead, blasted maid and child from the room with a volley of French, and stood there, her face twisting in fury. She turned and twirled the bottle around in the ice. Then she twisted off the wire, worked the cork out, and let it pop. She poured a mouthful and tasted. Then she filled both glasses, handed me mine, raised hers, and said "*Santé.*"

"To your very good health, Miss Tremaine."

"*Et succès, M'sieu Crandall-Quichotte.*"

She pushed me back into my chair, but didn't sit in my lap this time. Instead, she half-knelt on the floor, her elbows on my knees, her glass held under her nose. She said: "If I screamed, I ask pardon, please. The bill is indeed usual; the girl committed no fault. And I love gold, as you said. But you, *petit*, make me feel as *grande dame*, which I love too, and which does not occur every day." And then, sad, sipping: "*La joueuse* is *vraiment demimondaine*, half *dame*, half, *hélas*, madam. But, with you, I forget the one *et* become the other. So, *ci après*, if you please, attempt not to pay."

"Miss Tremaine, all I see is a lady."

"*Merci.* But to you may I be Marie?"

"I'd be honored to call you that."

"And how shall I call you?"

"My name is William."

But she laughed and told me: "This I cannot say." She tried to say it, and it came out a cross between *veal* and *bouillon*. She said: "I shall call you *Guillaume*."

"That'll please me no end."

She rested her glass on one of my knees, dropped her head on the other, and let some time go by without talking. The ice in the bucket looked clean, and I crunched a piece in my teeth. I said: "That's fine ice, Marie. Where's it from, if you know?"

"Minnesota. For two years it came from Canada, by sea, and was full of small creatures. But, *depuis* Vicksburg, the river boats can come down, and we get the lake ice once more."

"Where I come from the ice is no good."

"And where is this, Guillaume?"

By then, sweet as she was, and gallant, giving help when she didn't have to, I couldn't have lied any more, and in fact already hated I'd had to give her a false name. I said: "Maryland—it's tidewater, and whenever we cut ourselves ice, it's always brackish with salt."

"May I be *femme curieuse* and ask what you do?"

"Marie, I'm an engineer."

"Of railroads, *oui?*"

"No, hydraulic. My specialty is piles."

"Ah, *les pieux!*"

Now someone who drives piles kind of gets used to a smile when he says what his business is, and more or less smiles himself. But the way she took it, you'd have thought I sang in grand opera. She set her glass on the table, put her arms around me, and asked, very breathless: "You are *associé* with M'sieu Eads? You have been sent here by him?"

". . . Now how do *you* know about him?"

"Oh I know—I am *femme d'affaires* in New Orleans, and we of *affaires* know. He revives the de Pauget plan."

"The—what?"

"The plan of Adrien de Pauget, our great engineer, who wished long ago, perhaps one hundred years, to drive of *pieux* in the river, and compel it to cut its canal through the *barrière* to the Gulf. It should make of New Orleans a *capitale*, by opening her to big ships! It should open also Vicksburg, Memphis, *et* St. Louis—we shall have *pays cosmopolitain!* M'sieu Eads, so we hear, revives it, this de Pauget plan. You are of him, Guillaume?"

"Marie, I have to confess I don't know him—my father does, but I don't. And I never heard of de Pauget. But the channel is what brought me here, when Mr. Eads gets around to it. If I can get my business started, here on the spot in New Orleans, I hope to bid on the work—to be part of something big."

"*Ah, oui.* I could feel you were *poète.*"

"Marie, I wouldn't deceive you—I'm just a lad with a slide rule, a partner—kind of dumb but he does know tugboats—plenty of nerve, and one thing lacking."

"Money?"

"How did you guess it?"

"It *may not* be *difficile!*"

She kissed me once more, then jumped up and started checking over what we'd do with the girl. I got out the City Hotel key, the one to 301, gave it to her and said: "That room's in my name, but she can come right up, and I'll take another, in her name, and keep the key myself." We agreed on Eloise Brisson as a good name for the girl, and I wrote it down on paper I found in my pocket. I said: "If she'll come around seven, we can get the thing over quick, and she'll have the rest of the night to herself." Small details, we decided, could be settled with the girl. That seemed to be all, and Marie got my oilskin and hat, saying she'd see me out. In the lower hall, she stopped by the door across from the room I'd been in, opened it, and beckoned. My heart dropped into my shoes; I could see blue in there, on Union officers, and had a horrible fear one of them might know me and call me by name—by then I'd met quite a few. But the faces were strange and I circulated with her, admiring the various layouts. The girl I had seen was dealing blackjack, or *vingt-et-un* as it's also called, her little apron hugging her belly as it pressed against the table.

Other girls dealt other games, and one ran the dice pit, but a man ran the roulette wheel, and another sat on the high lookout's stool, a long black cane that surely had a sword inside it In his hand. She spoke to them all and to quite a few customers, some by name. In the hall she kissed me, saying: "The girl shall be there."

Outside, I was astonished to see my cab; I'd forgotten all about it. I drove to the City Hotel, registered Eloise Brisson, paid for her room, and took her key. The clerk winked as he handed it over, and I saw it was for 303, the room next to mine. I drove to Wagener's and did what I'd neglected to do previously: bought a tablet of the same cheap kind Burke had bought for his note. I got in the cab again, told the driver Lavadeau's. I was all excited to tell Mignon my latest news, the scraps I'd found in the basket, and how I meant to get them. Suddenly I thought: What do I say about Pierre? And then I thought: *What do I say about Marie?*

"Never mind Lavadeau's. The St. Charles," I said.

CHAPTER 7

I WENT UP TO MY SUITE, took a sheet of the tablet paper, printed something on it in pencil, then tore it into pieces the size of the scraps I'd seen in the basket. I put them in an envelope, tucked it into my pocket. I loaded my Moore & Pond and strapped it on. It was a gun I'd carried on pay day for my father's labor, keeping it on me as I went around with my satchel of cash. Originally, wanting it to be seen, I'd worn it in the usual belt holster. But one day as I was forming the men into line, an Italian grabbed it off me, threw me down, and made a dive for the cash. A colored blacksmith clipped him one on the jaw, so no great harm was done, but then I began wondering if a gun hanging out in the breeze was quite the idea I'd thought it was. So I had an armpit holster made, and that's what I put on now. A Moore & Pond is .36-caliber and nothing much for looks, being short and stubby. But it shoots a brass shell instead of paper cartridges and caps, which makes it handy. I buckled the straps in place, buttoned my coat high to hide them. The rain had stopped outside, so I hung my oilskin up and got my overcoat out. Then, at six, I went to dinner.

I ate in the Orleans House, a saloon across the street from the hotel so situated that by sitting next to the window I could see down Common Street. What I had I don't recollect, as I had my mind on the cab line down at the City Hotel. Pretty soon a victoria pulled out and came trotting up toward St. Charles. As it turned I glimpsed Burke. I strangled down the rest of my dinner, paid, and walked down to the City. The clerk spoke, and I went up to 303. It was indentical to 301 but, with the twilight settling down, looked indescribably gloomy, or shabby, or bleak, or something unpleasant. I tried my skeleton key in its lock, and it worked beautifully. I took off my coat and hat and stepped out to reconnoiter. Then I remembered: If I should be surprised, I had to look as though I'd just come in off the street. I went back, put on my coat and hat again, and strolled to 346. Inside, I could hear a man humming. I came back, hung up my things again and looked at my watch. It said 6:45. I closed my eyes, said the Lord's Prayer, the Twenty-third Psalm, and some Beatitudes, and counted to a hundred. When I looked again it was 6:48. But at last it came to seven o'clock, and nothing happened next door. I cursed myself for a sucker, to think that twenty dollars would buy such a date and that such a dumb scheme would work— all the time watching the minute hand as it crept to 7:01, 7:02, 7:03, 7:04. At 7:05, a key clicked in 301's door, and on the other side of the partition someone was moving around. Then, on my door, came a scratch. I opened and a girl was there, in dark gray dress with black braid darts on the jacket, black hat, black shawl, and black veil. I invited her in, so nervous my voice shook, thanked her for being so punctual, and asked her name. *"Alors,* perhaps you can guess," she said, lifting the veil.

"Marie!" I exclaimed.

"You did not know me, *petit?"*

"Well, you were wearing that veil, and——"

Actually, she seemed pleased at having fooled me, and pretty soon asked: "And our pigeon—he is in?"

"Yes. I just now checked."

"He is alone?"

"He's singing—must be to himself."

"Bon. Now I prepare me."

She ducked into the next room and was gone a couple of minutes. She came back looking half-boiled, her ringlets askew, her jacket off, her camisole mussed, so she looked terribly exciting. "One shall appear *séduisante,"* she whispered.

"There should be a law against it."

She laughed and stretched out on the bed. "It is not yet time," she said. "One must wait for the *gaz* in the hall, which the night maid shall light. One should not encounter her, when she comes."

"My God, I should say not."

"If we watch, the transom will tell."

She beckoned and I sat beside her, but she moved over for me to lie, and I lay. She snuggled against me, then felt the gun. She took it out, set it on the night table. I said: "I'm sorry, but to be safe, I thought—"

"But *oui.* I too."

She opened her pocketbook, and even in the murk I could see the brass sheen of a derringer. "One takes precautions," she said, "but your *pistolet* hurts!"

With the gun out of the way, she practically wrapped

herself around me, her skirt slipping up and most of her froufrou with it, so bare skin was touching me in all sorts of intimate places. She lined my lips with the tip of her tongue, then gave me a long, wet kiss. "One is not always *femme sérieuse*," she whispered, "or *grande dame*. Sometimes I amuse me."

"To say nothing of me," I whispered.

"How long will you be? In that room?"

"Why—no more than five minutes, I'm sure."

"*Alors?* Then we shall have the evening?"

". . . Ah—yes. Of course."

"We may dine? You like Antoine's?"

"I've never been to Antoine's. Sounds fine."

"Then theater? At the Variétés are vaudevilles."

"You can't beat vaudevilles."

"And then? We come here?"

"If you want to, Marie, that's fine."

"Or *chez vous*, perhaps? Where do you live, Guillaume?"

". . . At the St. Charles, for the time being."

"I think better *chez moi*."

"You have a very beautiful place."

She snuggled close, then rolled over on top of me and covered my face with little kisses. "It shall be *chez moi*," she whispered.

Light showed through the transom and she got up, even more rumpled than before. She asked: "Have I the appearance of some poor helpless one, who has brandy, for example, a bottle in her room, and no way to extract the cork?"

"Have you the booze is the question?"

"Oh I brought. Fear not."

"Then the appearance is overwhelming."

She said: "When you return from the *recherche*, please drop your stick on the floor, to *claquer*, as signal to me. I shall send him for glasses, then come to you here *vite*, and together we disappear." I said that would be perfect, and she put the gun back in my holster, helped me into my coat, and gave me my hat, saying: "You shall be ready to leave in one *coup*—I shall dress me as we go down." She stood, soft, sloppy, and mussed, then kissed me quick and went. While I watched, holding the door on a crack, she drifted down the hall and flitted around the angle. I heard a knock, then voices—hers and a man's, talking French. Then here she came back with Pierre, walking unsteadily, holding onto his arm. He was giggling, and carried a corkscrew in one hand. They went in 301, and when the door closed I tiptoed out.

I floated down the hall, turned the angle, stopped at 346, and got out my skeleton key. But when I put it in the hole and twisted, nothing happened. I twisted two or three times, and still the thing stuck. Then in kind of a panic, I twisted both ways, back and forth. On forth the thing turned. Then I realized the door was open—Pierre hadn't locked it when he went down the hall with Marie. I went in, found everything as it had been, except that a gaslight was on over the desk. The basket, when I picked it up, had all kinds of stuff in it, a newspaper, a crumpled-up cardboard box, some string, maybe papers, I don't recollect. But in the bottom were the same old scraps I'd come for. I took everything out and dumped them out on the rug. I sprinkled my own scraps in their place, put everything back as it had been, set the basket in its place. Then, on my knees, I gathered them up, two or three at a time, and dropped them into my envelope. How long it took I don't know, but it seemed at least an hour. I pocketed the envelope, opened the desk drawer, made sure the tablet was there, as well as a package of envelopes of the kind the note had been mailed in. I stepped to the door, got out my skeleton key to lock it, then remembered not to. I tiptoed back to 303.

I listened, and laughing came through the partition— Marie's laugh, and Pierre's, everything quite gay. I poised my stick on the strip of bare boards between the rug and the wall. I was all set to let it drop, when I thought to my- self: *Why?* You signal her, and you know what's going to happen, as you like her, plenty. I thought: Are you, after doing all this for one woman, going to ruin it by hopping in bed with another? I thought: How can you be such a rat, after the help you've been given by this brave, saucy little thing, as to leave her now in the lurch, without even telling her thanks? I thought: Rat or not, *that's what you have to do!* I shoved the stick under one arm, opened my wallet. I got out two twenties, dropped them on the bed. I put the wallet away, went to the bare boards, poised my stick again, and dropped it to make a clatter. Then I snatched it up, tiptoed quick to the hall, closed the door softly, and sneaked down the stairs, listening as I went.

On the second floor I sensed something.

I wheeled, and looking at me was another man with a stick, who had also apparently been listening. Suddenly I remembered him: Marie's guard, the one I'd seen on the high stool in her gambling room. I saw he remembered me, and went plunging down to the lobby and on out to the street. I tried to tell myself I needn't feel like a rat any more, that if this man had been brought to act as emergency guard that took all the danger out. I felt still more like a rat, a rat that had been caught.

CHAPTER 8

THAT DIDN'T GET RID OF THE FACT I had what I'd hoped to get, and as soon as I got back to my suite I worked like a wild man for the next couple of hours putting the scraps together. It wasn't too hard a job, once I got system in it. My first gain came when I realized that pieces along the outside must have a straight edge. By studying the ones with lines and other ones without, I was able to figure out which scraps went at the top, which ones at the sides, and which ones at the bottom. When I laid them out on my escritoire blotter, I came up with kind of a frame around a blank space in the middle. Now finding edges that fitted edges was just a question of patience, and pretty soon I had all the pieces in place. Then I got out my gum arabic, the little bottle I had in my draftsman's kit, and with that glued them in place, using hotel stationery as backing. At last I could read what they said, and it was damning so far as Burke was concerned. Because it was not only a trial draft, as I had

hoped it might turn out to be. It was that, but it was also a
translation from proper English, such as Burke always used,
into dumb lingo, the kind an illitorate wiites. In other words,
on odd lines was a note, decently spelled and punctuated,
giving details of the shoe shipment, while on even lines,
under words to correspond, was the rough, misspelled printing of a pretended ignoramus, even to the signature LORL
PATROT—everything in exactly the same style as the note
I'd seen at headquarters.

I was plenty excited about it, but had to figure how to
use it, and went down to the lobby to think. The point was
that though I could name the informer, I couldn't disprove
his evidence if the Army insisted on believing it meant anything, and I kept telling myself Burke was incidental; the
main thing was Mr. Landry and how to get him out. And
then I suddenly saw that my tactic lay not in fine points of
what proved what, but in taking the fun out of the Army's
self-righteous zeal for the sport of human sacrifice.

In a seat beside me watching the theater crowd enter
was a newspaperman, John Russell Young, who wrote for a
Philadelphia paper. After a moment or two he beckoned
and another reporter, Olsen, who wrote for New England
papers, came over. Young was just a boy, but Olsen was in
his thirties, a bit seedy, with yellow paper stuffed in his
pocket and a kind of hatchet face that squinted all the time.
I halfway knew them both, and spoke; I couldn't help
hearing what they said. It seemed Young was taking a trip
to field headquarters on the Teche and wanted Olsen to
cover him here in return for copies of the Franklin dis-
patches. They fixed it up quick, then Young said: "Olsen,
there's one thing I'm having a look at, and that's the camp
followers they have out there—the bevy of colored girls

who cook for the boys, as I hear, and press their pants, and do their laundry—and what else, would you say?"

"I couldn't imagine," said Olsen.

"I mean to find out," said John Russell Young.

That's when I remembered Dan's panic at what the press might hear. I leaned over and interrupted: "Mr. Olsen, how'd you like it if I had a story for you?"

"I'd like it fine, Mr. Cresap. What story?"

"About a client of mine, falsely accused."

"Not Adolphe Landry, by any chance?"

"I see you keep up with things."

"Keeping up is my business. But how is he falsely accused? The way they tell it at headquarters, he's practically a one-man Q.M. for Dick Taylor's Army."

"They tell it their own way," I said, pretty grim, "but if you'd like to hear it my way, why don't you have breakfast with me tomorrow, and I'll have it all lined up."

"Fine. Around eight-thirty, shall we say?"

"I'll be expecting you then."

I put in a call for 7:30, then went up and went back to work. I wrote a letter to the Commanding General, asking dismissal of the case on the ground of plain reason, but putting in other stuff too, like the motives the Army might have in being unduly severe, and other things the press could be interested in. I made two copies, and turned in around 1:30. In the morning, shaved and brushed and slicked, I went down to find Olsen waiting, and took him to the main dining room, as the bar wasn't open yet. When we'd ordered, I handed him one copy of the letter, telling him: "Keep it, I made it especially for you."

He whistled as soon as he'd read it, and said: "Hey, hey, hey—I'll say it's a story, Cresap. You've practically

accused this Army of inventing a false accusation in order
to earn a bribe—something we've known goes on but
haven't been able to prove, as you say you'll be able to do.
You mind my asking how?"

"Well—I'll reserve that for the confab."

"What confab, Cresap?"

"At headquarters, today. That's another thing I wanted
to ask you about. How'd you like to attend?"

"Attend, Cresap? Hell, they wouldn't let me."

"Who is 'they'? I'm this man's counsel."

"That's right, so you are. So you are."

He eyed me sharply then and read the letter again.
Then he said: "But suppose you don't have proof? This
letter alone is a bombshell, enough to bring in the Gooch
Committee. They'll find the proof, if it's there. And it has
to be there, of course! This whole Army's a mess of corruption, caused by cotton—graft, cumsha, and slipperoo,
straight down the line and straight *up* the line, as this letter
intimates. That's what'll interest Gooch."

"Who's Gooch, if I may ask?"

"Chairman of the committee in Congress that investi-
gates this kind of stuff, the conduct of the war."

"Oh yes, I've heard of him."

"He can't disregard *this*."

I let him run on, through orange, eggs, and coffee,
until he'd folded the letter up, tucked it in his pocket, and
patted it. Then I said: "Of course, I haven't submitted it
yet."

"What do you mean, you haven't submitted it?"

"But that's understood," I said.

"Not by me," he snapped, quite annoyed. "You hand
me a letter, a copy you say you made for me, and I supposed it had been sent."

"But I told you; I'm having a confab."

"Listen, Cresap, you're not in the newspaper business, so perhaps you don't get the point. This letter is news, but I can't touch it until it's sent—that's what makes it public, that's what puts it on the record."

"I do get the point. That's the idea."

"Well, thanks. *And* thanks."

"Mr. Olsen," I said very quietly, "I'm Mr. Landry's counsel, and I don't act for you, or the news, or the record. I act for him, and only him. If submitting the letter helps him, I submit. If not, if the confab says I shouldn't, I don't submit it. Now if you want to be present—"

"You know what this sounds like to me?"

"All right, Mr. Olsen, what?"

"Like you're using me for a cat's-paw."

"Then call it that."

"I call it what it is."

"So I'm using you for a cat's-paw, but if you don't want to be one, just hand me the copy back, and I'll find somebody else."

". . . What's the rest of it?"

"You asking as a cat's-paw?"

"As a cat's-paw, yes. What next?"

"It's very simple."

I told him there was another person I had to invite to the confab, and that all he had to do was meet me at headquarters in an hour and let nature take its course. By the way he nodded, I knew he would be there.

I walked down to the City Hotel, turned in the key of 303, and when I got to the third floor, opened the room with my skeleton for a quick look. It was all just as I'd left it, even to the rumpled bed, except the two twenties were gone. I locked up and kept on to 346. Pierre opened as usual, giving no sign he connected me with the goings-on of last night—though of course, except for his brief interlude with a lady, he had no reason to know there'd been any goings-on. While he was calling Burke I had a flash at the basket: it was empty. So there weren't any dangling ends, and Burke was surprised to see me. I told him: "I've been thinking things over since I saw you yesterday, and I'm making one last try on behalf of Mr. Landry, a direct appeal, man to man, to the Commanding General himself."

"Me boy, it does you credit."

But when he found out I'd already written the letter, he balked and demanded to see it. I said: "Mr. Burke, naturally I'd like your judgment, and I'd show it to you gladly, except for one thing: If I don't help Mr. Landry, if I actually worsen his case, you're the one hope he'll have to undo what I've done. But in that case, you must be able to say you had nothing to do with the letter, didn't even see it. And, naturally, you wouldn't say so if it weren't actually true."

". . . Naturally not."

"*But*, I'm reading it to them first."

"Reading to whom? And why?"

"To that bunch up there—those officers, up at headquarters. As a way of playing it safe, to see how it goes. If I've hit a sour note then I can tear it up, and perhaps you'll step in. But I think you ought to be there."

What I actually thought was: He dared not *not* be there. He stared, while the rheum in his eyes glittered, and then said: "Me boy, I find this peculiar."

"But if you don't want to go, Mr. Burke—"

"I must, but . . . What does this letter say?"

"What can it say? 'Please sir, let him out.'"

He asked more questions, but now that I knew he would come, I was gaining nerve, and gave him open-faced answers. In the end he had no choice and picked up his hat and coat. Outside I called up a hack, but as we got in he told the driver: "We're taking another passenger—stop at Lavadeau's costume shop."

At Lavadeau's, he hopped out and ducked inside, I suspected to find out what she knew about it. When he came out she was with him, her eyes big question marks. I had hopped out by that time too, and as we stood on the banquette I told her: "Mrs. Fournet, I hope you approve this thing I'm about to attempt—it'll be nice if all of us pull together. But, whether you approve or not, as counsel I must do as I think best. It's my responsibility."

"Well, since I don't know what you're doing—"

"You will, all in due time."

We both sounded cold, and he apparently didn't twig that we were doing an act. When he'd handed her into the cab and taken his place beside her, I took the facing seat, so her eyes could rove my face. They had a fishy look, or a good imitation thereof. At headquarters, he was for holding things up until we could get an order for the guard to fetch Mr. Landry, but that was completely forgotten when Olsen stepped out of the wire office. "We can't have the press in this," Burke roared in a kind of panic. "'Twould ruin us, me boy—the General makes the announcements! 'Tis how the thing is done!"

She said stuff of a similar kind, taking cue as I looked at her, but I shrugged it off. "Olsen's all right," I said. "He'll give us a fair report."

Then I led the way upstairs.

CHAPTER 9

Dan dorsey was surprised at the visitation, as I hadn't given him any notice, but sat us down politely, and when I told him what we were there for sent the orderly out for more chairs, then went across the hall himself and came back with Major Jenkins. We had the pleasantries, including introductions to Mignon. Then I said to the officers: "Gentlemen, as Mr. Landry's counsel, I've decided to make an appeal, a man-to-man thing, to the Commanding General himself, asking the release of a citizen who's broken no law, who's not even charged yet, who's done nothing whatever but help those very boys, discharged Confederate vets, this Army is trying to reconstruct."

"One moment," said the major. "If this is an appeal for clemency, it can't be from nothing—has to be from something, the verdict of a court. But no verdict's been rendered yet. And if he's going to plead, as you indicated he would, how can he make an appeal from his own admission of guilt? I find myself confused."

"It's an appeal to reason. To ordinary sense."

"On the basis of the evidence?"

"Now you've got it, Major."

"Evidence is for a court to pass upon."

"Major, the Commanding General's supreme, even overriding a court, certainly overriding you. Do you presume to decide what letters he may receive?"

That calmed things down somewhat, but my eye crossed hers and, perhaps thinking she saw a cue, she cut in, pretty sharp: "Just a moment! I want our lawyer in this!"

"Certainly," I said. "I mean to consult him, of course. But first I want to read my letter to these gentlemen, for phraseology, so your father has the benefit—"

"Then revise for final submission?" asked Dan.

"That's it—with the lawyer's help."

"Then all right," she said.

I glanced around, and everyone looked worried, each for a different reason, except Olsen, who seemed bored and to whom no one was paying attention. It was just about how I wanted it. I started reading the letter, and to the preliminaries like "your attention is respectfully invited," they hardly seemed to be listening. At my first real point, "intent is the heart of this case," the major yawned openly. But then suddenly he leaned forward, as very quietly I read: "While we don't deny that Mr. Landry shipped the shoes, or that some of them may have reached Taylor, we do insist that no proof has been brought that Mr. Landry foresaw this result, or in any way connived at it, and we emphatically take exception to the principle that a man can be held criminally responsible for acts the enemy commits. We would think it passing strange, esteemed Sir, if the President of our country placed you under arrest every time a Confederate guerrilla captured a few supplies."

"Hey, hey, hey!" said the major.

"That's getting kind of personal," said Dan.

"I want our lawyer," Mignon exploded.

"Then go get him," I told her.

She didn't move, of course, and the major barked at me: "You know what's good for you, you'll take the General out."

"Who's writing this letter?" I asked him.

"Bill!" said Dan. "You want our help or not?"

"On phraseology," I said. "Technicalities."

A chill crept in, and I gave it a moment to settle, knowing that after what I'd read no one was walking out. I went on: "Once intent be fairly examined, it becomes inconceivable that Mr. Landry would have acted disloyally. His record of cooperation with the Army of the Gulf in its policy of humane reconstruction, through his purchases of cotton from those whom reconstruction tries to reach, his resale through a partner acceptable to the Army of the Gulf, his cheerful disbursements to Army personnel to expedite cotton shipment—"

"I'll take that letter!" snapped the major.

"I haven't submitted it yet."

"You're practically alleging graft, and I warn you, once you registered as this man's counsel, you became subject to martial law, and I'll not hesitate to charge you."

"With what?" I asked.

"Insubordination. Give me that letter."

"Well," I said, seeming to think things over, "it may

save time, at that. Olsen has his copy, and as submission takes care of him, by putting it on the record—"

At last he saw the trap I was working him into, and when I extended the letter to him pulled back as from a red-hot poker. He jumped up, and kept retreating as I followed him around the room, holding the letter at him. I said, very coldly, as I went: "Tell me some more about martial law—and I'll tell you more about graft."

I'd been wondering when Burke would break, and now, sure enough, he did, blurting out: "May I answer the scut, Major?" And then, to me: "If one dime has iver been paid, be Adolphe Landry or me, to anyone in this Army, I hope you'll tell me when. Come on, me boy, speak up!"

"Yesterday," I said. "Glad you asked me."

". . . Yesterday, is it? To whom?"

"Our handsome friend here—the major."

After a long, bellowing pause: " 'Tis a lie, Cresap! Your own filthy fabrication!" Then, after another bellowing pause: "How much?"

"One hundred dollars, Mr. Burke."

"Why—that's ridiculous," said the major.

But there was no steam in it, and I took my time getting out my torn bill and waving it around. To Burke I said: "You'll observe it's the same torn C-note you offered me yesterday morning, in my suite at the St. Charles Hotel, to act as Mr. Laundry's counsel—the same C-note I declined until I'd done something to earn it." Then suddenly I wheeled on the major and said: "And *you'll* observe it's the same C-note you paid Mr. Lucan with to deliver booze to your billet." And to all and sundry I said: "You'll observe it's the same C-note I bought off Mr. Lucan for a hundred and one dollars, 'to have a big bill in my poke, to impress my friends with.' I hope you're all impressed."

I took my time returning the bill to my wallet, and was startled when a fist shook under my nose. As I jerked back Burke yelled: "Scut! Liar! 'Tis no appeal you're making, to reason or anything else! 'Tis a bold bid for scandal, and I'll not listen to't!" Then to her: "Lass! Come! Please! We must be going!" With that he broke for the door, but my stick got in his way, somehow slipping between his legs, so he sprawled on the floor. Big as he was, I jerked him up by the collar and flung him back in his chair. "Suppose you stay," I said. "You may be wanted to answer questions."

Orderlies gathered, the one on duty at the door and a couple from other offices. Dan dismissed them, brushed off Burke's trousers, and poured him a glass of water. Olsen was watching me, all excited now, and she was eyeing me too, as though not to miss any cue. But I was studying the major as he sat in a state of collapse, to figure how to handle him. He presented a problem. I'd smashed him all right, but my danger was, if I pressed my advantage too much, he'd begin lunging back and land us all in the soup, still hotter soup than this was, as of now. I wanted to put him together again, give him some self-respect, so the next blast I set off would blow him back to my side more or less in one piece, instead of slamming him around loose, wholly out of control. So, as he wiped his brow with his handkerchief, I said: "Major, I'd like to clear something up. *You* used the word graft, I didn't. You scaled this charge down on humane grounds, and in that case a little champagne, in ap-

preciation for your kindness, was no more than decent
manners."

"The whole thing's a lie!" roared Burke."

"I've admitted nothing," growled the major."

"It could have meant nothing," I said. "*Had* it."

". . . What the hell are you getting at now?"

"Major," I said, very quietly, "you were a dupe. Far
from giving a gift in appreciation of humane conduct, this
man was using you to subvert the Army's processes against
an innocent man—"

" 'Tis another lie!" screamed Burke.

"What motive could he have?" asked the major.

I ticked it off for him, the bearing it had on the partnership as an asset, but he cut me off pretty quick. "Naturally,"
he said, "any Reb in a godpappy case takes a chance with
his partner, but how could a plea profit Burke?"

"It would wind the case up at once."

"At that, it's better for Landry than prison. And what
proof do you have that that's what Burke was up to? My
God, we can't go on suspicion alone!"

"I have proof. You were made a sucker of."

"What proof? In heaven's name, say!"

"Burke wrote the informer notes."

"Oh come, come, come!"

"You don't believe it, Major? I don't blame you. I
wouldn't have believed it myself if I hadn't been compelled.
But you will believe it if you'll be kind enough to get
the latest note, the one that came in this morning naming
Rod Purrin of the steamer *Nebraska* and telling how the
shoes were shipped as Christmas gifts."

His jaw dropped, and at last he turned on Burke with
a venomous look. He went out and came back with the

same old envelope I'd seen on Mardi Gras. He undid the tapes, took out a sheet of the same cheap paper, and laid it on the table. It showed printing that read:

FEBY 10, 1864

GENL SIR:

ROD PURN NEBRASKA MATE PUT SHOES ASHUR MORGANZA IN GOONY SECS LIKE ADOLPHE LANDRY PUT THEM UP FOR HIM HE TELL NEBRASKA CAPIN WAS XMAS GIFFS FOR REB CHILLERN GENL SIR YOU DON HAF BLEE ME ASK CAPIN GOOL HE TELL YOU ABAT IT BUT TALOR HE GOT SHOES MORE SOON GENL

LORL PATRIOT

"Fine," I said, as everyone stepped up to read. "Now have a look at this—that I fished out of Burke's wastebasket, seven forty-five last night." And I put down my pasted-up scraps, which I had folded in my pocket. They read:

February 10, 1864
FEBY 10, 1864

General Sir:
GENL SIR:

Rod Purrin the *Nebraska* mate put the shoes ashore at
ROD PURN NEBRASKA MATE PUT SHOES ASHUR

Morganza in gunny sacks like Adolphe Landry put
MORGANZA IN GOONY SECS LIKE ADOLPHE LANDRY PUT

them up for him. He told the *Nebraska* captain they
THEM UP FOR HIM HE TELL NEBRASKA CAPIN WAS

were Christmas gifts for Reb children. General sir,
XMAS GIFTS FOR REB CHILDREN GENL SIR

you don't have to believe me. Ask Captain Gould, he'll
YOU DON HAF BLEE ME ASK CAPIN GOOL HE

tell you about it, but Taylor he got the shoes. More
TELL YOU ABAT IT BUT TALOR HE GOT SHOES MORE

soon, General.
SOON GENL

Loyal Patriot
LORL PATROT

"You win," said the major, sitting down very heavily.

"Then," I said, putting my exhibit back in my pocket, "if you'll have the prisoner brought and sign an order for his release, I'll tear up my letter to the General and forget the whole unfortunate incident."

". . . Afraid I can't do that."

"Why not, Major?"

"Identification of the informer puts a new light on the case, that's true. It doesn't change the evidence."

"Your evidence is worthless. It proves nothing."

"That's up to a court to decide."

"I'm sorry, sir. It's up to you to decide."

He looked startled, and I went on: "In the absence of habeas corpus, the Judge Advocate says if his evidence sustains the specification of a charge. I say your evidence doesn't."

"I say it does."

"There's also *my* evidence, Major."

". . . What do you mean, *your* evidence?"

"The bill I have in my wallet and this pasted-up note I just showed you are all I'll need to prove collusion on your part, for a hundred-dollar bribe, with a skunk, to his profit, in the manufacture of a case against an innocent man."

"I didn't! I tell you I didn't!"

"I know you didn't. *I'll prove it just the same!*"

"Keep it quiet, Bill!" said Dan.

"WHY SHOULD I KEEP IT QUIET?" I bellowed.

When he closed the door quick, the way he did that other time, I felt things going my way, so when he put his arms around me and started wrestling me into my chair, I let him. And I listened intently as he said: "Bill, after all, there's such a thing as showing some judgment. Your man's not out, he's in. And so long as he's in, wild talk from you can't help but hurt him. Now, are you going to be sensible, or aren't you?"

"I am, it's just what I want."

"All right—then let's start over."

"Fine, we can all relax."

I went over, patted her on the cheek. I kept on around, and patted Dan on the cheek. I patted Olsen on the cheek. I stood in front of the major, and when I saw that he would take it, patted him on the cheek. I went over to Burke and slapped him sharply on the cheek. Then I came back to my place and sat down. "So," I said, "in a calm and reasonable way, let's have a look at this thing. I'd call it a simple dilemma—with one horn and what we might call a handle. The handle is that the major, now that he knows the truth, can admit in a manly way that we all make mistakes and dismiss this case at once. The horn is that if he doesn't dismiss the case, I have to submit this letter—we mustn't forget that. The letter, once submitted, lets Olsen in, and also leaves him free to publish what's been said here. And that brings in the Gooch Committee—we mustn't forget them. And they bring in a Court of Inquiry—we mustn't forget *it*. That's as far as I'll take it now, but we all have to realize, now that we're being sensible, the backwash will

be unpleasant. Mind, I don't think the major was crooked—
he was too self-righteous for that. To me, he's an honest
man, fair to middling dumb, who got himself sucked in,
then couldn't take himself out. Unfortunately, we have to
go by the evidence, and my evidence—"

"Are you threatening me?" said the major.

"*Threatening* you?" I yelled. "Goddam it, am I talking English or am I talking Choctaw? You get Mr. Landry
up here, you dismiss this case right now, or *you stupid son
of a bitch* I'M SENDING YOU TO PRISON!"

"Bill, stop it!" yelled Dan.

"Try stopping me!" I yelled back.

"Then all right," whined the major. "I'll have the
case reviewed. You come back tomorrow, and—"

"I give you five minutes! Get Mr. Landry, or—"

"But I can't—"

"GET HIM!" barked Dan.

The major knifed out into the hall, and then things
began happening so fast they're all mixed up in my memory.
First she came running over, and in front of Dan, in front
of Burke, in front of Olsen, and in front of the orderly,
began kissing my hand. Then Mr. Landry was there, a
leather valise in his hand, and she flew to his arms, kissing
him and whispering to him in French. Then the major
came back with papers for me to sign, and I told her take
her father down and wait for me in the cab. They did, but
not before Burke got in it, snarling at them in French, and
she snarled back, but Mr. Landry answered quite mildly.
Then Olsen left, very solemn, bowing to me and saying:
"Your faithful cat's-paw salutes you." Then it was Burke,
me, the major, and Dan, but when Burke tried to go Dan

stepped over to block him, and told the major: "You're holding this man, I think. You'd better—if you know what's good for you." Then the major was taking Burke down to the detention room, the orderly going too.

Then it was Dan and me. I held out my hand to thank him for everything, but he didn't seem to see it. "Bill," he said, "I won't forget this day. I bring you in, I extend you courtesies out of personal regard—and then you play me tricks."

". . . I had a client to think of."

"Oh, he counts more than a friend?"

"Dan, you make me feel bad."

"Oh, please don't—I make allowance."

I supposed he was lining it up to take a crack at Mignon, and on purpose held my tongue so as not to give him the chance. He waited, and then when I said nothing went on: "You're now in Red River cotton, which messes up everything that it touches—and everyone."

"Oh no," I said, "I'm not."

"You think you're not but you are."

CHAPTER 10

Mr. LANDRY GOT OUT OF THE CAB in my honor and bowed me in, taking a seat on the other side of her, so she was in the middle. Their flat was on Royal Street, which is St. Charles extended, on the other side of Canal, so I told the driver take them there, "but stop first at the St. Charles Hotel, which is where I get out." It seemed to me, considering the stakes of the game, that she could have spoken up: "*And* me—I get out there too." But what she said was: "And before you get to the hotel, you stop at Lavadeau's— *I* get out *there*." And then to her father she added: "I have to go to work." He patted her hand, then told me, speaking across her: "Mr. Cresap, I haven't thanked nearly enough for what you did—and I still have no faintest idea how you did it. Mignon has tried to tell me, but law is not her forte."

"Nor mine," I said. "A reporter was the key."

"Ah! I begin to understand."

"But I'll be only too glad to explain. Why don't you and Mrs. Fournet have dinner with me tonight, and I'll give you the fine points?"

"Daughter?"

"Why—I'd like to. Yes."

"Mr. Cresap, we'll both be honored."

"Then I'll expect you around seven."

We rode along, the sun out for a change, and I remarked on how nice it was to think of something besides shoes, which caused her suddenly to ask him: "Why *did* you buy those shoes? Didn't you know they had to make trouble?"

"Daughter, they were cheap," he told her.

"And that was the only reason?"

"At twenty-five cents a pair, a storekeeper couldn't resist. They were Army rejects, mismated on size. But by taking a gross assorted, I was able to match them up, with only seven pair left over. At thirty-six dollars, plus burlap bags to ship in, plus freight, who wouldn't have helped out those boys?"

"Why couldn't you have told the Army that?"

"They didn't ask me."

"The idea, their saying Taylor got them!"

"So happens he did, some of them."

". . . *Taylor* got some? How?"

"They walked into his camp. Not all of those boys were paroled, and some of them, with shoes on, decided they wanted to fight. So they joined Taylor. I was scared to death, I can tell you, that one of them might get captured by some Union picket up there. *My* shoes on *his* feet could have hung me."

"My, I'm glad I didn't know it!"

"All's well that ends well," I said.

"Yes," he said, sounding rather strange. "Yes."

That brought us to Lavadeau's, and I hopped out to hand her down. She kissed him, then peeped down the back of his collar. "Your neck," she told him, "looks like an old crow's wing, and what causes that is *dirt!* You bathe when you get home! You hear me? You get in the tub and *bathe!*"

"Daughter, I've been confined."

"I said, you take a brush and *scrub!*"

"I will, but don't make personal remarks!"

I took her across the street, raised my hat, and went back for the rest of the block-and-a-half ride with him. He said: "Mr. Cresap, my daughter admires you extravagantly."

"I equally admire her."

"She's a fine, upstanding girl."

It was all pretty flat, not at all what I'd pictured in the way of a wild celebration of the triumph I'd hoped for and got. Still, he was her father, and I took things as they came. When the cab stopped, I shook hands, said I looked forward to seeing him that night, and stood waving as he rolled on toward Royal. Then I crossed the street and started into the hotel. I had my hand on the door when I heard running feet; looking, I saw her racing toward me and waving. I ran to her and caught her in my arms, as she stood on the banquette panting. She said: "I couldn't have him—know I was coming here—spending the day with you—can we go somewhere and sit?"

I took her into the ladies' parlor, and we sat till she'd caught her breath. Then I took her up to the suite, and when I'd put her things away, she sank down on the sofa and said: "I ran so hard, trying to catch you before you went in, I've got a stitch in my side."

"Want me to rub it?"

"Just hold your hand there, please."

I pretended her dress was in the way, and reached my hand up under it, expecting her to resist. But she reached her hand under too, and undid the knot of the tape, to loosen her pantalette waist so my hand could slip inside. It touched soft, warm skin and soft, warm fuzz. As I pressed the stitch, she relaxed in my other arm, and pretty soon whispered: "You were so wonderful, Willie! Just like a bull! Same as a rampaging bull!"

"I'm sorry about the cussing."

"I'm not! Oh, don't worry, I know all the words— and I loved it when you told him 'you stupid son of a bitch!' It was just thrilling to hear! Willie, I never knew a bull could mean something to me, but now I do! He can be the most beautiful thing there is! The most beautiful—" She broke off and started to cry.

"What's the matter?" I asked.

"Nothing! I'm just happy, that's all!"

For quite a while she sobbed, snuggled close, and kissed, so I inhaled her, the Russian Leather, her spit, and her tears, all in one fragrant cloud. Then I asked: "Stitch any better?"

"All gone! You made it well!"

I started to move my hand, but she grabbed it and held it to her. I picked her up and carried her to the bedroom.

The rest of the day was wild, if that's what I wanted, but it was other things too—sad, intimate, holy, and just plain silly. We lay close for a while and whispered, and then she started exploring—every part of me, including especially my scar. She wanted to know how I got it, something a soldier likes to forget, but I told her: my dive for the rear when the Rebs burst out of the woods, my stumble, the Reb's lunge with his saber, the pistol-shot in my ear as one of my men got him. She listened, kissed it, then snuggled to me, patting it. Then she jumped up, slipped bare feet in her shoes, and paraded in front of the pier glass. "You think," she said, "that it's you I came here for—that's a mistake. It's this full-length mirror, so I can see if I'm getting pot-gutted. Well?"

"No," I said, "you're not."

"You better say so."

"I can only speak the truth."

"Ever notice how a girl without *inny* clothes is nothing but a thing? Just a bunch of dabs, dewlaps, and dimples shaking up and down? But lift her heels with shoes and then you got a nymph—a regular stone nymph in a garden, pouring water out of a cup."

"I never saw a girl without any clothes."

"You've been missing something."

What I'd been missing was so beautiful I had to look, even though I felt I shouldn't. And it wasn't all full, round curves, but partly the way she moved. That, she said, came "from the way they beat it into me, at the convent in Grand Coteau—they make you walk like a lady, whether you want to or not, and won't have you walking like a camel." I asked if she was Catholic, and she said no, "but the sisters will take you in, whatever you are, *if* you're worth *taking*, and they seemed to think I was. I'm Episcopalian." She was pleased that I was Episcopalian too, and asked where I went to school. I told her St. John's College, and that started her on her childhood in Alexandria—especially Hilda Schmidt, the girl who'd lived next door to her, and how they had played, chasing each other around, "before she died of the fever, up and down the cistrens, over the roof, and down through the skylights." It seemed that her father's store was a double one, half of which, with the flat above it, he used himself, and half he rented to Mr. Schmidt, who had a sugar-mill supply place. Alexandria seemed to enchant her, and suddenly she asked: "Where you taking us?"

"Tonight? You know the places. Say."

"How about Galpin's, then?"

"Galpin's is fine."

"It's just a few steps from us, Willie, and after we've finished dinner we can all three go to the flat and I'll show you some pictures I have. Of Alexandria. Then you can see what it's like."

"I'd love it."

"Incidentally: I've been working today."

"At Lavadeau's, you mean you're telling your father?"

"That's it—I'm all tuckered out, but will go home to dress and we'll come to you. And, incidentally, if I'd known what was scheduled today, at headquarters and all, I'd have put something on. Better than what I'm wearing. At least I have a *few* things left from before the war."

"I haven't complained, have I?"

"No, but I have my pride."

She stared as I talked about her dress, giving the fine points on why I loved it. Then she kicked off her shoes and came close to hear more about it. I don't think she really believed all I said about its lines, and the way it swung so soft from the swell of her bottom, but how much I'd thought about it seemed to touch her. Around five she gave me one last kiss, then got up to dress.

"I hope they hang that Burke."

We'd had quite a dinner, with cocktails, a soup called crayfish bisque, some kind of chicken with white wine, and ice cream with brandied cherries—and as we ate we talked. I told Mr. Landry of the way I'd smashed up Jenkins by making use of Olsen, and he made acute observations, comprehending at once the tactics I'd had to employ. She filled in with details on the way I "whipped—that was the thing, he *whipped!*" I mentioned in passing the twenty-five thousand dollars I must find, but didn't get much reaction. He named a banker he'd take me to, but didn't really show much interest, and I saw the reason was that—to him as well as to her—a channel out to the Gulf cut by the river itself didn't mean a great deal. Alexandria was what they lived for, so Alexandria was what we looked at as soon as dinner was over. We walked a block to their flat, which was on the second floor of a house between two saloons, a toasty-warm little place from heat coming up through a register, because, she explained, "the landlord's wife has palsy, and he must keep the fire up for her." It had walnut-and-horsehair furnishing, a potted rubber tree, and framed mottoes on the walls. While he was lighting candles she was getting her album out, and then we sat with it in front of us on the table, she turning the pages.

She had photographs, water colors, and plats, and they both seemed to take a delight in pointing everything out—the four wharves the town had, ramps up the riverbank, with railed platforms up top, "nice, well-built structures," as he put it, "not like those Teche wharfboats, all full of bugs and rats, or those Mississippi levees, with their rum holes, gambling dives, and cathouses"; the "cistrens," as they called them, just visible through the trees, "as there's no wells in Alexandria—it's all rainwater, which we run off the roofs and valve to our various cisterns, these big ones that you see, which stand on trustles so they warm in the light of the sun, and the drinking ones underground, where the water keeps fresh and cool"; the big, new hotel, a three-story brick affair, "one of the finest in the land, except just as it was getting finished the dayum war hit, and their furniture never came"; most lovingly noticed of all, the line of stores on Front Street, looking out on the river, as the bank itself had no structures on it, with of course the Landry store, near the corner down from the hotel, so it faced the lower end of Biossat's, or the upper wharf, and its twin next door, the Schmidt van, pipe and kettle house; Mrs. Landry's grave, in Pineville, which seemed to be a little town across the river. When I'd got so I thought I knew Alexandria better than I knew Annapolis, he closed the album and mused: "What I miss most, living here in New Orleans, is the cleanliness of it—but of course that's a natural thing. Alexandria's where the Southwest begins."

"Southwest's cleaner than other places?" I asked.

"Mr. Cresap, I have to say—"

"Call him Bill," she cut in.

"Bill, I have to say it is. Texas may be dry. It may be dusty and poor. A Texas ranchhouse is just six skinned poles in front, holding up the porch, and no poles at all behind, as there's nothing back there to hold up—but it's big. And it's clean."

"I'll have to go there some time."

"You could do a lot worse."

Perhaps to draw me in it again, she recalled more points about the morning, and that was when she said what she did, about hoping they'd hang Burke. And then he downright astonished me. "I certainly hope they don't," he said, almost in the tone of a prayer.

"But why?" she asked him, bewildered.

"Daughter, he's still my partner."

"You'd still call him that? After what he did—"

"For sixty thousand bucks? I certainly would."

"But Father, how can you? How—"

"Mignon, we're chained! We're articled to one another! Everything's in his name, and if he doesn't claim my cotton, once the Army seizes it, I lose everything! All he need do is nothing, and that sinks me!"

"But he turned on you! He—"

"And what am I supposed to do? Turn on myself?"

"You could kill him!"

His face darkened, and his hands, still on the table, closed into two big fists. He said: "I could, that's true. He deserves it, and I imagine I'm able. But that would get me hung, and it would not file a claim for my cotton when it gets seized. And if they do something to him, saving me the trouble—like hanging him, or holding him in jail so he can't be present up there to take receipt for the seizure, that wrecks our claim too. Yes, I'd like nothing better than to see him swing from a gallows, but not—not, *not*, NOT—to the tune of sixty thousand bucks."

"Then what are you going to do?"

"I? Nothing. It's not up to me to do."

"You're certainly talking funny. And that explains something else: why you acted so meek when you saw

him up there today. The least you could have done was
punch him, and all you did was say hello."

"That's right. Very friendly."

"To that *rat!*"

"Daughter, once again: To that *partner*."

It was a twist I hadn't thought of, and though I could
see his point, walking back to the hotel I found myself
upset. And I wasn't much surprised to see Dan there in
the lobby, apparently waiting for me, beckoning me to
come over. I sat down with him on the same sofa I'd sat on
to start things off with Olsen. When I asked "What's the
good word?" he paid no attention, but piled in at once:
"Bill, be in my office tomorrow morning eleven o'clock, to
answer questions about Burke, these things you've accused
him of. Have Mr. Landry with you, and also Mrs. Fournet."

"Well I guess I can make it—fine."

"Don't do any guessing, Bill. You make it, or wish
you had. My reason for coming tonight is to preclude a
soldiers' visit to the Landry flat tomorrow, and a trip on
foot for those two up here, under guard. This way, if it's
known you all three will be there, no order will be issued."

"I thank you, Dan. I'm really grateful."

"You needn't thank me—I'm not doing it for you.
I wouldn't mind a bit seeing you marched through the
streets. But *she* seemed like a very nice girl."

"Then she'll thank you, I'm sure."

"How'd you like to go to hell?"

"I ignore your remark. I'll have her there."

"See that you do. *And don't bring Olsen.*"

CHAPTER II

I HAD HER THERE, with her father, and promptly at eleven
o'clock we were all in the selfsame places we'd been in the
day before—Dan, Jenkins, Burke, Mignon, Dan's orderly,
and I. But in addition, Mr. Landry was there, as well as a
lieutenant colonel named Rogers, from the Judge Advocate's office, a belted guard in charge of Burke, and Pierre,
Burke's gippo, in his reefer, his sailor hat in his hand. The
lieutenant colonel was senior, so everyone waited for him
to begin, which he did after taking his time and shuffling
papers around. He was a smallish man who looked like a
lawyer, and presently he said: "All right, let's take up first
this money which William Cresap alleges to have been paid
by the prisoner Burke to Major Jenkins of this staff. Mr.
Cresap, do you still have the hundred-dollar bill which you
say was passed?"

"I do." I took it out and showed it.

"You saw this bill passed?"

"No sir, I didn't."

"Then how do you know it was passed?"

"I saw it first when Burke offered it to me in payment for services and then an hour later, when Major Jenkins paid it out to a man for a case of champagne. To have it as evidence in the Landry case, I bought it for a hundred and one dollars."

"You're sure it's the same bill?"

"I am, definitely."

"By what means of identification?"

"This jag torn in one end."

"Mr. Cresap, since neither Burke nor Major Jenkins makes any admission regarding this bill, do you have any further identification?"

"No, Colonel Rogers, I have not."

"You realize any bill could have a jag?"

"No two would be jagged the same way."

"They could be! They could be—couldn't they?"

"Not so as to set up a *reasonable* doubt."

"Mr. Cresap, a jag is no identification at all."

"Nothing is—under a coat of whitewash."

"Whitewash, did you say? What do you mean by that?"

"You heard me, and you know what I mean."

My hackles were rising as I saw the drift of his questions, and I got up from my chair, but Mr. Landry came over and pushed me back, trying to keep me quiet. Colonel Rogers started to roar about people who made "wild, reckless charges, without a scintilla of proof," but I cut in to tell him: "Talk louder, Colonel—so maybe you'll believe what you're saying!" Then she got in it, screaming at him furiously: "You think he didn't take it, this money Burke paid him? Then why weren't you here yesterday, as I was, to see the look on his face when Mr. Cresap showed him that bill? Why was it he turned white as a sheet? What was he scared of, Colonel, if it wasn't the truth catching up?"

"Daughter! Please!" said Mr. Landry.

"Are you trying to shut me up?"

But he did shut her up, by putting his hand to her mouth and pushing her back in her chair, the way he'd pushed me. Colonel Rogers walked around, his face purple, trying to get control. At last he whispered: "Bribery charge dismissed."

"My, I'm surprised," I said.

"That'll be all!" he yelled at me.

If was five minutes before he calmed down, shuffled his papers some more, and started over. Then he asked for the trial draft of the informer's note, the one pasted together from scraps, and I got it out, laying it down in front of him. He studied it, then announced: "There can be no doubt at all, in any fair person's mind, that the last informer's note and this trial draft are by one and the same hand." He was pretty solemn about it, and his tone was cold, so it suddenly dawned on me that with his brother officer whitewashed, he wouldn't be so lenient as he had been. Or in other words, Jenkins-and-Burke was one thing, Burke alone a different kettle of fish. I caught her eye, and motioned she should keep quiet. She nodded and stared at him. He went on: "The next question is: Whose hand?"

"His!" said Burke, pointing at me.

"Quiet! . . . Mr. Cresap, you pasted up these scraps?"

"I did, yes sir."

"Where did you get them, please?"

"From Burke's room at the City Hotel."

Then, as he questioned me, I told of seeing the scraps by accident, of signing on as William Crandall, of having the skeleton key made, of searching the room that night, and of returning to the St. Charles, where I pasted up my exhibit. At first I spilled it freely, being just as annoyed as she was at Mr. Landry's strange behavior in shushing things up for Burke, and feeling exactly as she did that the point had already been reached where partnership had to end. But little by little, I smelled I was heading for trouble, and that the colonel probably knew I'd had help that night, and what kind. That's where I began to fence, to protect Marie; after what I'd done to her, I felt I couldn't involve her. Maybe, as a gambling-house proprietor, she didn't have much reputation, but I had made the point that to me she was a lady. Yet the questions kept boring in, and at last the colonel said: "Mr. Cresap, here's what we're driving at: Burke's man, Pierre Legrand, who sits here, insists he never left that room, that you couldn't have made a search, as he was there all the time to stop you. Now please search your memory well, as to whether you can prove he left the room that night. Have you a witness to it?"

". . . I have to say I have not."

"The hotel clerk has informed us that William Crandall, that day, took a room for one Eloise Brisson, and that a veiled woman checked in. Is this true?"

"I prefer not to say."

"You have to say, Mr. Cresap."

"I was seeking evidence as counsel, and as such my actions were privileged. I don't have to say."

"You do, to sustain your charge."

"Then consider my charge withdrawn."

"Mr. Cresap, charges aren't debts, to be canceled at one man's caprice—they allege crimes, in this case fabrication of false information, and once made they have to be gone into. Now *your* charge, if true, which we incline to believe, can be substantiated, we think, only by this woman, who was seen by the night maid whispering to Legrand at his door, and who may, as your decoy, have lured him out of that room. It's essential we question her—but neither police, provost guard, nor city directory has any record of an Eloise Brisson. Was this a false name, Mr. Cresap?"

"On that I have nothing to say."

"You don't deny it, then?"

"I make no statement of any kind."

"What's her true name, Mr. Cresap?"

"I wouldn't say if I knew."

"Can you bring her incog, for interrogation?"

"Whether I can or not, I won't."

Mignon, by now, had become her stone nymph in a garden, or at least had turned to marble, and I dared not meet her eye as she stared unwinking at me. But who got into it now was Mr. Landry, as he interrupted to say: "Colonel, could I put in a word? In behalf of getting this straightened out?" And as the colonel didn't stop him, he went on: "No one who knows Mr. Cresap could doubt his word, and the same goes for whoever knows Frank Burke. *But,* if those scraps were found in that basket, it doesn't say Frank put 'em there! Think, sir, how many people had passkeys on that floor, and could have planted this evidence, as a way of throwing the blame on Frank for the injury done to me! Think how many people wish me ill—not to go any further with it, the ones that owe me money, right here in New Orleans! I strongly urge on you, that all this could be true that's been spoken of here today, and at the same time prove nothing at all!"

"You're defending this man here?"

"Frank Burke is my friend."

"And your godpappy, no?"

"He's my trusted partner."

Burke, who had stared in astonishment, got the point at last and put out his hand, to squeeze Mr. Landry's arm. Then she got in it: "And another thing, Colonel Rogers," she said, very sweetly: "Frank leads a decent life—he wouldn't bring some woman in, a honey off the streets, to help with some sneaky search. How could he? Keeping this man in his rooms all the time?"

"God bless you, lass."

Burke put out his hand to her, and she took it, kissing it, then patting him on the cheek. The colonel watched, then turned again to me, asking: "You still refuse to name this woman?"

"I've already told you I won't."

"You spoke of a whitewash just now?"

". . . I thought I detected one."

"Of one of our officers here?"

"Of that officer there, Major Jenkins."

"But when it comes to someone else, like the godpappy of your client, you don't mind a whitewash, do you? You're perfectly willing to withhold the information we need to proceed against him?"

"That's not the idea, Colonel."

"What is the idea, then?"

That was Mignon, who jumped up, ran over, leaned close, and screamed: *"Who was this woman?* WHO WAS SHE?"

"Daughter, that'll be all."

Mr. Landry came over, took her by the arm, and led her back to her chair. The colonel, still disregarding them, said to me: "Whitewash is whitewash."

"Could depend on what's aimed at."

"I go by what's covered up."

He then lit into me so bitterly I knew that *he* knew his case had blown up. But Dan interrupted, asking permission to speak. When the colonel nodded, he said to me very coldly: "Bill, not one word that's been said here—by you, Mr. Landry, or Mrs. Fournet—is true; but we make allowance, as I told you before, for the Red River cotton, which makes people do queer things. But if you think, by suppressing information now, you're helping Burke, Mr. Landry, and Mrs. Fournet cash their chips, you were never so wrong in your life. Because, if you cooperate, if the three of you do, we could equalize, somehow. For example, those articles we found when we searched Burke's place last night, that partnership agreement, we might void for some reason—such as fraud figuring in. That would restore Mr. Landry his titles, and might lead to a handsome profit. Now that we know the shoes were a trumped-up thing, we'd be disposed to treat him kindly. But if the three of you keep on associating yourselves with Burke, it breaks the bank for you. It so happens I'll be in charge of the trading passes next month when the invasion starts to roll, and, I promise you, this oily, slippery, crooked Irishman will not be on board the boat. That'll extinguish all titles because, don't forget: The godpappy has to be there, in person, to claim his seizure receipt. Without it he can't litigate. Do you hear what I'm telling you, Bill?"

"I hear you, so far as that goes."

"But you still refuse to cooperate?"

"I have nothing more to say.

"You persist in shielding Burke?"

"I'm not shielding anyone."

"Yes he is, he's shielding a woman!"

"Madame, hold your tongue!"

The colonel snapped it out like the crack of a whip, and she shut up for a second or two. Then to Dan she said: "You think your old headquarters boat is the only way to Alexandria? Well, there's others."

"That's right, you can walk—or swim."

"We'll get Frank there, don't worry."

"Then I wish you luck."

After ordering the guard to quarters, the colonel told Burke: "You may go." Then, except for the military, we were all clumping downstairs. In the lower hall, Mr. Landry grabbed my arm, saying: "Bill, I'm sorry, but I couldn't throw away that money. I know Frank did me a grievous wrong, but to get back at him, I'd have to—"

"It's all right, business is business."

"I should have talked against him, perhaps, but——"

"Well, I didn't; why should you?"

"Bill, I may say you surprised me. That woman—"

"Oh, the hell you say!"

I ripped it out, very bitter, and in fact was perfectly furious that not only she but he, after what I'd accomplished for them, should have the gall to object to a thing already explained by the officers themselves—even the colonel had caught the reason for my bringing a woman in. At my tone he cut it off, and started mumbling about my fee for acting as his counsel, "which I should have brought up sooner, but didn't." To me, that was just a pain in the neck, and I started for the door. Then something hit me on the chin— warm, wet, and ticklish, and I realized she had spat from where she was standing nearby. The previous day, the smell of spit from her lips had been intoxicating to me, but now it made me so sick I thought I might lose my breakfast. I ducked out onto the street, and turned the corner before I got out my handkerchief and wiped the stuff off.

CHAPTER 12

At the hotel I washed my face, then went down for something to eat. Back in the suite again, I sat down and tried to take stock. I was rocked to the heels, I knew, by what she'd meant to me and by what she'd done to me—unreasonably, I thought. But there was no doubt in my mind as to what I should do about her. It was clear I had to forget her, root her out of my heart completely, so no trace of her would be left. After a while I concluded the best way to do it was to get back to the original tune, the twenty-five thousand dollars and how I would get it. Remembering the talk about bankers we'd had the night before, I began wondering if they weren't the answer and figuring how I might meet some. Then the numbness seemed to start wearing off, but I was deluding myself—more afterclaps were due, and my troubles had hardly started. Around three, I guess, a knock came on the door, but I waited a second or two before opening, to steel myself to be tough, in case she was there, taking back what she'd said and wanting to make up.

Who was there was Marie's guard.

He didn't wait for me to speak, but whipped out his sword, shoved his foot in the door, and called out in French, all in less than a second. Then Marie appeared, in the same little gray dress, with black darts and black shawl, she'd worn that night in the other hotel. He backed me into the room to the space between the windows, and when my head banged the wall told me "Reach." I did, and then she pushed in close, waving my three twenties in front of my eyes, pulling my mouth open, stuffing them in, and pushing my chin up. They weren't new bills, so they tasted indescribably filthy. Then she started to work me over, firing the first slap so hard my ears rang. I reached for her wrist automatically, but he jabbed the steel in my stomach, telling me: "Keep 'em up! Keep 'em up against the wall!" I did, and she kept on with her slapping, the licks coming so fast I sounded like a razor being stropped. The shawl slipped off and she flung it aside. The jacket came unbuttoned and she flung it aside. Her hat slipped over one eye and she flung that aside too, causing her ringlets to twist askew and hang over her face. Real, she was ten times the Jezebel she had been, pretending, to entice Pierre from his post. And at last, free of all encumbrance, she let me have it hard, pulling off one shoe and banging my cheekbones with it.

Then, exhausted, she told him: "*Assez, assez, assez,*" and he told me put down my hands. Then to me she said: "Wash you! Then hear me, what I shall say!" I started for the bath, but kept on to the bedroom, first spitting the bills out on the floor, then digging into my bag and coming up with my Moore & Pond. I went back holding it on them, and he dropped the sword cane, both parts at the same time. I put my foot on the blade, then lifted its hilt to snap it, and kicked stump, point, and scabbard against the sofa. When I looked up she was reaching for her purse. I remembered the derringer in it and kicked over the table she'd put it on. Then I picked it up and dropped it in my pocket. I said: "All right, now suppose you *git*. The two of you, march!"

She said: "I must dress me, please."

"Then *you* git," I told him. "Git and keep on gitting. If I open that door and you're there, it's the last place you'll be on this earth. Did you hear me?"

"I did."

"You did, *what?*"

"I did, sir."

"That's better. *Now—*"

But he was legging it for the stairs as I closed the door. When I turned, for the second time that day I felt a wet tickle on my chin, and from the look on her face knew blood must be running down. I took out my handkerchief, but she grabbed it and started to wipe. I knocked her down. Then I went to the bath to wash up, first rinsing out the horrible taste of the money. My face, when I looked in the glass, was so cut, bruised, and puffed that I hardly knew myself. But when I laved it with the witch hazel I used after shaving, it was better—not much, but a little.

When I went back to the sitting room, she was still there on the floor, a tiny heap of blonde ringlets, tousled froufrou, bare arms, and pretty, silk-stockinged legs. But one look and my insides collapsed, as the reaction set in, not only from this scene now, but the preceding ones too, in

Dan's office and in the headquarters hall. I'd worked up quite a sulk, but the bottom fell out of it, and I knelt beside her, picking her up, in a clumsy, laborious way staggering to my feet, and making it to the sofa. I sat down, snuggling her in my lap and having a look at her chin. It was beginning to swell, and of course that made me feel wonderful. I said: "I'm sorry, Marie."

"I too am sorry, Guillaume. I excuse me."

"I had it coming, if you mean the beating you gave me. The only surprising thing was I didn't get it sooner—that you took so long finding me."

"I found you the same night. It was not *difficile*, please believe me, for me to locate some—"

She hesitated, and I said: "Yank with a game leg?"

". . . *Ingénieur* with hair of gold."

"That's a very nice way to put it."

"I came yesterday morning—you were not here. I came last night—you were not here. I came for third time today——"

"And I kept the appointment."

"I have said, *I excuse me, please.*"

That seemed to mean she apologized, which was about all I could really ask. She put her feet up, then stretched her legs out full length, so practically everything showed. Then: "Guillaume, always it is the same, you are *gentil*, I *gamine*. Today, I confess it, I tell the truth: I tried to demean you, to make of you some creature—it was my reason to beat. To see the *élégance brisée. Et après?* You compel Emil to say *Sir*. There, in one word, was my *grand seigneur*. And what have we here, *aussi?*"

"All right, what?"

"*La créature, moi, regardez.*"

"Oh I wouldn't quite say that."

"*Ah oui*, I am nothing."

"Stop being silly with this kind of talk."

"*Petit*, I am *demi-mondaine!*"

Then suddenly in a torrent of tears she was kissing my face, every welt and bruise that she'd put there, winding up with my mouth, I kissing back and meaning it. She kept saying: "You make me feel as *grande dame*—as what I wanted to feel and *could* not." I kept whispering she *was* a *grande dame*, and should stop talking this way. She listened, and soon the weeping began to slack off, so it was just comfortable little sobs as she relaxed in my arms. Then she was loosening her clothes, and not objecting much when I began taking them off.

Pretty soon she was in pantalettes, stockings, pink garters, shoes, and not much else, except for a thin gauzy sling for her attachments above. I patted her, soothed her, and she purred almost like a kitten. Then, after a long time, she asked: "Guillaume, why did you not say? You did what you did for Mignon?"

". . . Mignon? You know her?"

"Mignon Fournet? But of course!"

"I hadn't realized."

"Not well, but—agreeably. Fournet I knew—too well. When he has lost everything in the war, he comes to me— and loses it *encore*. To him I have returned—all, all that he loses to me, at roulette, at *vingt-et-un*. I owe her nothing, and—"

"She means nothing to you?"

"*Ah oui, rien, rien!*"

"Then that's just what she means to me."

"Then why did she quarrel with you today?"

"So you heard about that too?"

"It is my business, as *joueuse*, to hear all, but I understand not why her father should reconcile with Burke."

The ins and outs of that had to be explained, and she listened closely. "The answer was tin," I said. "He made that plain last night—no matter *what* Burke had done to him, he couldn't afford to pass up sixty thousand dollars. Well, maybe she quarreled with me so Burke wouldn't quarrel with her and spoil her father's game."

"To me, this is not really clear."

"To me either—*but she means nothing to me.*"

"Why did you leave me, then?"

"If I hadn't, you know what would have happened?"

"We said dinner, *non?* At Antoine's? And—"

"Marie, I'd have spent the night in your bed."

"*... Alors? Alors?*"

"I had work to do that night."

I told of the paste-up job, the letter, the two copies, the arrangements I made with Olsen. I said: "It had to be done that night, *everything*—or I couldn't take Burke by surprise."

"But this you could have explained."

"I was afraid."

"Of me, Guillaume?"

"Of myself."

"Why did you not explain me? By—letter?"

"To be honest, I was ashamed to."

"*Did you go to her that night?*"

"I swear to you, Marie, I did not."

She thought that over, lying there in my arms, with the look in her eye of a stud-poker player who knows how to

read your mind, then asked: "Have you spoken to her of
les pieux?"

"Yes—last night, after dinner, to her and her father
both. They didn't take much interest. I have to say, if it
had been a Red River job, I think it might have been different—their reaction, I mean."

"Fournet made this complaint."

She went into some detail about this boy from the
Teche who had started a law practice here, married Mignon,
and then found out that all she could get her mind on was
stuff about Red River. Then suddenly: "She is *folle*."

"Well? Aren't we all, more or less?"

"She makes combinations—which prevail not."

"I've had a few flukes myself, Marie."

"She put Fournet in *coton de la guerre*."

"And—she put her father in, so she says."

"For Fournet it was a catastrophe."

"For Mr. Landry it may turn out better."

"He is in—not yet out, *petit*."

"At least he's out of jail."

"Thanks to you, not to her, *pourtant*."

There may have been more about Fournet, his moral
collapse after the cotton broke him, his gambling, his enlist-
ment, and death; it seems to me there must have been because I wound up knowing a great deal about him, but
then, very solemnly, she asked me: "Guillaume, do you love
her?"

"I swear to you I don't."

"Your *demi-mondaine* could love."

"I know no *demi-mondaine*." And then, pretty solemn
myself, I added: "If a certain *grande dame* could love, then
an engineer could, too."

"She could venture twenty-five thousand bucks."

She called it *bocks*, very funny, and my heart gave quite a twitch. Then the full force of what she meant to say hit me, and my heart gave a real, shaking thump, which caused a lump in my throat. I said: "For that I'd owe you some kisses."

"And—anything else, *petit?*"

"Are you talking about marriage, Marie?"

"To *demi-mondaine* it means much."

"Consider yourself proposed to."

"I am *Épiscopalienne*, as you are."

"And not Jewish, as I thought you said."

Recollection of that made her laugh, and suddenly she kissed me and jumped up. "But, kisses first, *petit!* May I look at my chin in your bath?"

"Help yourself, it's right in there."

She went in and a minute or two later came out without a stitch on, holding her shoes and things in one hand. Blowing a kiss at me, she went on into the bedroom. I started gathering the rest of her clothes; for all I knew someone might come, and at least I'd have the sitting room clear of telltale duds. And then suddenly there she was, still with no clothes on but walking like an old woman, and slumped down in a chair. "What's the matter?" I asked. "Marie, what in the name of God is it?"

". . . Guillaume, you lied to me."

"I didn't, I swear!"

In my heart I hadn't been lying, at least to be conscious of it, as I'd made tremendous decisions, and in the light of them what had happened the previous day, which was all I'd really omitted, hadn't seemed important. Or, if it had been important once, it wasn't any more. So I went right on talking, saying the same things over, and she kept sitting there, paying not the slightest attention. Then she got her things from the bedroom, came back, and put them on. Pretty soon she was all dressed, pulling her veil in place. Then, very dignified, she said: "Guillaume, I was happy to go to your bed, and thought only of the kisses I meant to give. Then her scent came as a *coup*. I mistake not the Russian Leather, it is as her *marque de fabrique*, and your bed is full of it. It has made me *malade*, for example. I suppose I understand why you lied—but how can one speak of the scent? It is too much, I must go."

"She quarreled with me over you."

"And—you protected me, as I know."

"They wanted your name. I refused it."

"There spoke my *chevalier*." And then, very quietly: "To him I must keep my word. You shall have the twenty-five thousand—"

"Will you forget the goddam tin?"

"My banker shall call. And now, *adieu*."

CHAPTER 13

So HE DID, the next morning, a Mr. Dumont, connected with the Louisiana Bank, but I wouldn't let him in and talked through a crack in the door, telling him come some other time. That was because by then my face looked like liver—purple, blue, black, and yellow all at the same time—as well as being swollen twice its size. So I wasn't seeing anyone, even waiters bringing my food. I had them leave it outside the door, then pulled the tray in after they'd gone. So I put Mr. Dumont off, and wasn't any too sure, I admit, I wanted to see him at all. But at night I'd go downstairs, and without going through the lobby, slip out the back way, up Gravier to Carondelet, over to Canal, then down to Royal and on to the Landry flat. I'd skulk around outside, trying to see Mignon, torturing myself by spying on what she was doing. I found out all right. One night, as I stood in the shadows across the street, a cab drove up, and out of it popped Burke. Then he handed her down, and told the cabman to wait. She was laughing gaily, and the two of them went in. How long he stayed I don't know, whether alone with her I don't know. I slunk back to the hotel and in by Gravier again, like some cur hit with a whip. But next night I was out there as usual, seeing nothing.

In four or five days, call it a week after Mardi Gras, here came Marie, tapping on the door, saying she had to see me. I let her in, and she asked if Emil could "excuse him," as "he feels very bad, and wants to be friends with you." I said I'd accept his apologies through her, and she called in French through the crack.

"*Bon*," she said. "He is gone—and feels better now." She held my face to the light, and made little whistling noises. But when she sat down I asked her: "Yes? What do you want, Marie, that you 'had' to see me?"

"You might say you are glad I am here."

"I might—if I was sure I am."

"La-la. La-la."

Actually I wasn't, as those nights had warned me my success in the root-out operation had fallen short of what I'd assumed it was, and that all my bitter decisions weren't so final as they might have been. Still, there was no doubt in my mind that they ought to be final at any rate, so I gave her a little pat. That wasn't difficult; she looked most fetching in a little blue silk dress, red straw hat, red shoes, red gloves, and red shawl, obviously put on to please me. I said: "All right, I'm glad."

"Guillaume, I have spent some dark nights."

"With me, it's been just the opposite—the bright days are what I minded, the way they lit up my face. By night I looked better."

She went to a wall mirror, touched her chin with one finger. It had a black-and-blue spot on it where my fist had clipped her, though a dab of rice powder hid it. She said: "I too have a face, but at night one communes with the heart."

"If I bruised that I didn't mean to."

". . . *Donc*, you have not seen her."

"Oh? You've been keeping track?"

"Keeping track, Guillaume, is easy for me in my business—I send Emil, he speaks with some night maid, he pays a bock, he learns what I wish to know. . . . She sees Burke —much, every night."

"It's a free country, Marie."

"Perhaps you have not lied."

"Let's not start that up again. I lied."

". . . *Alors, alors.* You lied."

"But, my reasons were not unfriendly—to you, I'm talking about—and if you still feel friendly to me, then——"

I went over and lifted her face to kiss it, having by that time arrived once more in my mind at the inescapable conclusion that she meant salvation to me. But she pulled away abruptly, and I backed off, sitting down on the sofa. I said: "I'm sorry, Marie—I keep forgetting this face, and how unappetizing it must be."

She took off her hat, shawl, and gloves, and tossed them on the table. Then she came over, knelt on the sofa beside me, took my face in both hands, and covered it with soft, quick kisses. She said: "The face *could* not unappetize me! I l-l-loave your face."

"Red-white-and-blue and all? And yellow?"

"And green."

She kissed a spot under one eye.

"Hold still!" I said. "*I* want some kisses, *too!*"

"*Non, non, non!*" she whispered, holding me off at arm's length. "Your kisses, *petit*, must wait. They must! It devolves!"

"Devolves? On what?"

"Many things—my heart, for example. And one must know—if one has business partner—in which case *les affaires* must prevail—or if one has something more—in which case—"

"An affair might be in order?"

"*Petit*, it cannot be!"

"My mistake, it was just an idea."

"After these dark nights I have had—"

"It devolves that we know where we're at?"

"It is what brings me today, *petit*."

"All right, but how?"

". . . You received some invitation to the *bal?*"

"*Bal?* What ball?"

"That the General gives next week?"

"Oh—this Washington's Birthday thing? To commemorate the election he's holding that day? Yes—some kind of bid came in. Apparently I got put on the list by a friend before he decided my name was mud. It's around here some place. Why?"

"*Alors.* You ask me why?"

"You'd like to go? Is that it?"

"If you are ashamed of some *demi-mondaine*——" She got up, her face twisting, and started pulling on her gloves.

"*Will you stop talking like that?*"

I reached out, grabbed her arm and yanked it, pulling her back to her place on the sofa. I said: "How can you say such a thing?"

"You hesitate, *pourtant?*"

"I certainly do—in the first place, I don't dance very well, and in the second place, I don't get the connection—what it proves, that's all."

"It is not that someone may turn me away?"

"How, turn you away?"

"From the door?"

"If so, he won't live until dawn."

Suddenly she folded me in her arms, pressed her mouth to mine, whispered: "One little kiss you may have! . . . For this, one little kiss I must have!"

"Is that how we go about proving it? With pistols for two? In—where's the dueling ground here?"

"No, *petit*, I forbid! You might hang, and this would be too much. But I love this spirit, that might kill someone for me."

"All right, but get to the point."

"She will be there, *petit*."

". . . Who?"

"Mignon. With Burke."

"I see. I see. I see."

"Already ice fills your heart, *petit?*"

"No—I see what you mean, that's all."

"You may renege, if you wish."

"Not at all. I think we'd better go."

"This confrontation shall tell me."

"To say nothing of me."

So we did go. It was held in the French Opera House, a big theater in the Quarter, and everyone was there, not only the Union officers and their ladies, but New Orleans society too, especially the ones cozening up to the North—of whom there were more than you'd think. I went in full evening regalia, which Marie rented for me at a costume place on Poydras, around the corner from Lavadeau's: clawhammer suit, puff-bosom shirt, cape, and silk hat. But from the way she was got up, no question could arise that she would be turned away. She looked like the Duchess of El Dorado in a white ermine cloak, scarlet satin gown, cut so low she was bare halfway to her navel, gold shoes, gold purse, and gold fillet on her hair. In addition, she wore diamonds wherever you looked—at her neck in a pendant, on her wrists in bracelets, and on her fingers with various rings. She glittered like an igloo in the midnight sun; I was proud of her in a way, yet I wanted to laugh. She caught my look, and instead of being angry, started to laugh too. "*Alors?*" she said, as our cab pulled away from the gambling house. "Am I *grande dame* now?"

"So grand I feel like a pigmy."

"I hope I am creditable."

What was causing my stomach to twitch wasn't concern at her being thrown out, but who would be waiting for us once we were let in. For some time, though I searched the place with my eye, taking in flags, bunting, smilax, and the band up on the stage, I didn't see her. We got into the receiving line and I had a bad moment when we came to Dan Dorsey, who was presenting the guests. He was in dress uniform, with epaulets, braid, sword, knots, and white gloves, and when he saw Marie his face turned to stone. But he didn't hesitate, and sang out loud and clear: "Mr. William Cresap, Miss Marie Tremaine!" The General's lady, I imagine, had never heard of Marie; she smiled graciously and offered her hand. Marie, after dropping a graceful, comic little continental curtsey, took it. I took it. We shook hands with the General, passed on, and that was that. "*Voilà*, I am in!" said Marie, pleased as a child.

"The honor is theirs," I assured her.

We stood around and I kept on looking. The band struck up the Grand March, and after we had sashayed around there came a long intermission while programs were filled out. All kinds of people wanted to dance with Marie, but she kept saying: "Lancers and quadrilles only—I care not for polkas and galops." That touched me, as it really meant she knew I couldn't dance round dances, and was willing to pretend she preferred to sit them out. So I marked them all X on her card, but accepted quite a few couples to make up sets for the square dances. And then, in the middle of it, I saw by the change in her face, from little French dancing partner to cold, calculating gambler, that Mignon had entered the room. I turned, and she was just crossing to the receiving stand on Burke's arm, Mr. Landry on the other side. She had on a black dress, whether left over from her palmier days or lent her by Lavadeau's I didn't know and don't know now. Over her shoulders was a mantilla, with a pattern of small gold spangles, and I remember a twinge of relief that her big, beautiful bulges wouldn't be seen by everyone. When the three of them had been received, Mr. Landry went skipping off and then reappeared in a box near the stage, where Mignon and Burke went to keep him company, though they stayed out on the floor. "*Alors*," whispered Marie. "I must speak; it devolves, let us go."

Her grip on my arm meant business, and for my part I steeled myself, feeling I might just as well get it over with. "Mignon," called Marie brightly as she rustled over the floor, "*bon jour, bon chance, salut.*"

"Marie," said Mignon, "*comment ça va?*"

She said it very coldly, staring down at Marie's bare shoulders, and then Burke took notice of us. "Why," he said, "if it isn't the sneak thieves themselves—the girl who enticed me gippo to her bed, the sly minx—and the boy—"

"Burke," I said, "retract."

His eyes moved around in their rheum as he took in my grip on the stick, and he said: "I may have spoken in haste."

"Apologize."

"I regret me impulsive words."

"Then fine. Hereafter speak when you're spoken to."

Marie's hand on my arms gave a quick, grateful squeeze, and then she went on: "Mignon, I have business with you, we have an *affaire*—but first may I present my fiancé, M'sieu Guillaume Cresap?"

Mignon flinched as though hit with a whip, and started to answer in French. Then she remembered and said: "I congratulate you, truly. I didn't know you were engaged."

"I didn't either," I said, sounding silly.

Now if, on that, Mignon had burst out laughing and said: "Willie, let's be going," my story would be over. And if Marie had slapped me and left me, it would be over, too. But neither of them did, the two of them standing there, Mignon as though turned to marble, Marie as though turned to flame. It was Marie who said: "*Alors?* I excuse me, then. One may be mistaken, it seems."

"Oh, I wouldn't say that," I told her.

"What would you say? *Jouez*, if you please?"

". . . Count me in. My chip's on the table."

"I congratulate me."

There was quite a long pause, with nobody saying anything, especially Burke. Then Mignon said: "And now may I present *my* fiancé, Mr. Frank Burke."

"*Enchantée*," said Marie

Burke bowed. I tried to say something and couldn't. Mignon went on: "Marie, what business have you with me? What affair can we possibly have?"

"*Ah bon*, you shall see."

She dug in the little gold purse and came up with pieces of paper that had been folded, then rolled. She stretched them like shavings off a board, held them up to Mignon, and said: "See! Here I have some *billets*, signed by Raoul Fournet!"

"Signed by—*whom?*" whispered Mignon.

"Raoul, your husband, who died."

"Let me see those notes!"

"Certainly—I have returned the money Raoul lost to me, but these *billets* I forgot. Here are two for four hundred, one for two hundred, one for six hundred—four in all, for total of sixteen hundred dollars. But, did you not know about them?"

"No, I knew nothing at all."

"I am distressed if you are upset."

". . . File your claim is all I can tell you, Marie. The estate's not settled yet—there's quite a lot owing, beside this."

"But a gambling debt claims not."

"Then what do you want of me?"

"Nothing. I thought you might like to have."

"In return for what, Marie?"

"*Alors*—you dance in my lancers, perhaps?"

"What lancers?"

"Here. Now. Tonight."

"Takes more than two for a lancers."

"*Oui*—you, I, your fiancé, my fiancé, friends."

After a long time Mignon said: "I accept."

Marie tore the notes in half and handed them over, and five minutes later we were all marching the lancers, Mignon like a ghost in the graceful way she moved, Marie more like a doll in that comic way *she* moved, as though spinning around on a music box. But there was no doubt in anyone's mind as to who had bowed the head to whom.

At supper, Mr. Dumont joined us, a mousy little man with gray hair—the first time I'd actually seen him, though we had talked through my door. He gave a report on the *hypothèques*, which I took to mean mortgages, that Marie was going to assume to raise my twenty-five thousand dollars. They involved considerable talk, not only with him but also with other men who dropped by, most of it in French, with Marie jabbering it pretty coldly. But in the middle of it, Mr. Dumont whispered to me: "You're getting a wonderful partner, Mr. Cresap. This woman can see a dollar farther and grab it quicker than anyone I know. Count yourself lucky, sir." When the music started again she decided she wanted to leave; going home in the cab she told me: "M'sieu Dumont accepts you, Guillaume. He thinks you *homme de bien*, and *ingénieur versé*."

"He said nice things about you."

"Were you pleased with our evening, *petit?*"

"I was. Are you asking me in?"

"... *Are* we *fiancé?*"

"Of course! What makes you think we're not?"

"The *mot* you said, to her."

"That was a joke! You caught me by surprise!"

"On this subject one makes no joke."

"Then—I take it back. *Are you asking me in?*"

She hesitated, snuggled close, and kissed me once or twice. Then: "I am tempted, this I confess, *ah oui*, so much. And yet—I trust you not, *petit*. Perhaps you still love her." And then, as I protested that this was ridiculous, that all that was finished, over, and done with, she kissed me again and thought it over again. But once more she said: "*Non!* Guillaume, we are partners in business—this I promise, the money shall be advanced. We shall also be married, I hope, and at last you can make a *grande dame* of me. If *then* there shall be more—*bon!* I shall give you children of me, *jolis* babies with hair of gold, as ours. But this must wait—until of you I am sure."

"I could make you sure tonight."

"Later, later, *petit*."

CHAPTER 14

So I HAD EVERYTHING in my grasp, the capital I needed, the construction firm I wanted, a woman I thought the world of, and the days began sliding by. Dumont forged ahead, though the *hypothèques* took time: appraisals had to be made, titles searched, and easements squared of the properties she was plastering. They were five houses on Rampart Street that she didn't want to sell but was willing to borrow on. And what hung things up worst was the easements—old grants, to places up the street, of carriage-entrance rights, something the bank didn't like. It was just a question of buying them up, but people are pretty grasping, and the haggle went on for some time. In between, she and I went around—to restaurants, to church, to the theater, and I met quite a few of her friends. What pleased her most, I think, was the way they treated her at Mrs. Beauregard's funeral, which was held one day in the rain. It was a damned impressive thing, and pathetic too because Beauregard wasn't there—hadn't even heard of the death, being off in the field commanding Reb armies in Virginia. We rode in a cab, but most of the people marched, a slow, sad procession of thousands trudging along, their heads bowed in the downpour. But at the foot of Canal Street, we stood around with the rest, while the body was carried on board the steamer to be taken upriver for burial. Many people spoke, and she whispered to me: "So you see? Perhaps I have friends."

"Who ever thought you didn't?"

"*Alors*, SHE was *grande dame*."

Later the same day, we went to the inauguration of a man named Hahn as governor, the one elected on Washington's Birthday. It was indeed quite a thing, with six thousand children singing the "Anvil Chorus" from *Il Trovatore*, one hundred anvils banging, and fifty cannon shooting, all in time to the music. But in the middle of it she said: "Shall we go, *petit?* I find it *sottise, non?*" So we drove to Christ Church to set the date of our wedding and make the various arrangements. She insisted on Dr. Bacon, the church's regular rector, and would have none of the other one—the one the Union had named, nobody knew why. We discussed several dates, and decided on March 29, the Tuesday after Easter. She seemed pleased, and I took her home. By that time, though I wasn't asked upstairs, she would bring me into the parlor, close the door, and forget herself a little. She brought me in there this day, but waiting for her was a man, an article named Murdock, with a blue chin, fat stomach, and New England way of talking. I was startled to learn he was bidding on the establishment, getting ready to buy her out. She quoted a hundred thousand dollars without batting an eye; he said seventy-five thousand with kind of a rasp on his voice. She said, very ugly: "*Allez, allez, out*—please do not waste of my time!"

"All right," he said, "eighty."

"Will you please go—*now!*"

He went, growling, and she said, very sweetly: "He will be back, I think." And then: "Does it please you, *petit*, that I shall be *joueuse* no more?"

"I like you the way you are."

"*Merci*, but—you would prefer *femme sérieuse?*"

"If you insist on asking, I would."

"*Alors*, you shall have."

So it all got better and better, the only trouble being I spent hours in cabs watching Lavadeau's, and at night, going back to the hotel, always went by way of Royal so I could see Mignon's windows. I saw her a number of times—occasionally by night coming home with Burke, more often by day going to work. Each time my heart would strangle me, the worst being when she'd have on that dress, the little black one I loved, which was getting so bedraggled now it made me want to cry. I would go back to the hotel then, walk around, beat on the wall with my fists, and curse. I'd tell myself cut it off, stop an insane game of self-torture, act as though I were bright. It would seem as though I would, that after a session like that I could return to my senses. And then the same night I'd be there, out in the dark again, staring as though demented, seeing what I could see.

And then one night I saw nothing: her windows were dark. The next night and the night after it was the same, and by day I didn't see her go to Lavadeau's. By then, it was coming on for the middle of March and all traffic had

disappeared from the river, the boats having been com-
mandeered to haul the invasion. It was the main topic of
talk in the bars all over town, and in fact had already
started, rumor had it, the Teche units having moved. If the
dark windows meant she had moved too with her father
and Burke for Alexandria, to be there for the cotton seizure,
it was a blow, of course, but a kind of relief too, because it
brought things to a head, affording the break I needed to
put her out of my mind and get on with my life. And that,
I think, is how it might have turned out if I hadn't run into
Lavadeau. Until then, though we'd nodded a few times,
he'd paid no attention to me, and I had no reason to think
he concerned himself about me. But one day on Gravier
Street, as I was taking a walk, here he came carrying a box,
and stopped as soon as he saw me. "Mr. Cresap," he said,
not even bothering to say hello, "I don't know if I'm speaking to you or not. How could you let her do that?"

"Let who do what?" I asked him.

"Mignon—go to Alexandria with Burke?"

". . . Then she went, with *him?*"

"Oh, Papa went too—and that ape Pierre. They all
went, Thursday morning, by ferry to Algiers, with two
wagons to load on the cars for Brashear, and then on the
steamer for Franklin, and then to drive the rest of the way.
But Burke's head man, and she's riding *his* wagon with *him.*
Mr. Cresap, why did you let her?"

"Who says I could have stopped her?"

"I do! She told me so!"

He caught my lapels then, and began to pour it out—
about how she had come into the shop last week, and wept
and wailed and made a show of herself; about how she
hated Burke and didn't want to go. She was doing it for

her father, the stake he has in cotton, but even for him wouldn't have gone if I had told her not to.

"She said that? To you, Mr. Lavadeau?"

"I swear she did, Mr. Cresap!"

"Did she say how she spit on me?"

"Oh, that—she knows now she did wrong, knows everything about why you did what you did; she made a mistake, she sees, and would be willing to start over, if only you'd come in to say you'd be willing too. If only she could be sure this other woman doesn't mean anything to you. If——"

"Why couldn't she come to *me?*"

"Sir, she did."

"I'm sorry. She didn't."

But he smiled, and told how he'd brought her to me that very same afternoon, upstairs to my St. Charles suite: "She had her hand raised to knock, and then wouldn't."

"Why not, for instance?"

"For fear of who might be there."

Up until then he'd been bitter, but now, having blown off steam, calmed down and stood there mumbling in French to himself. Then, to me, very friendly: "Well, it's too late now."

He left me, and kept on down Gravier to St. Charles and the shop. I kept on up Gravier to Carondelet, but not to resume my walk. I turned the corner, and stumped along as fast as I could, to headquarters.

"Dan, can I come in?"

"All right, but don't abuse my welcome."

"What welcome?"

I stood in front of his table, took off my hat, held it

in my hand, and tried to think how to begin. He burst out:
"Goddam it, quit bowing and scraping."

"Just trying to show my respect."

"I hate cringing. Sit down!"

He jumped up and grabbed a chair, shoving me down into it as though I were the ram in a bilge pump. I thanked him, then asked: "Dan, how have you been?"

"Rotten."

"Why don't you ask me how *I've* been?"

"I know how you've been. You've been fine."

"Well—that would seem to cover that."

"What do you want, Bill?"

". . . Dan, has your headquarters boat left?"

"Left? For where?"

"The invasion. You said there'd be one."

"It's not even chartered yet."

"Oh. I heard the movement had started, and——"

"It *has* started—but *we* haven't, not this headquarters, *yet*. We've been electing a governor. And holding an inauguration. And a ball. Couple of balls. All kinds of various things, more important than taking the field. Why?"

"I want to be taken on board."

"In what capacity?"

"As—trader. In cotton."

"*You?* Are going to buy cotton, Bill?"

"That's the idea, Dan. I haven't told you all about what brought me to town." I then sketched it out quick, the plan I'd made with Sandy and my need for twenty-five thousand dollars. I went on: "From all that I hear around, the quickest way to get money is to join this Red River thing—seems to be like picking the stuff off trees. *If* you can get on this boat."

"And *if* you tell me no lies."

"But—what lies have I been telling?"

"That you're taking this trip to make money."

"Well, what other reason could I have?"

"That girl. *She* left for Red River last week."

"But listen: I need twenty-five thousand dollars."

"I know you do, Bill—I know all about it."

"Then where does the lie come in?"

"Bill, ever hear of a man named Dumont?"

". . . The banker? I know him, yes."

"He was in, asking about you—said Miss Tremaine, the lady you brought to the ball, was fixing to marry you, then sell her business out and back you in another with the money you needed. He was for it, if you were an honest man—but if you already have the twenty-five thousand promised it proves you're lying, doesn't it?"

"What did you say about me?"

"Nice stuff—he went away quite happy."

"Could be I'd rather make that tin myself."

"And could be you'd rather have Mrs. Fournet."

But I clung to my story, and when he interrupted to know how I could make *any* tin, knowing nothing about cotton at all, I said: "What's to know, Dan? I go on your boat as a trader, I pile off at Alexandria along with the other traders, I buy stock off a Reb, which I still have money to do, I write up my receipt, listing bales by mark, number, and weight, I present it to the Q.M. officer making the seizure for him to sign. The rest is up to the lawyers. Is any of that beyond my comprehension?"

"Bill, I've told you that cotton is hooded."

"Hoodooed? This is not Hallowe'en."

"I'm not talking about Hallowe'en, or anything superstitious. All right, call it attaindered. But I'm telling you, it'll ruin whoever touches it, including you, including Burke, including Landry, including Mrs. Fournet—who's a damned pretty girl mixed up in a damned ugly business. Bill, we're trying—the Union is trying, this Army is trying —to *buy* a piece of this war to pay for our invasion by taking traders along, by letting them put out tin for the cotton the Rebs have in storage. I'm telling you, it can't be done! There's one piece of land that's never yet been up for sale, and that's the half-acre you need to plant a flagpole on. *That* you have to *take!* It's a people's maidenhead—it won't give in by itself, and its price is blood. It's what we're forgetting, but we'll pay the price, *that* price, or I'm badly mistaken. Oh, our motives are good—why the hell wouldn't they be, what motive's not better than war? The idea, Washington thinks, is to kill three birds with one stone: Block the Reb government from shipping the cotton abroad and buying guns with it, give some individual Rebs a lick at the sugar pot and win them back to their allegiance, get the Northern mills some stock to make shirts with for our soldiers. All right, but the only time *I* ever let go at three birds on a limb, I broke the dining-room window, cut my grandfather's head, and landed a rock in my mother's soup. But this will be worse: it's treason. Why? It takes two to make a sale, and in a war that means dealing with the enemy. The Reb army, if they let that cotton lay, if they fail to burn it when they evacuate Alexandria, have already heard the word as it's been passed up the line. And we, if we pass the wink to the owners, those Rebs licking up sugar as we make the confiscation—we're dealing with the enemy too. But, you say, not much—just a little bit. But I say, remember that maidenhead: there's no such thing as one that's been slightly took. And there's going to be trouble, I promise you. . . . Do you understand now why I say that cotton is hooded? Do I have to say more?"

"I thought you were my friend, Dan."

"I'm talking *as* your friend."

"You don't sound much like it."

"I'll prove it. My orders are to pass you."

"Pass me? You mean to go on that boat?"

"Yes, that's what I mean."

"Well, why don't you?"

"Bill, do you know what impressed Mr. Dumont? Not your Annapolis life—which I didn't know too much about, if I have to tell you the truth. But what you did right here, *that* brought him out of his chair."

"For Landry, are you talking about?"

"That's right—and it impressed us, too."

"Who is *us?*"

"This whole headquarters. They hated it, of course, but they respected you for it. And they feared you, as the one man who could and unfortunately might, blow this whole ship out of water. So the word came to me, pass this man in if he wants."

"Well? If I'm supposed to be rewarded——"

"I didn't say *rewarded.*"

"Well what's the point of it, then?"

"As a way of shutting you up."

I saw at last what he was driving at, and some time went by without either of us speaking. Then he said: "Bill, I've hacked at you, and—fact of the matter—you made me sore. Just the same, I knew an honest man was in town. Now, though, if you make a grab for that cotton, I have to let you on the boat—but I won't feel the same. *Bill, don't make me change!*"

After a long time I said: "I want on."

"So be it."

I took Marie everywhere—to dinner, to church the following Sunday, to drive in the park with the smell of spring in the air. I helped address the wedding announcements, as soon as they came from the engraver. When my pass for the boat came to the hotel one day, I told myself it meant nothing, that I had no intention of using it, that I'd just been blowing off steam. But the following Monday night we went to see *Richard III* at the St. Charles Theatre. The actor was John Wilkes Booth. He's from Maryland too, and maybe he's kind to dogs, and drops coins in the blind man's cup. But in that play he has death in his eyes, and watching him I knew I meant to go, and knew what I meant to do. I had death in my heart—that was the real answer. Whose death I didn't yet know, but the following day, March 22, 1864, for the second time I ran out on a woman who loved me.

CHAPTER 15

ALEXANDRIA WAS JUST LIKE THE PICTURES except for the rain drizzling down, the invasion fleet of steamers tied up at the bank, and the hoodoo on top of the courthouse—which I hadn't believed in before, but now was beginning to, on account of something that happened on the boat coming up. We'd left from the foot of Canal Street, twelve noon two days before, on a sidewheeler called the *Black Hawk*. We carried on the boiler deck General, staff, headquarters noncoms, and headquarters orderlies; on the main deck horses, Louisiana volunteers, newspapermen, and traders; wherever they could fit waiters, hostlers, and hangers-on. It was kind of a tight squeeze, but I made out all right since I'd brought what the trip called for. After kissing Marie good night with the Judas taste on my mouth, I'd spent the small hours packing, and divided my stuff in two bags. One I checked with the hotel, the other I filled with field stuff, including sandwiches I had the hotel put up and my gun. I wore my corduroys, and with the blankets I'd bought for the sea voyage plus a canteen at my belt I figured to do all right, and did.

I bunked in, or wedged in, with the traders, aft of the shaft, in the passage leading back to the fantail. They were a strange bunch, half of them sharpshooter businessmen, the rest politicians, all full of windy guff, like the pair holding Lincoln passes, those two slips of paper that muxed everything up, causing headquarters, as it did, to accept them as a tip-off of what Washington really wanted—unlimited trade in cotton as a matter of public policy. Some had brought bagging, rope, and gear on board the boat, and piled it up so there was hardly room to step; they were so hungry for cotton they expected to bale the loose stuff on plantations after the regular stock in storage had all been bought up. But nobody made complaint, and we all shook down very friendly, standing around in the afternoon, pitching banana skins in the wake, watching the swamps go by, or crossing to the other side of the engine room to visit the newspapermen. But as dark was settling down and the crew was lighting lamps, Dan showed up to ask me how things were going. By then, bottles were being passed and jokes were being cracked, so he took a look and beckoned me forward. We ducked under the shaft and went up into the bow, where the horses were, and the hostlers had rigged a tarp to shield them from the breeze. We stood by the rail, and after Dan had done his manners with me, he stared at the shore, very gloomy. When I asked what the trouble was, he answered: "Nothing, Bill—and everything. This damned invasion, mainly."

"Did something go wrong? I thought it was on."

"It *is* on—it started two weeks ago. By now the advance must be in Alexandria. But Bill, it's a queer; it keeps me awake at night."

"In what way, a queer?"

"Look, it's in three prongs, as I guess you know—Army, Navy, and Bummers. Sherman's lending us ten thousand men, but those bastards always mean trouble. Besides, there's no real chain of command."

"But isn't the General in charge?"

"Well, is he? Or isn't he? And if so, *how?*"

"Dan, I don't have answers for you."

"*If* he's in charge, he's in charge too many ways. No man can hold an election, dance the polka, inaugurate Hahn, dabble in cotton, and command a campaign all at the same time. They're asking too much of him! And he should have been there! At Alexandria, for the rendezvous. It was set for March seventeenth, when the three prongs should meet, but how could he be there, with these other things to do?"

"But has something gone wrong?"

"Not actually—at least not that I know of."

"Has there been any fighting so far?"

"Little. The Bummers took a fort."

"Well Dan? If they took it—"

"Bill, this bunch you're with is no help."

"They're what's really griping you, aren't they?"

"The cotton is. It's what really scares me."

"But why, if this hoodoo is all you have to go on? Or some theoretical attainder—that can't amount to much, if Lincoln's given his blessing."

"Lincoln's not here."

"But you've nothing definite to go on?"

"No—I'm scared and don't know why."

"It's a funny way to be scared."

"It's the worst way there is."

He found out why soon enough, before we even got to Alexandria. We stopped next day at Port Hudson, which is a levee, a bluff, and some houses, where the General reviewed some troops—colored men who'd distinguished themselves at the siege the previous year. Everyone went ashore, including me, but not caring to climb the bluff I passed up the review, went back on board, and stood in the bow chatting with a mate. Then everyone came back— the General, the staff, the enlisted men, the correspondents, and last of all the traders. But *their* faces, previously wreathed in grins from the money they hoped to make, now black with scowls, told me something was wrong; at once I started to follow them back to their part of the boat to find out what it was. But I had to stand aside while the deckhands pulled in the hawser after the boat cast off. While I was waiting Dan came down the stairs from the main saloon. He beckoned me to the same spot by the rail we'd stood at the night before and went on, almost as though there'd been no break. "Well," he said, "the hoodoo's on."

"Yes?" I said. "How?"

"The Navy's got the cotton."

"You mean, *they* made the confiscation?"

"Not quite. *They* made the *capture*."

"I don't quite get the distinction."

"Navy doesn't operate under the Confiscation Act, but under the Law of Prize—they keep all the money, they divide it between themselves, but a prize has to be captured.

And you don't give receipts to a capture. So no claim can be made for that cotton; it can't be litigated." As I nodded, getting the point, he went on: "Kind of funny, at that, how they worked it. They were telling us here at Port Hudson, some boys who got shipped downriver, on account of their time being up. The rendezvous, as I told you, was set for the seventeenth, but the Navy beat the gun. They got there the fifteenth, and the town—to be helpful—sent the mayor out in a boat to make the surrender. Boy, he didn't even get his painter taken on board—they fended him off like smallpox, for fear of what it would mean if they even heard the word *surrender*. Next morning, a detachment from the *Eastport*—your friend Sandy's boat— marched up to the warehouse and smashed in the door with rifle butts. The owner was right there, waving the keys in their face— but they had to use force to make it stick as a capture."

"Well, we live and we learn."

"From the Navy, we all learn plenty."

"But at least, *you're* out from under."

"You mean this Army? Bill, I'm not so sure."

"But if the Navy has the cotton?"

"Listen, Bill, the handshake was passed—and the Rebs left us the cotton when they pulled out of the town. Then the Navy stole it off us. All right, so that leaves these traders holding the bag. But the Rebs don't get paid, and it was *our* handshake."

"What are you leading to, Dan?"

"How do I know? But I smell still more trouble."

"Well, at worst we'll have to fight."

"Yes, Bill, but *can* we?"

He said what a poor army it was, a lot of the boys having enlisted as settlers in Texas, the rest of them soft from an idle winter, from laying up with colored girls, and from foraging for rum. He repeated: "And there's no proper chain of command." And then, turning to look at me: "Bill, you don't seem much upset."

". . . Why should I be?"

"That twenty-five thousand dollars. Losing it must be tough."

"I'd almost forgotten about it."

"Then you *were* lying, weren't you?"

"Well? I had to get me to Alexandria."

"At least, you're still an honest man—but I've known that all along, or I wouldn't be down here talking with you. And she *is* a damned nice girl."

"*If* she is, she is."

"Meaning, Bill?"

"It's what I'm on my way to find out."

"In other words, whether she's sleeping with Burke?"

I recoiled as though I'd been hit, and knew that was how he intended it. He watched my face, drilling me with his eyes, and then went on: "Bill, don't you go shooting that Irishman, for her. I'm telling you, don't you do it! Right now, *he's* a case of smallpox, with everyone afraid to give him a kind word for fear of being mixed up in some of his schemes. But dead, so nothing more can be proved, he'll have a thousand friends—and that town's under martial law. We'll try the case, and we have jurisdiction over murder. I'm trying to tell you you'll hang."

"I must play the hand as it's dealt."

"It's what I'm asking of you."

"*Suppose she is sleeping with Burke?*"

"She's still a nice girl, damn it—she wouldn't be the first to do just exactly that! But isn't it enough for you to give her the big hee-haw, for getting the little end of the stick? And Burke the big hee-haw? And Landry the

big hee-haw—specially him, because if he'd renounced the
tin, she wouldn't be up there now. Isn't laughing cheaper
than lead?"

"Is it better than lead is the question."

"It's better than rope, goddam it."

When I argued no more about it, he studied me and
then left, perhaps detecting I'd weakened, because the
truth was that once the full meaning of what the Navy had
done had soaked in I'd begun to have twitches of hope
along the lines he'd spoken of—I would picture myself
laughing, and then picture her turning to me, now the
scheme had blown up, and asking my forgiveness, and pictured myself taking her in my arms and telling her our love
was all that mattered. And so the long afternoon wore on.
We spoke the station ship, a walking-beam boat of the kind
we have back home. We ran past her, came about, then ran
down into Lower Old River. After six or eight miles of
that, racing with the current, we nosed into the Red. Night
began settling down, and in the morning it started to rain.
After miles of desolate country blighted by the war, suddenly here came the cotton, thousands of bales on a barge,
under the arm of a Navy steamer. It passed so close we
could almost touch it, and the traders watched it and cursed.
Ahead was Alexandria, all brick, green, iron lace, and driz-
zle. Then we were swinging into Alexandria's upper wharf
and crashing into the Navy's flag boat, a big three-decker
called the *Black Hawk*. No, I didn't make a mistake. Their
flag was on the *Black Hawk* and our headquarters on the
Black Hawk—two boats with the same name, lying side
by side, spreading nothing but mux. It was that kind of
invasion.

CHAPTER 16

"Yes, gentlemen, it *is* a big hotel, and one of the best, we hope. Nevertheless, appearance can be deceiving, and we don't have any room. The first floor, as you see, has lobby, bar, lounge, dining room, and drugstore—but no place to sleep. The third floor's a theater—no place to sleep up there. The second floor, it's true, has twenty-four rooms, but unfortunately, when you inflicted your war on us, we had just finished building and our inventory never came. They're big, beautiful rooms, but except for a few, already taken, they're empty—no beds, no rugs, no basins, no anything. Just goes to show you should have thought twice before starting to shoot. However, we're kindly disposed, and will do what we can for you. For meals, you may come and we'll see that you're fed. For lodging, we have houses for rent belonging to people who went upriver when they heard your invasion was coming—and *I* don't blame them, do you? They've left their keys with me, and if you'll kindly pay attention, I'll call out who they are, the kind of house they have, and how many it will accommodate—terms cash. Cash in advance to the first of the month, and cash in advance for each month thereafter! May I repeat, in advance? No refunds!"

He began picking up keys and reading stuff off tickets they had tied to them, and voices would call out, from the bunch of traders, correspondents, and hangers-on standing around the lobby, which was big, with leather chairs and settees, as well as desks that had signs on them like RED RIVER DEMOCRAT and GREAT EASTERN AND WESTERN STAGE LINES. Mostly, they bespoke by twos, threes, and fours, depending on how many wanted to share the accommodation, but pretty soon he hit a snag, offering a place with no takers: "Over-the-store flat on Front Street, clean fine place with bang-up space for four." As he repeated his spiel I came alert when I happened to catch the name, Schmidt. I sang out: "*Yo!*" and he slapped the key down in front of me, saying: "That'll be fifty dollars to the first of April." I paid, and then was clumping down the street, my bedroll over one shoulder, my bag in my hand, past a town I knew like a book from the talk I'd heard about it that night at the Landry flat and the pictures I'd been shown of it. Sure enough, below the corner, its windows looking out at the stern of the flag boat, I came to the store, its windows lettered *A. Landry & Cie.*, and a few steps further on to a place with vats inside, its windows lettered *Friedrich Schmidt, Sugar Mill Supplies.* Beside each place was a little green gate, and back of that a small alley. I went up the exterior stairway to a little platform, used my key, and went in. I stepped into a hallway, crosswise the flat, which led to another hallway at right angles to the crosshall. This was apparently the common wall between the two flats, and would have been dark except for the skylight, the one she'd talked about.

To the right, at the end of that hall, was a front sitting room, which I went into after dropping my stuff, and raised the shades to look at. It was as dreary a place as I'd ever seen. On the floor was coconut matting, which the whole place smelled of, like some unventilated Sunday School room. The construction was tongue-and-groove board, the paint mustard-color, the furniture carved oak with cushions tied on, and the pictures were steel engravings of what looked like German kings. The decorations were china dogs, china steins, china jars with gilded cattails in them, china heads that grinned at you, and meerschaum pipes in racks. The heads, which were life-size, were tobacco jars and had tops with sponges in them.

Back through the hall again, past the skylight, I peeped into doors, finding bedrooms, a bath with tub hung to the wall but no water connection, a dining room, kitchen, and pantry. The pantry had shelves with cooking things on them, a trap door in the floor, and a short stepladder, apparently for the skylight. The kitchen had a range, wood-bin, sink, and pump. Out the window, when I opened it, was the bath cistern she had spoken of, on its trestle. From the roof, spouting led down, now tinkling with water running through, and on it I spotted the valve, an arrangement attached by a screw sleeve and worked with a wooden handle. I put in about all these things so it won't be all mixed up when I tell what happened that night, but the truth is I only half-noticed them now. My mind was completely on her, not on what I saw. I left the window up for air, took my stuff into a bedroom, and sat down for a moment to get ready for what I'd do next. But the beat of my heart told me, without my having to think. After what Lavadeau had said and what the Navy had done, I had every reason to play it friendly, without giving way to the thoughts I'd struggled with after seeing John Wilkes Booth. So, when I had myself under control, I straightened up my oilskin, went down the stairs to the alley, around in front of the stores, and up the other stairs which led from the banquette of the street to another second-floor platform. I knocked and she opened, still in her little black dress that by now was downright shabby. "Oh," she said, with a small icy smile, though not in the least surprised, "I heard someone stumping around in the other flat, and I thought it might be you. You're the only cripple I knew of that it might be."

"Yes," I said, "I rented the Schmidt place."

Then, stepping out to the platform rail and staring down at the street: "Did Marie come with you?"

"No, she's still in New Orleans."

"Well, I was going to say, little as she has on whenever I see her, she must be cold down there in the rain and might want to come in."

"I doubt if she would, but thanks."

"I hear she's backing your firm?"

"There's been talk about it, that's true."

"She's awful rich. Or *filthy rich*, I've heard said."

"But sixteen hundred dollars poorer than she was."

That crack about the notes Marie had torn up hit the mark. She stepped back out of the wet, her face getting red and her eyes shining, and snapped: "What did you come for? What do you want?"

"Nothing," I said, my friendliness slightly evaporated

by now, "except to commiserate—for your selling your backside off and getting nothing for it."

"*What are you talking about?*"

"The cotton—that you did it all for, and then saw snatched away. Oh, I heard; the Navy gave no receipts. Is your father in? I'd like to condole with *him* too, for making a pimp of himself, renting his daughter out to the same rotten harp as stabbed him in the back, and then having nothing to show."

But instead of slamming the door, as I fully expected her to, she stared and changed her expression to the same icy smile as she'd had when she opened it. "Father's out," she said very sweetly. "We eat a lot of vension these days, and he stepped down the road to see the Indian who brings it in. But there's no reason at all to condole—*our* receipt is already signed. Of course," she went on, in a quiet, reasonable way, "I don't say they'd have signed for every pipsqueak here in town, like some poor hippity-hop, working women to back his company—but when a *man* showed up with his paper, someone big, like we'll say Mr. Burke, they get out their pen, pretty quick. We don't need any sympathy, but of course thanks just the same."

"Well then, congratulations."

"Will there be anything else?"

"Not that I think of at this time."

"Then, as we'll be taking the first boat out when the Army gets to Shreveport, can we say goodbye now?"

"Certainly. Goodbye."

"Give my love to Marie."

So I came, I saw, and I certainly did not conquer. I didn't do anything, even remember John Wilkes Booth, and it didn't help any, when I got back to my horrible sitting room, that I was all atremble just from seeing her, hearing her and, worst of all, smelling her. But then, little by little, it began to dig at me there was something funny about it—that receipt, I mean. Because, although Burke might once have been big with the Army, I knew of no heft he had with the Navy, and it was the Navy that had grabbed the cotton. And the legal aspect of it, from what Dan had said, was so peculiar it seemed incredible they would have waived it in any way. It also seemed incredible, considering that icy smile, that if Burke had thought of some shyster trick, or her father had, or she had, she wouldn't have walloped me with it, just for fun. And yet I was mortally certain, from the bragging way she had acted, that the receipt *had* been signed, and so the question was: How could it have been, and at the same time not have been? I didn't have the answer, but did have someone to go to for background information that might throw light on the subject. That was Sandy Gregg, whose ship, the *Eastport*, had made the cotton "capture," according to Dan.

By then the rain had stopped, so I piled out on the street again, asked my way of a bluejacket, and off the lower end of the town spotted an ironclad lying out in midstream. Her texas and staterooms had all been stripped away, and she was dented, scarred, and scaly, but did answer my hail. Then there was Sandy, at one of the gunports, staring in disbelief. He's a trim, dark, medium-sized lad, fairly good-looking, but right now in his old blues almost as rusty as his ship. However, he called to the cutter lying at the wharf I was talking from and had them bring me out. He welcomed me aboard cordially, and introduced me to three or four friends, but the whole time he was shaking hands kept asking over and over: "Bill, what are you doing here? What the *hell* are you doing here?"

Well, what *was* I doing there?

The truth, supposing I even knew it, was the last thing I wanted to own, so I fell back on my original story, the one I'd told to Dan before he smoked me out. "Well," I said, pretty testy, "*you* ought to know what I'm doing here. *We* need twenty-five thousand dollars, and this looked like the quickest place to get it." And then, not giving him time to speak: "And I can get it, I think, if the parties I've been referred to as having cotton to sell me show up as they're supposed to. But what worries me is this: If I do buy their titles, can I get a receipt?"

"You're here as a trader then?"

"I came up on the *Black Hawk* today."

"And the cotton you're after was stored?"

"In Rachal's Warehouse, I believe it's called."

"Bill, we captured that cotton last week."

"Oh I know about that—I saw it; we passed the barge coming up. But condemnation rests with a court, and fact of the matter, the battle hasn't started till a court calls the case in New Orleans."

"Springfield."

". . . Springfield?"

"Illinois. That cotton's headed for Cairo."

"Oh, I didn't know that."

"Bill, if you buy titles, you're sunk."

"You mean, on-the-bottom sunk?"

"I mean, in-the-mud sunk. We're *both* sunk."

"But tell me: Have any receipts been signed?"

"No, Bill, none."

"If any had been, would you know it?"

"Detail from this ship made the capture—I wasn't in command, but was there, and if receipts had been signed, I'd know it."

But one of the boys he'd introduced me to, who was in earshot as we talked on the bow, said something, and Sandy corrected himself: "Oh that's right, I forgot. One of our officers, Lieutenant Powell, could have signed something; of that we can't be sure. He did shore duty evenings, up at the Ice House Hotel, hearing civilian complaints—and got plugged by a skulker one night as he stepped out of the hotel to come back to the ship."

"Why doesn't Cresap talk to Ball?"

That was the boy who had interrupted, and Sandy said: "That's right, Ball would know. He's on that duty now, and has all Powell's notes."

"Can I see him?"

"He's asleep, but he'll be at the hotel tonight."

"Then—I'll talk to him there."

"Now, Bill, let's get back."

". . . Back? To what?"

"The twenty-five thousand dollars."

I was in the unfortunate position, I discovered, that he'd swallowed my whole yarn. He took the twenty-five thousand dollars very seriously, feeling he was to blame, not only for our needing it but, still worse, for our not having it. So for an hour I had to fence, while he asked all kinds of questions about who my "parties" were. Finally, when I admitted I had no idea, he looked so utterly baffled I had to do something, quick. I slipped off a bill from the roll I had in my pocket, tore it in two with my fingertips, then came up with one half and said: "All I know is, they're to present me with identification, the matching half of this. Until they do, I don't know them from Adam, and can't even guess who they are. And maybe, from your account of the seizure, or capture as you call it, they won't even show at all." It satisfied him, but I went back to my flat more shaken than before, if such a thing was possible. I was no nearer the answer to my riddle, but quite a lot nearer the poorhouse. I had supposed, when I tore the bill, that I was wrecking a twenty, but saw when I looked it was fifty. Perhaps, I told myself, it would be just as good as new if pasted together again, but as I fingered and folded and eyed it, it was one more silly thing in a dreary, complete fiasco.

I'd done better than I knew.

CHAPTER 17

WHATEVER I HAD OR HADN'T FOUND OUT, I still had to eat, so around 6:30 I walked up to the hotel. It was jammed, and I didn't get a seat until the third or fourth table. But I bought my ticket, and then saw Dan come in and beckon to the newspapermen. When they'd gathered around him, he gave them the latest: the Army was moving up, being now in Natchitoches—"Nackitosh," he called it; the Navy was having some trouble from low water on the falls, the stretch of rapid water just above the town, but several boats were up, and no serious delay had been caused. In other words, everything was moving according to schedule. But when he'd finished with them and dropped into a chair beside me, he had nothing to say and seemed in a sour humor. I said: "Why all the gloom if the sun is shining so bright?" He said: "It is, in a pig's eye," and then, mysterious: "You want to see something, Bill? Meet me out back."

So I did, slipping out past the desk in under the stairs, through a door between the dining room and a big lounge with a stove in it. In a moment, there he was, in among the hotel's steam boiler, gas tank, and cistern, pointing. I looked; in the gathering dark, the sky back of town was pink. He said: "That glow is cotton they're burning out there— from some plantation gin on the Opelousas Road. They've been doing it, I'm told, every night since the Navy crossed them. We hear they hate our guts."

"Yes, but since when did they love us?"

"They were all ready to think things over."

"You're hipped on that hoodoo, Dan."

"I'm telling you, it's going to dog us."

"The cotton's gone—it's on it's way to Cairo for condemnation in Springfield. The rest is a new deal."

"We haven't heard the end."

When I didn't respond he got sore, and circled the tailor shop at one side to return to the headquarters boat without going back through the hotel. I went in and at last got a place for dinner, which wasn't too bad: corned beef, cabbage, potato, rice pudding with rum sauce, and real coffee—the first sign of a change when the Union comes to town. When I went out into the lobby again, Ball was back of the stagecoach desk, a grizzled, seamy two-striper who looked like an old river pilot, which is probably what he was. He was talking to a woman about her son who'd been captured, but spotted me and called me over, telling her to wait. He shook hands, saying: "Mr. Cresap, Sandy Gregg said you'd come—I know you by his description."

"I'm easy described," I said, waving the stick.

"He never mentioned it. He spoke only about your

beauty—*and* that torn fifty-dollar bill you have. Could I see it just once, Mr. Cresap?"

I got one half of it out, and when he loved it as though it was alive I realized I had a pass, by just a crazy accident, to a lodge I'd never heard of. He said: "It's the old smuggler's talisman, and my, how that carries me back. Mr. Cresap, before annexation, and the tariff changes of Forty-six, everything was protected—from jumping jacks to sewing machines—and the smuggling that went on, especially here in the South, had to be seen to be believed. Jefferson, Texas, was the Lone-Star port of entry, and Shreveport of course was ours. We had, and still have, the long, narrow steamers, and what they took through the bayous—Twelve-Mile Bayou to Lake Caddo, and Big Bayou to Red River—ran into the millions, sir. And with every dummy manifest, I'd be given this same bill—a fifty torn once, to match a piece I had in my wallet. Well, when you show me this I know you have real friends, and I may as well tell you the truth—or they will. *So*: Our orders, here in the Navy, are to receipt for *loyal* cotton, whether *captured* or not. But which Red River cotton *is* loyal? As we hear, there's *none*. It's all been impressed, we've been told, by the Confederate bureau at Shreveport, for export—you know how they do? Haul to Texas, then ship through Mexico?"

I said I knew about it, and he went on: "So much for what we heard. There's also the element of confusion. Did Sandy speak of the stencil?"

". . . Stencil? I don't think so."

"When we capture a bale we stencil it *USN* to keep things straight. And the boys—no order was given, it was strictly a fo'c'sle idea—they put an extra stencil on, *CSA* —all perfectly honest, since it meant Cotton Stealing Association, U.S. Navy. But a court could easy conclude it meant Confederate States of America. Well now, couldn't it? But why, you may ask, couldn't a court open its mouth and *inquire* what the stencil meant? All right, since you ask, I'll say. Under the law of prize, if the prize bears any marks, 'sufficient to its adjudification'—that's what he said, *adjudification*—that closes the case, no more evidence can be heard. So the court *can't* inquire, the law don't permit it! So you, Mr. Cresap, are sitting in the soup, so far as cotton's concerned that was stored in Rachal's Warehouse, and that's offered you for sale. Am I making the point clear?"

"I think I get it, yes."

"CSA—CSA, they're one and the same."

"We could say, like *Black Hawk—Black Hawk*."

"That's it! War is war!"

Then, leaning close: "I ask you right out, Mr. Cresap: Have you bought in on this cotton or haven't you?"

"Not actually, Lieutenant Ball."

"Then don't! Save your tin!"

"I'll remember what you say. Thanks."

He called the woman over, took the name of her son, and said he'd do what he could to get the boy released. Then he leaned back and started in again about the old days of the smugglers, in the time of the Texas Republic, when all of a sudden he stopped, as a man in moleskins, jackboots, and felt hat leaned over toward him. We were seated facing each other, he behind the desk, I beside it, my back to the lobby. He looked up, said: "Mr. Burke, I'm sorry I have no news—we're taking nobody upriver until the occupation is complete."

"But I *must* get to Shreveport," said the familiar voice, "*before* I leave for Springfield, to see to me interests there."

I've a tremenjous opportunity to buy a parcel of cotton on the Sabine, back of the town—"

"The Pulaski dump?"

"Aye, a cache of five thousand bales, *no less!*"

"But the Army has boats too. Why not see them?"

"The Army and I have our differences."

"Well with this Army, who wouldn't have differences —we have a few ourselves. But for two million in cotton, *I* wouldn't be too damned proud. Why don't you hop a wagon? You don't need a pass for that."

" 'Tis an idea; I'll think it over."

They batted it back and forth, and perhaps to change the subject, Ball suddenly asked: "Did the little lady cross? To visit that grave in Pineville? Her mother's, I think you said?"

"She's—been a bit under the weather."

"She still has Powell's pass?"

"Aye—she remembers'm in her prayers."

"Whenever she's ready, any cutter'll take her."

"And she's grateful, have no doubt of it."

"Funny, Mr. Burke, I've often thought about it: How could they lay out this town so neat, with no place to bury people? No cemeteries here, you know. What's the idea? Do they figure to live forever?"

"As they tell it, many of'm do."

"Not Powell, unfortunately."

"Have you word of the wretch who killed'm?"

"Not yet. But God help him when we catch up."

"To that a brace of amens."

They came back to her again, Burke saying how "slimsy" she'd felt today, "especially with the rain." How long it went on, I don't know, but more than just a few seconds, as I had my back to the lobby, and Burke couldn't see who was there—and long enough for stuff to go through my head. I thought: Since when was she "slimsy" today? She hadn't looked slimsy to me, and in fact was chock full of mean, rotten ginger. Then I thought: If she wasn't slimsy, why should he say she was? To cover not using her pass, but then I thought: Why hasn't she used it, for instance? I thought all that without caring too much. But then suddenly it hit me like a sledge: Suppose she's not going to use it? Suppose it was just a trick to get Powell's specimen signature, so Burke could forge the receipt the Navy wouldn't give? And suppose that's why Powell got killed, so he couldn't deny his name in court? For one heartbeat, she was guilty as hell to me and one heartbeat again, I felt the same feeling as Booth had had in his eyes. But then, as always, came the excuse I made for her: Suppose, I thought, she knew nothing about the pass? Suppose he'd got it for her so he could forge the receipt, and conveniently forgot to tell her? That would tie in with the way she'd acted with me, bragging about the receipt, and certainly believing he had one. It would also put her, as soon as the Navy caught up—and figured why Powell was shot—right on the gallows step. Because, when they searched Burke's papers, they'd find the pass in her name, the receipt with identical signature, and nothing to show she hadn't been in on the trick.

By the time he looked down and saw me, I was well on my way, I knew, to solving two or three mysteries, all in one fell swoop. "Hello, Burke," I said.

". . . What are you doing here, Cresap?"

"*Was* talking to the lieutenant. *Am* talking to you."

"What business have you with me?"

"You'll find out. Thanks, Lieutenant Ball."

As Ball, kind of puzzled, gave me a wary wave, I led to the DEMOCRAT desk and took my seat behind it, but then saw that Burke hadn't moved. "Of course," I called, "IF YOU WANT THE NAVY TO HEAR——"

He'd heard me bellow before, and came in five quick steps, pulling up a chair so he could sit close. But I kicked it out from under him. I said: "Stand when talking to me."

"Talking to you? About what?"

"Couldn't we say a slight case of murder?"

"Are you out of your mind? Whose?"

"Lieutenant Powell's, perhaps—whose name you got on a pass, so *she* could cross the river; then used his specimen signature, to forge one on the receipt, the Navy's receipt for your cotton, as you forged the informer notes last month down in New Orleans; and then *you killed him so he couldn't deny it in court!*"

"Cresap, I think you're crazy."

"I don't, that's the difference—and the question is, what do we do about it? I wasn't here, I didn't see it, I don't have to turn you in—it all hinges on the other people involved, the ones named in your written agreements, as to whether they're guilty too. If not, I can't turn you in, but I can destroy your papers, to cut you out, and them out, of every dime of the hundred-twenty thousand you thought you'd make from this crime. If they are as guilty as you are, I'm turning you all three in—you, your partner, and *her*. I don't care how pretty she is, or whether you love her or not, or whether anyone does, *she's going to swing!*" I let that soak in as he stood there licking his lips, then went on: "So that's what we're doing now—going into it, to see what's what, and who gets his neck broke. Come on, we're paying them a call—*now*."

" 'Twill suit me very well."

"Then fine, let's go."

"But I've a suggestion, me boy—when we've explained the thing to Adolphe, and to Mignon Fournet, of course, why don't we all go to my house—after all, me papers are there. 'Tis quite a decent place I took on Second Street in the block below the market, back of Adolphe's store—we can make ourselves comfortable there, and I'll prove to you once and for all how mistaken you are."

"If they agree, your house sounds fine."

"Then 'tis settled, and let's be off!"

It was settled—a little too much. Because I'd worked myself out on a limb and was neatly sawing it off. To own the truth, I'd come without my gun, not supposing I'd need it. And how far I was going to get, walking down the street in the company of this man I was sure had killed the lieutenant, I didn't like to think. With the stored-up venom I'd had, I had let myself go regardless, but now I had the cold sweaty feeling of someone about to fall. However, that venom saved me, as everyone there stopped talking and turned my way, and the clerk, the same stiff-necked one who had rented the houses out, got so concerned, as my vicious whispering kept on, that he strolled to the door, stepped out, and called: "Corporal of the Guard! Corporal of the Provost Guard!"

In a moment a soldier was there, not a corporal but a private, belted for duty with sidearms, who took things in with one look and came over to Burke and me. "What's going on here?" he wanted to know. "What seems to be the trouble?"

"Nothing," I said. "Just a nice, sociable brawl that's nobody's business but ours." But then, thinking fast, I added: "But I feel my life in some danger, going home tonight, and if you'd ask your corporal, or whoever's in command, to provide me with an escort, I'd feel myself obliged."

"Where do you live, sir?"

"Schmidt store, block and a half down."

"It's on my post. I'll take you there myself."

"*And* me," said Burke. "Me life's in danger too."

That got a laugh, for some reason, and we got a laugh and a hand when the boy formed us up, Burke and me in front, he bringing up the rear, and we marched out the door. Even Ball was laughing, but for once that day I didn't feel like a dolt.

We were quite a noisy parade, going down the street, the guard's heels clopping, my stick clicking, my corduroys whining, and Burke's jackboots whispering like a deck of cards being riffled. When we got to our corner I told Burke to rouse out Mr. Landry and Mrs. Fournet while I got some stuff I'd need, and then, after thanking the guard, I went through the little gate, up the stairs to the platform, and into my flat with my key. I was no sooner in than I scrambled fast to the bedroom, clawed into the bag, and after scattering all kinds of stuff—sandwiches, clothes, and gear—I got my hooks on the gun. I dropped it in my pocket, not bothering with the harness, then went down to the street again. The guard was still on the corner, looking up at the Landry flat, where Burke was on the platform, beating on the door, and calling loudly in French. Not a sound came from inside, and no light showed. "They don't answer," he said peevishly.

"I bet they don't," I said, "after you told them not to, in that trick language you speak with them. They'll answer me, though."

"Hey, *you!*"

That was the guard, snapping it out as I started up, and stopping me in my tracks. He called Burke down, and gave us both a bawling out, ordering us "to your billets, or you'll spend the night in the clink." I told Burke: "You be at my place in the morning, with them, *both* of them, do you hear—at nine, *sharp*." Then I watched him march off in the dark, thanked the guard once again, and went back up to my flat. I bolted the door, lit a half candle that was there in an iron stick, hung up my clothes in the armoire in the bedroom, put on my nightshirt, and went to bed. As I reached for the candle to blow it out, there grinning at me from the night table was one of the china heads. I said: "My friend, for once, the joke is not on me, and you haven't seen anything yet. Just you wait till tomorrow, and you may really have something to laugh at."

CHAPTER 18

I HAD SLEPT A LONG TIME, several hours from the way I felt, then awoke all of a sudden with a prickle up my back that told me I wasn't alone. Whether I heard anything I don't know, but I could have, as I was so well-slept-out the slightest sound would have reached me. I stared at the dark, wondering how anyone, short of a conjure trick, could have slid those bolts on the door to get in. Then I remembered the window, the one by the cistern, that I'd opened and forgotten about. From the wall, the tongue-and-groove partition between room and hall, came a sound—the faint, trembling rub that a hand would make feeling its way along from the rear of the flat. I groped for where I'd hung the gun in its harness on the bedpost. When I had it I lay there for a moment, but at the sound of another rub began to feel like a sitting duck. I slid out, grabbed one of the pillows and shoved it under the covers in such way that it made a bulge, then took the china head and pressed it down on the other pillow. Suddenly a man was there, sleeping. I crouched down with the gun by the side of the bed, out of sight, waiting.

The rub was repeated again, still closer to the door. Then the latch clicked and the hinge spoke. The door opened by inches and a dark shadow was there. I wanted to growl "Hands up," but made myself bite it back, to give this shadow its chance to move farther into the room, so I could jump between it and the door and cut off any retreat. I had no doubt it was Burke; if I could hold him at gun's point, then I could go ahead without turning him in yet or starting something I couldn't stop. I could beat on the wall between flats, get Mignon and her father over, and have my showdown at once: find out who was guilty of what. If she had connived at that pass, letting Burke bespeak it for her as a preliminary to murdering Powell, I meant to turn them all in—her no less than the others. If that seems unduly mean, all I can say is that I could still smell her spit, and she'd done nothing the day before to make me forget its aroma. But if she hadn't known of the pass, if she'd become an unwitting accessory, then I meant to stand pat until somebody brought me the papers. When I'd stuffed them into the stove and made her touch them off with a match, then I'd feel myself hunk and be able to take a new start—hie me back to New Orleans, begin again looking for twenty-five thousand dollars, perhaps take up with Marie, if she was still speaking to me.

That, some kind of way but fairly clearly, I think, is what went through my mind as I crouched there holding my breath. But then, in one blazing second, it all got out of hand, and the smoke that filled the room could not be stuffed back in the shells. The shadow darted. It was suddenly close to the bed. Then the room filled with light and there came a crash—the ear-splitting crash a gun makes when it's fired indoors. And then self-preservation, which seems to be stronger somehow than any plan you can make—for getting hunk or otherwise—got into it. While china still clattered around from the shot smashing the head, I fired by reflex action, not knowing I would. Then I fired again, on purpose. You can't sight a gun in the dark, but your hand will do it for you, and the thud on the floor told me I'd found my mark. I circled the bed, felt around with my bare toe, touched a gun. I picked it up, shook what was lying there to see if it still lived. It didn't move, so I knew *I* had to—and move by the book, quick. I made my way to the sitting room, threw up the window, and called: "Corporal of the Guard, *help!*" I did it three times, each time banging a shot in the night, in the prescribed military way. Then I got a military answer: "Corporal of the Guard— *yo!* We hear you! Who are you who call? Locate yourself and we'll come!"

"Schmidt store, second floor, Front Street!"

"On our way, coming up!"

I ducked for the bedroom again, but in the hall came a whisper from the dark: "Willie! Are you all right?"

"Mignon! For God's sake, where are you?"

"Here! Can't you see?"

Something touched my head, and when I grabbed it it was her hand, reaching down from the skylight. For a moment, one tremendous moment, her fingers locked with mine, and then she repeated, "Willie! *Are you all right?*"

"Yes, but will you go? I've had to kill a man, Burke, I

think. The Provost Guard's on its way—and they must not find you here!"

"I almost died when I heard those shots!"

"*Heard* them? Where the hell have you been?"

"Home! Where do you think?"

"Then why didn't you answer Burke's knock?"

"With Father not home? I wouldn't answer *anyone's* knock! It's the one protection I have, and—"

"You answered my knock, though."

"Well? I knew it was you. . . . As for Frank—"

"Never mind about him. He's dead."

"I've been trying to tell you: I don't care."

I shook her hand, as a mother shakes a child, to make it listen. I said: "Mignon, you *have* to care, or everything's in the soup! Things have been going on that I can't take time to explain—terrible things that you can't know about, or you wouldn't be talking this way! Things that can land you on the gallows, and not only you but your father! We have to cover up! I do, you do, your father does, especially about those papers in Burke's house! So if you hear me talking funny, don't you undercut me, don't you get in it, giving your two cents' worth! I'll have my reasons, and your life is at stake! Mignon, do you hear what I say?"

"My, but you sound funny."

"Do you understand?"

"Yes, Willie, but *are* you all right?"

"I am! Now, will you *go?*"

"You don't even sound like yourself."

"Mignon, here comes the Provost Guard!"

At last, she pulled back her head and lowered the frame as footsteps sounded outside. My heart raced as I went to the door, and my head was spinning around because, of course, from her failure to answer Burke and the way she acted with me, she'd never lived up with him and had had no part of his scheme—at least any scheme leading to Powell's murder. It put a different light on everything.

I opened to the corporal, who was carrying a bull's-eye lantern, and two of his men, then led at once to the bedroom. But when he threw his beam I got my first jolt. The thing on the floor wasn't Burke, but Pierre Legrand, the gippo. The corporal took both guns, which by then I had in one hand, sniffed them, and put them on the night table. Then he opened Pierre's reefer and felt around in his pockets, perhaps for some identification. He didn't seem to find any, which suddenly tipped me off that he wasn't known to soldiers just recently here, and mightn't be, at least right away, if I played my cards right. So when I was asked, I told everything just as it happened, except that I used the word *prowler* and gave no clue that could be followed up. In other words, I told the truth, but not quite all of the truth. The corporal shook his head, said "This damned place is so full of jayhawkers, bushwhackers, and swine of all different kinds, they'd steal our goddam boats if they wasn't tied fast to the bank." He posted a man to stand guard, said he'd get the captain, told me dress if I wanted to, but there was really no need, "as give us a half hour, and we ought to be off your neck, with *him* outen the way too."

He was all ready to leave when suddenly, at the door, he turned to his other man, asked: "You see what I see, soldier?"

"Well Corporal, gimme some light."

"That hat, under the bed!"

"Brother!"

He strode over, picked it up, and stared at the red pompon. "It's him," he whispered, "the one that killed Lieutenant Powell! That's what the bosun said, the one on duty with him—he saw the man's hat plain, it was one like the French Navy wears and had a red tassel on it!"

"That there's a tuft, not a tassel."

"Whatever it is, it's red."

"Corporal, you could be letting the Navy know."

"You bet I'm letting the Navy know."

In so short a time that I barely had my clothes on, I was a bigger hero than I'd ever been in my life, and I've had my share of praise. The Navy got there: Ball, Sandy, and three ensigns from the *Eastport*; a two-striper from the flag boat, and seamen from other boats. They piled in with a Captain Hager from the Provost Guard, the corporal, more privates, a stretcher, and so many bull's-eye lanterns the place was bright as day. They closed in on the corpse like staghounds, and all kowtowed to me as the one who had made the kill. None of them, as yet, seemed to know who Pierre was, except that he'd murdered Powell, and I certainly didn't enlighten them, though I avoided direct statements, one way or the other, by pretending "a bad reaction—don't ask me to look at this man." Hager, though, when he made me admit I was the one who had asked for a bodyguard earlier on in the evening, at once began boring in, but I told him: "*That* was just a precaution I felt I should take, from carrying a large sum of money, and had no connection with this—that I know of, unless this fellow had heard rumors about me." That seemed to satisfy him; he even returned me my gun. "Obviously," he said, "under the circumstances, in this godawful, lawless place, you may need it."

Then he had the privates clean the room up, and Ball ordered the seamen to help. They found a pan and brooms in the kitchen, and swept up the china that was crunching underfoot, then brushed off the bed and made it up fresh. They did a bang-up policing job, and while it was going on, Sandy drew me into the hall. "Boy!" he growled. "Did you fall into the cream pot!"

". . . Cream pot? What are you talking about?"

"Your receipt! We'll have to sign it now!"

"Sandy! I don't have a receipt!"

"I know you don't! You don't even have any cotton, but this is your chance to get it! Bill, don't you see? The Navy couldn't refuse you now and still look you in the eye—and we wouldn't *want* to! After all, we look out for our friends, and you've just settled the hash of the killer we were looking for! *You get some cotton, Bill!* From your hombre if you can—the one holding the other half of your torn fifty-dollar bill! But if he doesn't show, forget him—go buy up stock of your own, from whoever holds any titles to that cotton we took from the warehouse! You're the only one who can get a receipt, you got a monopoly, you'll be the only bidder, they'll have to take what you offer, you can get hold of that stock for a song! Don't you see, Bill? *Stop arguing with me!* Here I've been racking my brains all night for some scheme you could pull to make that twenty-five thousand dollars, and now when it's right in your hand, you stand there—"

"I haven't said a goddam word."

"All right then, why *don't* you say something?"

"I'll think it over, I certainly will."

At last they went, carrying the corpse with them, and after I'd closed the window and bolted the door, I started back to bed. But for a moment I stood in the hall, trying to gather my wits, to think what to do next, about Burke and his deadly papers, and how to do it in time, before Pierre's identification, when the cat would be out of the bag. And then, from above, came the whisper: "Willie, have they gone?"

"Thank God, they have."

"Get the ladder. I'm coming down."

"Have you been up there all this time?"

"I held the skylight on a crack."

I got the ladder, and then she was sliding down through my arms, in nightie, slippers, robe, and beautiful smell. Then bare skin was on my hands, and time stood still as our mouths came together. I carried her into the bedroom, and nothing was there but the hunger we had for each other. Then she was up on one elbow, asking about the dead man. She said: "That wasn't Burke they took out, it was Pierre. I saw him plain."

"I made a mistake. I told you wrong."

"What was Sandy talking about?"

"Oh—cockeyed scheme he cooked up."

"I heard him say cotton."

"Yes, he did mention something about it."

"Willie, if I ever hear the end of *that*, that's when I leap up and holler. And if you ever get yourself in it, that's when I wring your neck. Now what *was* this scheme of his?"

I told her, not going into any details, and when I was done she said: "It's out! I never want to *look* at cotton again as long as I live. Do you hear me?"

"I do, and cotton doesn't attract me."

"Because listen, Willie Cresap—"

But I still hadn't got to the main point, and I cut her

off with a kiss, telling her: "Mignon Fournet, you listen to me!"

I said our time was short, and that I had to explain some things that could mean her life as well as her father's. I took it from the beginning—why I'd left New Orleans, what Dan had said on the boat, what I'd really meant when I came the day before, calling on her in the rain, what had gone through my mind when she told me their receipt had been signed. I told of my trip to the *Eastport*, and the faked-up story I'd told about the torn fifty-dollar bill. I told of my trip to the hotel, the answers I'd got from Ball, and Burke's sudden appearance. But when I mentioned the pass, she cut in quick: "But I never asked for a pass!"

"I figured that out, myself."

"But what was Frank thinking about?"

Her eyes, opening with disbelief, became two big black moons as I told about the receipt, how I was sure it was forged from the name on her pass, its connection with Powell's murder, and what it would mean if found with Burke's papers, once it became known who Pierre really was—"you're tied in through the pass, and your father's tied in through his articles of partnership." And then, as an afterclap of the bitterness I'd lived with so long: "Not that he doesn't have it coming, after what he did, using you as bait—"

"Using me as *what?*"

"You heard me! As bait, to Burke."

"Oh, how wrong can anyone be!"

She said the bait was "the Pulaski cotton, the chance to buy it in a tremendous big cache on the Sabine River, that we had to dangle at Frank, to keep him from burning his papers just from pure spite. And where I came in, why

I had to be on Red River, was that I was the one who knew them, those people in Texas, those growers who hold the titles, through Raoul, before the war." Of course, that corresponded with what Burke had said when he first started talking with Ball, and I hauled in my horns quick, especially after hearing point-blank, out of her own mouth, that she hadn't been close to Burke. But when she started going on with more about her father, I cut it off by asking: "Where is he, by the way? I have to see him, and quick."

"I told you yesterday. He went for vension, to the Ransdell place back of town. But sometimes, when the Indian who brings in the deer is late, he has to stay overnight, and—"

"When'll he be back?"

"Won't be too long after sunup."

"Then I can see him in time—we hope."

". . . The dawn's early light. I have to go."

"Hold on, Mignon, not so fast—let's get back to Powell and why he was killed. If you don't believe it's true, my notion about that pass—"

"Willie, I know it's true."

She got up, and in the graying dark started putting on the robe. She said: "And I know what has to be done. So if my father, with Pierre out of the way, doesn't go to Frank with a gun, take that receipt and burn it, along with every title to every bale of cotton we ever *thought* was ours, you know who's going to do it?"

"I am."

"No, Willie. I am."

CHAPTER 19

She let me in in a red-checked gingham dress, the first time I'd ever seen her wearing anything but black. It was just a morning dress, but went with her color somehow, and she seemed pleased when I said how well it became her. Then she brought me into a flat that was the duplicate, in reverse, of the one I was living in, and yet was as different from it as day is from night. In place of the coconut matting, the halls had Axminster runners; in place of the mustard paint was decent wallpaper, with lords and ladies and dogs; in place of the Sunday-School smell was her smell, the smell of books, and the smell of ham frying; in place of the Prussian kings in the sitting room were books—hundreds of them, in shelves as high as your head almost covering the wall. On top, stuck around every which way, were all kinds of pictures and stuff, from photographs of her as a child to old dance programs, filled out. The furniture was old-fashioned, but nicely upholstered in tapestry. At one side was a Steinway grand, at the other a long table, with an iron stand on it, supporting a wash-boiler, with a muslin skirt on it and a spirit lamp underneath, taking the chill off. When I asked who played, she sat down and clattered the keys, saying: "That's Mozart—Father loves *Don Giovanni.*"

But then: "I have to watch my meat," and I followed her back to the kitchen. It was like mine, but looked used and had sacks and bins and canisters. She had a fire going, and in a skillet pieces of ham that she speared with a fork and turned over. She seemed proud of how she could cook, explaining: "I learned it in the convent at Grand Coteau. We were studying to be ladies, but when the war began to come on, the Reverend Mother insisted we study to be cooks." She gave me breakfast in the dining room: stewed prunes, ham, eggs, and hominy; when I marveled at the menu, how good it was in a place overrun by the war, she said: "Don't forget, Father keeps store. He knows where stuff is, and how to get it in." But as I finished my coffee she held up her hand. "That's Father," she said. We went into the pantry; she drew the bolts of the trapdoor, I gripped it by the holes and raised it. Mr. Landry came up, dressed roughly, half a skinned deer on one shoulder. He needed a shave and was thinner, but for some reason he seemed younger than I remembered him—it could have been the way he handled the deer. Once again, I noted how strong he must be.

When he saw me, he shook hands, very quiet—not surprised, not upset, and not glad. I said I had business with him, and he said: "Very well, sir—I'll be with you as soon as I take this carcass apart and get it down in the cistern, where it'll be cool." When I told him there wasn't time for that, he looked at me sharply, dumped the meat on the kitchen table, sat in the chair beside it, and waited. I gave it to him quick, everything he needed to know, down to my killing of Pierre. I said: "They'll identify him, sure. When they do they'll go to Burke—they'll question him, they'll fine-tooth-comb his place. You're in mortal danger, as Mignon is, for the reason—"

"I can see the reason, please."

"Where does Burke live?"

He pointed beyond the back fence to a brick house facing Second Street, cater-cornered across from the market Burke had mentioned, now all shuttered up. I asked: "Can you go in the back way?"

"I have the key, as Frank has to my store."

"Then, you have to move fast, or else—"

"I *know* I have to move fast!"

He shriveled me with his tone, then sat there, not looking young any more but horribly old. He passed a hand over his face, then said: "So." And then, after some moments: "Here I am, at the end of the line."

"That's right," I said, my old bitterness speaking once more. "After chasing that will-o'-the-wisp, that pot of gold you thought was under the rainbow, to hell-and-gone and back, up the river and down the lake, here you are, right where you started from, with every bale of that cotton lost —because once you burn that receipt, the rest of it's nothing but paper. It's what you get, my friend, for hooking up with that skunk, the one who turned on you for the sake of making some tin. There're other things, occasionally, more important than tin."

"Sir, by what right do you censure me?"

"The right of a man who wouldn't be here if it hadn't been for you. When you brought Mignon, I had to come too—I hated it, I tried to shuffle it off, to pretend there was no need. But here I am, and I'm telling you, if it wasn't for what you did, we'd all three be in New Orleans, she and I would be married, and life would go on. Instead of which, you stand, and not only you but her, in the gallows' shadow, and—"

"It may not be so simple as that."

"It's exactly as simple as that."

"That cotton was made over to me by people in desperate need, people I'd helped in one way or another. They're proud, and it was their way of paying. But they're still in desperate need, and if there was any way I could cash in, so perhaps they could share——"

"Oh my, listen at Santa Claus!"

"I did share, as you yourself can tell."

"And when was this noble deed?"

"I bought those boys shoes. You defended me for it."

". . . I'm sorry. I forgot."

"What else could I do for these people?"

"Fight for their country, maybe—and yours."

"I'm sorry, that's impossible."

"I hear different, Mr. Landry—very different."

"Our country's Louisiana. War's over here."

"Taylor's fighting for Louisiana."

"Taylor's a fool. I look down on, I despise him, *any man that asks boys to die for a cause already lost!* I don't call that patriotism, I just call it dumbness! But if, by using a trick, I don't care how crooked, I can break out of this hell we're in, this half-war they've inflicted upon us where they won't let us fight and won't give us peace, I can get some of their tin, to divide up with my long-suffering people, I'll do it, I don't care *who* I have to hook up with. So it's Burke, and he turned on me, you tell me. So he did, and I'd kill him, give me the chance. But did he, any worse than the rest? Which of them didn't turn—on me, on all of us here? I'd kill 'em all! I hate their bluebelly guts, and—"

"But not Willie, Father!"

She stood there in front of him, and he swallowed once, then said: "All right, not Willie."

"He saved you, don't forget."

". . . How's Miss Tremaine?" he asked me.

"But when I opened my mouth to answer, she closed it with her hand. "Are you going?" she asked him.

"Of course I'm going. I have to."

But he still sat there, apparently gathering his courage, and she said I should cut up the meat. She got a knife, steel, and cleaver from a drawer, and told me: "First you take off the haunch, then the loin, then the foreleg, then the neck, then the chuck, which leaves the rib in one piece—then it'll all fit in the tub. But first, before anything else, take off the shanks—I can use them tonight for soup." But while I was whetting the knife, he suddenly pointed outside, and that ended the meat for a while. On Second Street, up by the market, Burke was coming down, walking slow, peering around. "He's looking for Pierre!" whispered Mr. Landry. "He must not have heard he's dead!" As the three of us stood by the window, Burke reached the corner, which he had all to himself at this hour, looked in all four directions, and kept on. He disappeared beyond his house, but in a few seconds popped out from the back door into the yard. Then, after snooping into the outhouses, he ducked through the gates in the fences, headed for our back door. "He'll come in with his key," she said to her father. "You talk, and talk right—have him come up, and don't give any sign."

To me she whispered: "You cover him."

By then she'd seen the gun, which I'd reloaded before coming over and strapped on under my coat. I drew it, and took position with her just by the kitchen door. Mr. Landry went to the pantry and called. It had its own partition, but was really a continuation of the hall, and the kitchen door was alongside. Burke answered, and we heard him come up the stairs, heard the trap close as Mr. Landry lowered it to cut off retreat. We looked at each other as Burke said: "Adolphe, I'm scared to death—Pierre's not in the house, hasn't been in all night. And—did you know?—Cresap's in town! And I heard shots in the night! And with Pierre detesting'm so, it could mean, God forbid—"

"Real trouble, couldn't it?"

I stepped out, chocking the gun in his ribs, slapping him up quick, and taking a Colt Navy gun that he had in one coat pocket. I handed it to her, motioned him into the kitchen, and sat him down by the table in the chair Mr. Landry had used. I told him put down his hands. "We have some talking to do. And just to start it off friendly, cast it out of your mind, all worry about Pierre Legrand. He's dead."

". . . You lie."

"No. I killed him. After he tried to kill me. Who told him to, I don't know—but shooting a man asleep is a dirty Irish trick no Frenchman would ever think of."

"Where is he?"

"I don't know. Ask the Provost Guard."

"And what do you want of me?"

"As to that, I'll let Mr. Landry say."

"Adolphe! Don't tell me you're in with this thug?"

"Frank, there's things I have to ask you."

"But your home, that you bade me come to, that you invited me into just now, no more than a moment ago, and that I entered all in good faith—where's the sanctity of't?"

"That bothers me, I own that up. But this is life and death. Frank, what about that receipt, the one the Navy gave you, for this cotton I made over to you?"

"Well *what* about't? I *have't!*"

"Mr. Cresap thinks you forged the signature."

"I forged't? Is the fellow daft on this subject?"

"What about that pass for Mignon?"

"Well! 'Twas to be a pleasant surprise, and . . ."

"*Pleasant?* A trip to her mother's grave? And who gave you leave, Frank, to mess into it?" Burke's gall in daring to use this sacred thing seemed to infuriate him more than all the rest put together, and I had to remind him it had nothing to do with the case. He hardly seemed to hear me, but he did get off the subject. "And you had Pierre kill Powell, didn't you," he went on in his merciless driving at Burke.

"But Adolphe, how could you think such a thing?"

"The Navy saw him, that's how!"

"They saw—Pierre?"

Mr. Landry wheeled, said "Tell him, Mr. Cresap, what the boys said in your flat!" I repeated about the red pompon, but Burke, even when hit with the truth, would keep on screaming "Lie!"—and that's what he did now. However, we'd got to the meat of the matter, and time was going on. I said: "Burke, put your keys on the table."

"I have a key," said Mr. Landry. "To his back door."

"He may have a lockbox or something."

And to Burke again: *"Put 'em out!"*

He obeyed, pretty quick, pitching a ring on the table, with quite a few keys on it, of assorted sizes. I reached out to pull it toward me, still holding the gun, hooking it with my little finger to pull it to me. By then, my stick was second nature, and I hardly thought about it as my other hand held it, supporting my weight. But the sneaky Irishman did. He twitched it with his feet, just a little, but that was enough. He shot it out from under me, and as I lost balance and fell, he smashed one hand at my gun, the other at her face, so she fell and his gun flew out of her hand. He grabbed it and leveled both guns. "Stay where you are," he commanded, "and listen to me, the three of you!" Then he started in, as Landry stood where he was and she and I lay on the floor, pouring out what he felt. It quickly became clear that we weren't the only ones with pent-up ugly feelings. It was shocking, the language he used, not only to her and her father, but most of all, to me. He swore he was going to kill me, and I had a horrible feeling he meant it. But pretty soon Mr. Landry broke in: "Quit it, Frank, *quit it!*"

"I repeat every word I've said!"

"You want to hang? Because that's what you'll do, that's what we all will do, unless I get that receipt before the Navy gets it."

He held up his hand at Burke, slipped his hands under Mignon's arms, lifted her to her feet and kissed her. Then he started for me, to help me up. But, as though doing first things first, he turned to hand me the stick that still lay on the floor. The rest was all one motion. He picked it up by the small end and swung it—in an arc as a batter swings a bat, so hard it whined through the air. The crack was sharp, and Burke fell like a pole-axed steer, toppling from his chair. I grabbed the guns as they fell, shoving the Moore & Pond into the holster, handing the other to Mr. Landry. He took it but without paying attention, as he was staring down at Burke with a wild, venomous look. She was staring too, but at *him*, as though he was something holy. I guess I stared too, and maybe mumbled my thanks for the quick-witted thing he had done. Then at last he looked up, patted the Colt, and took the keys. He said: "I want him—left where he is, till I dispose of him later. While I'm searching that house—get this meat cut up—put it down, out of sight. If somebody comes—let them in—act natural—talk. If they're looking for him—all you know is—he was due to leave—for Shreveport. Tell them nothing—above all, don't bring them back here."

"Yes," she said.

"Right," I agreed.

"I'll be back as soon as I can."

He went, down through the store, through the gates in the fences, and in through Burke's back door.

CHAPTER 20

S<small>HE SCRAMBLED DOWN</small> and spread newspapers out on the floor at the foot of the stairs, directly below the trapdoor. Then she came back, standing by as I hacked at the meat, taking each piece as I got it off and dropping it down on the paper. It was a new kind of job to me and made me pretty sick, though whether it was the bloody meat that got me or the sight of Burke on the floor, I can't rightly say—maybe a little of both. But before very long I was done, and as soon as I wiped off the table and washed up the tools and myself, I went down with her to the locked-up store, with its empty shelves, musty smell, and cobwebs. The meat had to go in a tub, which was already down in the old cistern, but to reach it boards had to be moved; these she pried up with tire iron. The cistern was dry enough, but the bottom was covered with duckboards, and the tub sat on them. It was half full of other meat, including a picked chicken she said we would have for dinner. I handed it up and she passed the venison down. I put it in with the other meat, replaced all the boards, and followed her upstairs.

She was a few seconds ahead of me, and when I got to the kitchen, she was standing face to the wall, her head on her arms. When I asked what the trouble was, she pointed to Burke and said: "Willie, I was glad at him being dead—I was proud of Father for hitting him. But he's not dead! He's breathing!"

I listened, and he certainly was, with a rattle in his throat, his face a purplish red. I said: "He won't be for long, I imagine."

"Willie! I'm not glad any more! I'm scared!"

"So what do I do? Shoot him?"

"No!" Then: "He's getting a knot on his head!"

"Well he was cracked on the conk, you know."

"But it shows! It proves how long we left him lay!"

". . . I guess that's not so good."

"It knocks in the head any story we tell—about its being self-defense, or anything of that kind. Willie, if he dies or he doesn't die, there's that knot to prove that what we say is not true! Because if it was self-defense, why didn't we give one yelp for help when we needed help? Why did we let all that time go by while that knot was swelling up? And if it was not self-defense, what was it?"

"Take it easy. Let's figure on it."

To tell the truth, I was beginning to be just as scared as she was, now I was seeing things as they were, not as I thought they were going to be. While we were cutting the meat to get it out of the way and have the place shipshape, I'd been putting first things first and postponing everything else until Mr. Landry's return, when I supposed he'd take the lead—it was his responsibility, he had swung the stick. But that was on the assumption he would only be a few minutes, and once the papers were burned we could decide what to say, with our corpse still not cold. But here it was almost an hour, and instead of a corpse there was Burke on the floor, not even really alive. What to do about him I was too panicked to think. I may as well own up I was tempted to settle his hash, give him a tap with the peen of a hatchet that was on top of the woodbox. But I didn't quite have the nerve.

All of a sudden she pointed, and there was Mr. Landry, coming through the gates, stuffing papers into his coat pocket. But instead of entering the store, he raced to the Schmidt place, and then from under my flat we heard metal banging. Then there he was back in the yard, carrying a tremendous can, one I'd seen through the window, in among the sugar-mill stuff. He opened the door below, and we heard the can banging, down at the foot of the stairs. Then he was climbing up through the trapdoor, his face white, his eyes bright the way hers were sometimes, with a wild, fanatical shine. He said: "Sorry, Mignon; sorry, Bill, to be so long, but I was forever finding that tin box he had to keep his papers in. It was inside the square piano! However, it may have been just as well, as it gave me time to think what to do with him. He's going in a can I borrowed from Friedrich Schmidt—we wire the top on, load it on the dolly, roll it across Front Street, and dump it into Red River— right in front of their eyes, now, in broad daylight!"

"We're not!" she said. "No such!"

"Daughter, we dare not report this death."

"He's not dead!"

"... *What?*"
"All right, go look for yourself!"

He looked, listened to Burke's breathing, and sat down at the table. "This complicates things," he said. His eyes lost their shine, and I could see him doing what I did: lose his nerve and fall apart at the change from high excitement to dull, stupid danger that wasn't the less dangerous from being halfway under the gate, and stuck there. He licked his lips, and then pretty soon looked up. "At least," he said, "I've brought the can in—it's down there, in the store. When it happens, we'll have it ready." To that nobody said anything, but it was plain, from the silent treatment she gave it, that she didn't enthuse at all to that *we* he'd got off so glibly. After some minutes, he pulled himself together a little, took the papers out of his pocket—some on legal-cap, tied at the top with tape that had wax seals on the knots, some on printed forms with RACHAL's at the top, some just plain foolscap with columns of letters and numbers. He said: "At least, we can get these out of the way, so we can breathe safely," and started for the stove, where some embers were still glowing. I watched him lift the lid, then suddenly bellowed: "*Hold it!*"

I stumped over, snatched the papers from his hand.

"Mr. Cresap," he said, very peevishly "you were the one who insisted this stuff must be burned! Here it is, just as you said, the forged Navy receipt, with the signature traced on, identical with the one signed to the pass, that thing he got for Mignon. I even found his tracing outfit, the stand, the glass, the mirror for reflecting light—the thing is completely damning. What's the matter now? Why did you grab those papers? Why shouldn't they be destroyed?"

"Suppose it *doesn't* happen?"

"You mean, suppose he doesn't *die?*"

"Yes—for the hell of it, *just* suppose."

"Well all the more reason, I'd think—"

"Think again, Mr. Landry. Found by a party searching Burke's house, that stuff could hang you—and probably hang Mignon—as accessories to Powell's murder; they'd tie you in, close enough. But found, by *you*, and duly presented to them, it would be your exoneration—not only of any connection with Powell, *but for this fracas today, as well!* When I came in just now, with news of last night's shooting and with what I'd been told by Ball up at the hotel earlier, you began to have your suspicions, and when Burke came, you asked some sharp questions. He didn't answer, but tried to shoot you, and when he pulled his gun, you smashed him with the stick. Then you took his keys, went over, and made your search. *You* think it clears everything up—and they'll have to think so too. It'll take care of what worries Mignon, why we let time go by, without even calling a doctor. To you, I think you can say, it seemed more important to check this evidence over, though it might take a while, than to worry too much about a skunk who wasn't worth saving *anyhow.*"

"Thank God!" she said. "Willie has the answer!"

". . . Bill, you could be right."

We went over it two or three times, to have it clear and straight, especially about Pierre and how we'd bring *him* in. Because it was all right the night before for *me* not to recognize him, as no one could rightly say whether I knew him or not, but now for Mr. Landry not to have a suspicion when I told of the shooting would have a fishy look. We decided suspicion was really the key, that for him it was one more thing he wanted Burke to explain, but not something he was sure of to the extent he'd have to report what he thought. That way he wouldn't look dumb, and at the same time he'd be in the position a sensible man would take, of hesitating quite a while before shooting off his mouth with charges he couldn't prove. All that seemed rock-ribbed enough, especially since Burke could not contradict—we'd assumed, for some reason, that he was due to die, if not there in the kitchen with us, then later somewhere, in custody. So with things pretty well settled, I put the papers away in the grand piano, there in the sitting room, taking a tip from Burke. When I went back to the kitchen, it was all in the soup, every last thing we'd cooked up.

Burke had started to groan.

The three of us looked at each other, then looked away in consternation. "He's coming to," said Mignon.

". . . What now?" her father groaned.

"By me," I said. "I'm stumped."

However, I wasn't too stumped to give Burke a kick, a hard one, right in the rump, and he let out a muffled yell. Then he sat up. Then, dragging himself to a spot near the wall, where he could lean his head against it, he touched his knot with one hand, while he leaned on the other and cussed. He called me scut, crud, and dirty son of a bitch. He called Mr. Landry a Judas. He called her whore, drab, queen of the swampland strumpets. He called on the Holy Mother of God to be his witness what a fine hombre he was, and told all the good he'd done, from Nicaragua to Mexico and back, as well as special good deeds in Limerick. He kept it up for some time, until I began wondering why any of us had to listen. I went over and gave him another kick. He shut up and lay there panting. And then suddenly, from over on Second Street somewhere, I heard: "Column, *halt!*"

I looked, and in front of Burke's house the whole bunch had halted—Hager, Dan, Sandy, Ball, four or five Navy ensigns, some seamen, and a detail from the Provost Guard. I heard my mouth say to Burke: "Skunk, they've identified their corpse, and they're looking for you at your house. They'll be here, and listen what I'm telling you: We have all that cotton stuff, including the forged receipt. Mr. Landry found it, in your square piano. It can hang you, do you hear?"

"What are you getting at, scut?"

"We can show them that receipt. We don't mind."

"Then show't, and be damned to you!"

"We prefer not. We'd enjoy seeing you hang, but the thing could ramify against these two wonderful people that you've got into this mess—especially if you dragged them in, trying to save yourself. So we're *not* showing it to them! At least, not *yet*. To get the curtain down, to close the case, to hush up the real truth, we're giving you your chance to tell it your own way. So when they come, see that you talk right."

"Tell him," wailed Mr. Landry, "what he's to say!"

"Well, what is he to say?" I asked.

"We—have to think of something, *now!*"

"I've completely run out of think. And besides," I went on, somewhat annoyed, "who the hell are we to be teaching a liar how to cook up a lie?"

"*Here they come!*"

There was panic in her voice, and when I looked out the window, here came the column of twos, Dan and Hager in front, marching down the side street.

CHAPTER 21

BUT NO ONE CAME to the door, and it wasn't until a knock sounded on the other side of the building that I realized that Burke, the last he'd been seen by the guard, was being ordered by me to report to my flat in the morning. So I went down and around to answer. Hager was up on the stoop, with Dan, Ball, and Sandy, banging to get in, the rest down below, standing around in the alley. I spoke, and when they said they were looking for Burke, I explained where he was and said: "We're having our talk over there." Then Dan said: "Good morning, Bill," and said he'd been detailed "to sit in as Headquarters observer, on this shooting thing, whatever it amounts to." I said a dead man, especially one that I killed, amounted to plenty with me, and that I'd give any help that I could, if more information was wanted. Then I led the way around, and Mignon opened the door. I introduced Hager and Ball, reminding her:

"You know Captain Dan Dorsey, and also, I think, Lieutenant Gregg." Sandy stared when he saw her, but took her hand when she gave it, and called her Mrs. Fournet. Then Burke appeared behind her, but balked when Hager told him he was wanted at the courthouse for questioning. "I'm not feeling too well," he said. "I don't care for marching about."

"And what seems to be the trouble?" asked Hager.

"The wallop I took on my head."

He pointed at the knot, and while Hager was peering at it, said: "I was out, looking for me gippo, and banged me head at the market on the awning over a stall."

"It's your gippo that brings us here."

"I've deduced as much, Captain."

"He's dead."

"Aye."

Adolphe Landry got in it then, appearing beside Mignon and asking everyone in. The ensigns and enlisted men were told to stand by below, while Hager, Dan, Ball, and Sandy came in. Hager camped on the sitting-room settee, looking much like a judge, while Mignon, Dan, Ball, and Burke occupied the chairs, and Adolphe, Sandy, and I stood, our backs to one of the bookshelves. Hager got at it immediately, saying: "Mr. Burke, a man was killed last night, in the flat next door, by Mr. Cresap here, identified as Pierre Legrand, your personal servant or, as you call him, your gippo. What do you know about it?"

"Nothing, of course, Captain."

"Did you know he tried to kill Cresap?"

"Not until Cresap mentioned it."

"That your man shot at him?"

"That someone did, he didn't know who. I twigged't."

That covered, in a way I had to admire, my failure to identify Pierre, so nothing had been joggled in a way I would have to explain. But I put in, on my own, that I'd only seen this Pierre once, for the barest glance, in New Orleans, and wouldn't have known him from Adam. Burke asked: "Who made the identification, if I may make so bold as to inquire?" Hager told him: "Two sutlers and a cook at the Ice House Hotel." Burke nodded and said: "That explains't—Pierre always bought our food." Then Hager got back to the point, and asked Burke very sharp: "Did you send this man to kill Cresap?"

"God forbid! Why should I?"

"Did you send him to kill Powell?"

"No. . . . You think he killed Powell?"

"*We know he killed Powell.*"

Hager was murderously cold, and walked over to where Burke sat by the piano to stare down at him, hard. But Burke was strangely unfussed. "I may say it doesn't surprise me," he said in a quiet way, as if hearing gossip of an interesting kind.

". . . Why not?" asked Hager, caught off balance.

"The bad blood between 'em," said Burke.

"Bad blood? Between Powell? And—*this* man?"

"I don't care for that remark," roared Burke, with a snarl. "It seems to imply, Captain, that as between a fine gentleman such as Powell and a midge such as Pierre, bad blood couldn't exist, as the officer wouldn't deign and the varlet wouldn't dare. Know then, the gentleman *did* deign, in a vulgar, ungentlemanly way, and the varlet did dare, in a way even *you* might respect. He had his pride, he was a man."

"And when was all this, Burke?"

"Last summer. Last June."

"And where?"

"Bagdad, Mexico."

Hager, whose reaction to surprise had been to rip at Burke, was now set back on his heels even worse than before, and to cover up, pretended disgust. Returning to his place on the settee, he said in a lofty way: "Let's get back to Cresap."

"Let's not," said Burke.

Then *he* got up and went over, so he could stare down at Hager. "At the Hotel DeGlobe in Bagdad," he rumbled slowly, "Pierre had got'm a job, after his discharge from the Berthollet, serving drinks in the bar. And there every night came Powell. He was on the *Itasca* then, the steam schooner on blockade duty, and would come ashore at night, to inquire about cotton shipments—and to drink. To swill booze, carouse, and quarrel with Pierre in the bar, holding the boy up to ridicule, taunting'm, plaguing'm, mocking'm. It got to the point where to head off something dreadful, I took a hand with Pierre, and brought'm to Matamoros by *diligencia* one day. And then, in me growing affection for'm, I hired'm on as boy, as valet, as gippo." His voice had risen a little, and he turned suddenly on Ball. "Am I right, Lieutenant?" he asked. "Isn't it true? Every word that I've said?"

"I've never been to Mexico."

"You've been to the Ice House Hotel—you followed Powell on that duty, right here in Alexandria. How did he conduct himself in that bar?"

"In exemplary fashion, sir."

"Then he reformed himself, I may say."

How much of it was true, I didn't of course know, though some of it had to be, especially the *Itasca* part, or Ball would have contradicted. But true or false, it was a mile away from himself and any motive he might have had for ordering Powell killed, and though I hated myself for it, I had to be on his side, as I had sicked him on. He smelled advantage, and in a reasonable tone resumed: "Or in other words, Captain—"

"Never mind the other words," snapped Hager. "Let's get back to you. Why, in the light of all that, didn't you once open your mouth when Lieutenant Powell was killed?"

"I? Inform on me own gippo?"

"If you knew he'd committed a crime?"

"Captain! I didn't know it!"

"Don't quibble! You knew about the grudge!"

"I knew of twenty thousand grudges."

". . . What do you mean by that?"

"Your own among the rest!"

"*My* grudge, Burke? *My grudge?*"

"Aye—you bore'm a grudge, you bear'm a grudge as you sit there, as this whole Army does, against the Mississippi Squadron of the United States Navy, for the rape of the cotton last week—you hate the Navy's guts, so don't single me out for failing to open me mouth on a matter that could have involved every man in this town—except the boys afloat! *Who didn't bear'm a grudge?* Tell me who didn't, and I'll tell *him*, not you, why I didn't speak up!"

Clammy silence settled down, and it was some moments before Hager asked: "Why would this man try to kill Cresap?"

"I don't know, he didn't discuss't with me."

"What would be your conjecture?"

"Why don't you ask Cresap?"

"We did. He didn't know. I'm asking you."

"Why wouldn't he try to kill Cresap? A man who

blackened his character, did infamous things to him, only last month in New Orleans? Who attempted to make it appear the boy deserted his post in my rooms at the City Hotel, so a pretended search could be made and evidence discovered which 'twas said that I manufactured against a friend and mentor and partner, who sits here in front of your eyes, Adolphe Landry, no other, and who can throw the lie in me teeth, if I wander one inch from the truth! When all the time 'twas himself, this same clever Cresap, who forged the documents up, in the hope of discrediting me, and in that way enriching himself!" He came over and smiled in my face, so I knew what to expect, if the forged receipt came out—by hook, crook, or trick, it would be hung on me. He turned to Hager again and went on, very pious: "Pierre was plain, rude, and ignorant, and no doubt given to violence, as such boys usually are. But false to a duty he was not—*he never deserted a post!* And perhaps he brooded a bit at me own troubled spirit, when I returned to the house last night."

"What troubled your spirit, if any?"

Hager was quite sarcastic, but didn't ask about New Orleans, which told me he knew what had happened there, and if it told me it told Burke, he not being dumb on such things. "His rapacious demands," he answered.

"Cresap's, you mean?"

"For's fee."

"What fee?"

"That I promised'm, two hundred and fifty dollars. To free Adolphe."

"Well? He freed him, didn't he?"

"Aye, but look what he did to me! Got me accused, unjustly, so I spent a night confined, as a common thug, in a cell! I refused to pay'm a cent, and last night he renewed his demands—Lieutenant Ball will bear witness for me, how he called me aside in the hotel, wanting payment, and your guard will corroborate that he ordered me, on the street, to report here today, else bear the consequence—he made threats against me."

"What threats?"

"He questioned me passes, Captain."

It all matched up, it didn't sound collusive, and it concealed real motive. It was a masterly job of lying, and I had to get in step. When Hager turned to me, I said: "I doubted, and still doubt, if this man has proper permission to be here —he came when the Reb Army was here, and a Reb permit isn't valid, it means nothing to a Union marshal. However, that's not for me to decide. As to what he says in general, allowing for distortion, self-pity, and overpraise of the gentle Pierre, I would say he's pretty well covered the ground. Now that I know who I killed, I admit he had grounds to dislike me."

"The passes, Burke? Let's see them."

Burke got them out, from the same old stuffed-up wallet—letters, from prominent Rebs in New Orleans, that he'd used on the trip up the Teche to enter the Confederate lines; stuff concerning Pierre, including his French discharge; and a U.S. custom-house permit for the importation of cotton, covering, Burke said, "right of access to me property"—meaning, his presence in Alexandria. While Hager was reading them over, small things happened. Ball, who had snickered at "the gentle Pierre," looked over and threw me a wink. Sandy leaned close and whispered: "This Mignon package—you like her?"

"Yes, I guess so," I whispered back.

"I was hoping to lift her skirt."

"*I* hope to make her my wife."

"*Ouch*—I didn't say it; you misunderstood me!" And then, for a real fast switch: "Bill, did you notice Ball? How friendly he's acting toward you? You're still hot!"

"So? What then?"

"You can still get that receipt!"

"For what?"

"For cotton, stupid!"

"I don't have any cotton!"

"Goddam it, get some!"

Next off, Hager, Ball, and Dan had their heads together, and just once Dan shrugged. Then Hager reached out and handed Burke back his papers. It was over, with the officers marching out after saluting Mignon and thanking Mr. Landry for his kindness in asking them in. Then there we were, Mr. Landry, Burke, Mignon, and I, drawing trembling breaths. And then: "Frank," said Mr. Landry, "I couldn't ever forget what you did just now, in the way of what could be called, I suppose, convenient prevarication. And I *hope* I never forget the horrible reason for it."

"The horrible reason," I told him, "was that knowing a skunk for a skunk, you still partnered with him—for the money. So if you don't like how he smells, you may smell the same way, yourself."

"Willie," she snapped, "don't be ornery."

"Sometimes," I said, "orneriness clears the air."

"And well the air needs't," Burke flung at me with a sneer. "As the author of the idea, you smell a bit yourself."

"Perhaps," I agreed. "No doubt."

"But in a wholesome, mephitic way!"

"Damn it, I owned up to it, didn't I?"

I sounded hysterical, and slammed out of there.

CHAPTER 22

In my flat, I had a bad reaction and lay down for a while to think. It was going on noon, and I'd decided to visit the hotel for lunch when a tap came on the door, and I got up to let her in. She had a platter of ham, cornbread, and lentils, all warmed up very nice and covered with a napkin, and a pail of hot coffee. She served us in the dining room, using Schmidt dishes, and as we ate she talked, mainly about Burke and how he'd leave soon, as soon as his head didn't hurt, for the Sabine to buy in the cotton. She said she'd written a letter for him, addressed to people out there, giving him a "character," and that her father had written him one, addressed to Kirby Smith, the Reb commander in chief, "as of course that whole country is still in the Secesh lines." She talked of various things, as though nothing had happened at all, and I found myself wondering if anything really had. She made me eat up every speck, so she could wash the things in cold water, and then when she'd put them away, led on up the hall. But instead of turning off to go out, she kept on to the sitting room and, though I took a seat, kept on marching around, restless. I said again how pretty she looked in the gingham, and she said: "I like red—and it likes me, I think. It's my color, kind of."

And then: "What was Sandy saying to you?"

"Why," I said, "he wanted to know if I liked you. He let drop he'd been hoping to lift your skirt."

"Well he tried! Did he let drop about *that?*"

"No, and you didn't either."

"Well? In one of the fitting rooms, there at Lavadeau's, he commenced messing around. It didn't amount to much."

"Just practically nothing at all?"

". . . What else did he have to say?"

"Nothing. Just this, that, and the other."

"He was nagging at you about something. What?"

". . . I don't just now recollect."

"It was the cotton, wasn't it? What he spoke about before, this morning there in the hall. And how you could get a receipt, after killing Powell's murderer. That's what it was, isn't it?"

"All right, but I don't have any cotton."

"Yes, but we have."

"Who is *we?*"

"Father and I, Willie."

"Did Mr. Landry send you to me?"

"No, certainly not—he's over at Frank's, packing him up to leave, trying to get him started, he wants him out of the way. And Frank's going—he thinks, now that that forgery didn't work, those titles he had are worthless, so the cotton on the Sabine is all that's left for him. He doesn't know what we know, that you can get a receipt, that the Navy will give you one. So all we have to do is tear up the papers in his name and copy new ones off, in the name of Willie Cresap. And then, lo and behold, it's a hundred and twenty thousand dollars!"

"Mignon, I'm sick of this cotton."

"Well, wasn't I? Didn't I say I was?"

"Then what makes you change?"

"You, that's what. So long as Frank was in it, I was scared to death. I learned to fear him as I'd never feared anyone. But you, Willie, are honest."

"Dan says this cotton is hoodooed."

"Hoodoo wasn't the trouble. Crookedness was."

"Whatever it was, I'm still sick of it."

"What about the twenty-five thousand dollars?"

". . . It's what Sandy's worrying about."

"You still have to get it, Willie."

"I don't care to get it that way."

"But you do care to get it from her?"

She had nestled into my lap, but now got up and faced me, and when I just sat there and stared, caught utterly by surprise, she charged back into the dining room, then came up the hall with her platter in one hand and her little tin pail in the other. When I barred her way at the crosshall, she banged me with the pail, so it flew out of her hands and clattered to the floor. To keep it from getting broken, I took the platter away from her, then took her by the wrist and dragged her into the bedroom. When I'd flung her on the bed, I said: "Calm down for a change, why don't you? What's the idea, flying off the handle this way?"

"You can get other things from her, too!"

"Well, I never did, but—"

"You never did! Well, you've been missing something, that's all I have to say. Because she's willing, that I promise you!"

"So happens, was the other way around."

"You asked and she said no?"

"That was it, exactly."

"Why? What made her act so noble?"

"Whiff of Russian Leather."

Some things have the ring of truth, and I saw from the flick of her eye that she knew this was one of them. She stared up at the ceiling, and her mouth began to twist. I'm sure that of all the things that happened to her that day, none meant to her quite what those four little words had said. Some little time went by as she lay there, trying not to cry, her dress rumpled, her white petticoat flared out, her pantalettes hiked up, her beautiful legs showing as far as the garters. I put the platter down, set the pail beside it, and went over to her. I undid tapes and buttons, and she didn't seem to help, but didn't stop me either, and pretty soon there she was, without a stitch on. Only then did she whisper: "My favorite costume, it seems."

"And very becoming, too."

"Willie, stop trying to *switch*."

"I'm not. I guess Burke called it on me— I *am* in, whether I like it or not, and might as well make it pay. How long will this write-up take?"

"Couple of days, no more."

"The *Eastport* could be gone by then with the rest of the invasion—headed for Shreveport. Upriver."

"No, Willie. Great big boat like her can't get up the falls in a hurry—she has to be drug. They learned their lesson from another one, the *Woodford*, that they got careless with. She's sitting on bottom right now up at the head of the falls, a hole punched in her hull. This boat will take some days, and in that time we'll do our writing—I'll help with it. What takes the time is the bale markings. Cotton's not like corn, which is so many bushels and one bushel's just like another. With cotton, it must be this particular bale, and every one has to be listed, by mark, number, and weight. And that list goes on all papers. We'll write the deed up first, the bill of sale from Father, conveying the cotton to you, which is the proof you give the Navy that the cotton belongs to you, a loyal godpappy. That should be ready tomorrow, for recording down in the courthouse. Then the receipt itself, which you can take to the Navy on Sunday, I would expect. Then the partnership articles, they can be written up last, as there's no hurry about them. You really mean to, Willie?"

"If your father's agreeable, I am."

"Kiss me then, nice."

Not that Mr. Landry, when she told him in their sitting room later that afternoon, exactly jumped up and cracked his heels. He was bitter against me for telling him that he stank, and full of justification for the relations he'd had with Burke. "I deny it was my fault!" he speechified at me, walking up and down. "I deny it was anyone's fault, except the Union's fault, and the fault of this hell-on-earth they've put on us! *War's over in Louisiana*—but do they give us peace? No! They keep tramping us down with this half-war, half-peace they bring with them, worse than that life-in-death of the Ancient Mariner, neither one thing nor the other! And if I did what I *had* to, to give, to help others live, I don't apologize, and I won't have it I stink! All right, Frank's a skunk—I was the first to say it, and I tried to kill him for it! But I used him, he didn't use me! And I had my decent reasons! It was the only way open to me to get back at this bluebelly bunch, to get a chunk of their tin, to make them pay through the nose for what they've done to me, and what they've done to mine! Because, at least I meant to share a little, if any profits accrued, with these people here, my people, the ones who've suffered the most!"

"This I find most astonishing."

"I've already shared with these people—I bought them shoes, and you defended me for it. Didn't you?"

". . . Yes. I retract."

I'd been hoping, I guess, that by plaguing him, even though I owed him my life, I'd force him to reject me as a partner and I'd be out from under. But when I said: "If you don't want this deal, just say so," he wheeled on me quick and answered: "I didn't say that, Mr. Cresap. I would assume, however, that first before anything else, you'd want to be assured you're not hooking up with a skunk."

"Then, you're not a skunk," I said.

"You two could shake hands," she told us.

Down in the store was an office partitioned off in one corner, with a high bookkeeper's desk, a safe, and shelves piled up with ledgers. Landry worked there the rest of the day, and by candlelight into the night, getting the bill of sale up, making it correspond with the markings on the papers I'd stuffed in the piano. Next day he signed it over and took me down with it to the courthouse, where we went past Hager's desk to the Clerk of Court's office and had it recorded. Then, with Mignon right beside him calling the data off, he wrote up the Navy receipt, and next day I took it to Sandy. I found him on his boat, which was celebrating Easter Sunday by battling her way up the falls. The falls was really a rapid a mile or so long above town, and no place for boats at all, let alone a tub like the *Eastport*. She was there at the lower end, tugs behind her pushing, tugs ahead of her hauling, and tugs alongside lifting. From a tree dead ahead a hawser ran to her capstan, and on command the steam would hit it, and it would turn with a clank while the paddles churned the water. Then everything would stall, and on command, stop. It wasn't a pretty show, as the boat was plated with iron which was rusty and scaly and dented, with stuff rubbing off on the men. But, at least to a hard-rock man, it was interesting, and I watched it a while before waving my paper at Sandy, in charge of things on shore at the tree. He waved back, but it was some time before a whistle blew, they all sat down for a rest, and he was able to join me. He took the receipt and read while a cook went around with a pot and ladled coffee into mess cups. Pretty soon he asked: "Landry? Isn't that the man I met? Mrs. Fournet's father, who asked us in to question Burke?"

"That's right," I said. "He didn't make himself known, as the cotton-owner, that is, until I happened to mention what you said to me—matter of fact, she saw you whispering and asked what it meant. He had supposed his cotton lost when the Navy took it over, and hadn't wanted to embarrass me by bringing the subject up. But, when he learned I could get a receipt, or at least had a chance of getting one, he came up with this quick."

I flashed half of my fifty-dollar bill, then took out the other half and fitted the pieces together. He blinked, then said: "Bill, I own up three hundred twenty-seven bales is more than I bargained for. I thought you might be able to swing—well, say a hundred bales—but this——"

"I'm in it with him, share-and-share alike."

"You mean later? Right now, he didn't ask cash?"

"That's it. That's how I'm able to do it."

". . . I'll have to get Lieutenant Ball."

He hailed the ship, and Ball showed at a gun port in undershirt, dungarees, and straw hat, and had himself rowed ashore in a gig that dangled alongside. He too whistled when he saw the number of bales, then whistled again. "Listen at this," he told Sandy: ". . . '327 bales, bearing the following marks *and no other marks*.' That makes this valid in court, as it nullifies that CSA stencil! Did that hombre know his cotton, the one who drew this up!"

"Still," said Sandy, "the hombre who killed Legrand—"

"That doesn't figure!" barked Ball, "in any way, shape, or form! Our orders are all that concern us, and our orders were receipt for loyal cotton. So far, we haven't found any. But if you know Cresap is loyal—"

"I have my Army discharge," I said.

"And if the cotton's lawfully acquired—"

"I have a bill of sale covering that."

I got out discharge, bill of sale stamped by the Clerk of the Court, torn bill, and I don't know what else, and let him look them over. He asked to borrow them briefly, and went out to the ship. Then a belted seaman came ashore, carrying an oilskin package, and I took him for a courier on his way with my stuff for the flag boat. He legged it down through the woods, and I waited at least an hour, while work on the falls resumed. Then here he came back and boarded the ship again. Then Ball came back in the gig, the package in his hand. He handed it over, saying. "All right, Cresap, here you are, everything signed up. It's an awful lot of prize for the Navy to give up, but orders are orders, even when they hurt."

"I thank the Navy," I told him. "I thank you."

"It's money in the bank."

"Good luck with it, Bill," whispered Sandy, leaning close as he shook hands, trying to hide from Ball how excited he was.

That night, by candlelight, we celebrated our luck, Mignon, Mr. Landry, and I, with three rum toddies. She was quiet, her eyes dreamy, but he wanted to talk and, as he said, make a clean, fresh start. He kept insisting: "I'd like to make clear, it's more than the money, sir. It's also you, what you mean to Mignon, and if you'll allow me to say so, what you mean to me. I've been very concerned about you—I mean, what Frank might try to do in his vicious, vindictive way. But, with him going west, and you bound for Springfield, I would say the danger is past, so I can sleep nights."

"When does he leave?" I asked him.

"He has left. He went today—on foot. Sometimes it can be the quickest way. I gave him back his gun, as he's carrying lots of cash, and—he took himself off."

"Can't we forget about him?" she wanted to know.

"We *can* forget him; that's all I'm trying to say."

"Then *let's*."

CHAPTER 23

So BEGAN THE QUEER THREE WEEKS of sitting around all the time, waiting for a boat to go out on. At first I'd go down each day to see Hager at the courthouse; he'd promised a pass for the three of us when navigation resumed. But then she began going alone, because Dan paid me a call to warn me off the streets. The traders, he said, were being rounded up for shipment back to New Orleans on the *Empire Parish*, under arrest. If I got caught out, I'd be shipped back, too. It seemed a strange reward for saviors of their country, as they'd been assured they were, but that's how the thing was handled, now that they weren't saviors any more but nuisances. So that's how it came about that I stayed indoors all the time, waiting, waiting, and waiting. She'd come in the morning, bringing my breakfast over, and when I'd finished she'd help me dress, which always took some time and seemed to involve kisses. Then we'd take the tray back together, ducking across the back yards, and she'd make some lunch. Then the three of us would sit, under the books in the sitting room, through the afternoon and evening.

I would crack jokes, if, as, and when I remembered some. She would spend the money, all kinds of different ways: on a house in New Orleans; on mahogany, silver, and cut glass for our dining room; on a carriage with matched grays—but not often on clothes, for some reason. He would go around, touching the backs of books and talking about literature, especially Casanova, who he said was the greatest literary figure of the eighteenth century, "the father of many more fiction characters than of illegitimate children—of D'Artagnan, Jean Valjean, a whole endless gallery." Then he'd make her play *Don Giovanni*, who he said was Casanova in disguise, "as the librettist knew him well—and it all corresponds to *him*, not with Don Juan of Seville." I got curious about it, and took down the memoirs one time, Volume I, to have a peep. But it was in French, and I could hardly understand a word. It all surprised me; I'd heard of Casanova as lover but didn't know he wrote anything. I can't say I quite got the point, as I hadn't read enough, but I felt it was educational, and was always glad to listen.

And while we talked and talked, and sipped our nightly grog, the invasion rolled upriver, all the Army and most of the Navy, until nothing was left in town but freight boats, the Guard, and the Q.M. Things had quieted down, and you felt they would soon be normal. Bees buzzed, flowers bloomed, perfume filled the air, and townspeople ventured out—the few who were still left and hadn't skedaddled upriver before the invasion came in. When the *Empire Parish* went down, I ventured out too, to resume asking for my pass. Captain Hager shook hands, said it was "just a matter of days, with regular river schedules, as soon as we get to Shreveport." I reported the news, and we celebrated a bit with an extra grog that night.

And then one day, as we raced up the stairs with my breakfast dishes, the door opened in front of us and her father was there in the hall, a solemn look on his face. I supposed her visits to me were the reason and braced myself to argue, to say she was grown up now, that we meant to be married, that if she wanted to come it was none of his business. But that didn't seem to be it. He led to the sitting room, and there on the floor were a rucksack, blanket roll, overcoat, and hat, all in a neat pile. She stared, then asked: "Are you going away—or what?" And then: "Oh! Our passes have come? Is that it?"

"Sit down, Daughter, Mr. Cresap."

He was very quiet, but also dramatic, and when we had sat he went on: "I'm going to join up. Turns out Taylor wasn't the idiot. I was."

"All right," she said, "but what's he done?"

"He's *whipped*, that's what!"

"Whipped? Whipped who?"

"The Union! *War's not over in Louisiana!*"

"Well you don't have to snap my head off, do you?"

"Daughter! It's not over. For me, or for you."

"*Me?* I don't even *yet* know what happened!"

"He smashed 'em! In the woods, just this side of Mansfield, he cut 'em to pieces, this whole Army of the Gulf! It was a shambles, a slaughter, a rout! Two of his scouts got through; they're up at the hotel now. They never saw anything like it! It couldn't happen, and it did! But that's just the beginning. They're in a race now, he and the Union Army, for this place, for Alexandria. They're in full flight to get out, and he doesn't mean to let 'em. He's shutting 'em up, he's out to capture every man—and that's where I come in! I'm late, God forgive me; I thought it was all over, but better late than never, the eleventh hour in the vineyard, and there's things I can do! I'm on my way to report!"

He began to talk, then, reviling himself for giving up too soon, and then went back to her. "Daughter," he told her very solemnly, "don't forget, when I'm gone, that *you* must do something *too*. As a Reb, as a loyal Confederate, you have to! You—"

She cut in: "I'll do what I can, of course!"

"Daughter, that's not enough."

"How does anyone do *more* than they can?"

"It has to be *something*, not just good intentions!"

"Listen, you speak for your *own* self!"

"Don't worry. I will."

He slung the rucksack over his shoulder, then held his hand out to me with a friendly, elegant smile, and saying something about "my regret we now have to be enemies." But I said, not seeing his hand: "Sit down, Mr. Landry. We haven't quite finished our talk—you haven't included me, so far, but I'm in anyway, you may be surprised to learn."

"I don't understand you, sir."

"What about our cotton?"

". . . I assume you're an honorable man."

"You mean, Mr. Landry, you assume you can go traipsing off to jump on Taylor's bandwagon, now it's no longer a sinking ship, and that I won't mind at all, but will cut you in just the same for your full share of what I make at Springfield? Haven't you forgotten that as a Reb, in arms against your country, you'll have no standing in court? You're putting yourself once more in the spot you found yourself in when Burke informed on you in New Orleans."

"That seems to say you'd euchre me, too."

"Not quite. You've forgotten other things, too."

"What are you getting at now?"

"Your Union allegiance, Mr. Landry."

"It was coerced from me. I never took any oath."

"You took your freedom, though."

"I was born free!"

"You were set free when I proclaimed you loyal. *Then loyal you're going to be!* Take off your bag, Mr. Landry. You're not going anywhere."

"I'm going. And I warn you I'm armed."

"I know you're armed—I can see the bulge in your pocket. I didn't myself think necessary to strap on my Moore and Pond. But you start out of this place, I'm following you down to the street, I'm hailing the guard at Biossat's, I'm having you taken in, and I'm charging you as a spy!"

"Then, my departure must wait on yours."

"Meaning, I'm to leave your house?"

"I hope you don't make me say it."

"I don't go till I have your parole."

"Parole? *Parole?*"

"Your word to me you're going to stay put!"

"Mr. Cresap, I think you forget yourself."

"Mr. Landry, I must have your promise."

"Sir, I will not accept dictation—"

"Goddam it, Mr. Landry, do you think I'm playing games? *Speak, and speak now, or I will!* I'll *not* let you up easy, and they *will* break your neck!"

". . . Sir, you leave me no choice."

"Say it."

"I pledge myself not to join—"

"—the enemies of my country—"

"—the Confederate States of America."

"I'll accept that."

"Then, sir?"

"Leaving now, Mr. Landry."

I turned on my heel, walked out of there, and returned to my own flat. I went to the front room, peered out on the street, and everything looked the same. I wondered if it was true, the news that Landry had heard. I tried to think what it would mean to me. I was still trying when the knock came on the door. I let her in and followed her into the sitting room, but got kind of annoyed when all she did was stare. "What's the matter?" I growled. "Something *on* me?"

"Willie, I don't know you any more."

"Don't worry, it's me, the same old one."

"But how could you talk to him like that?"

"You don't see the reason?"

"I certainly don't."

"Then maybe you need talking to, too."

She started to rake me over for how ungrateful I was, "after the way he's treated you, almost as a son, asking you in all the time, letting me give you your meals, putting you in on the cotton . . ."

"*I'm sick of that damned cotton!*"

"Well, it's *his*, you know!"

"Listen, I don't know what's his, what's mine, or what's the Navy's any more, but I know this: He's been deceiving himself, with all this talk of his about the half-war–half-peace we've got, the life-in-death that was inflicted on the Ancient Mariner. Don't you know what that life-in-death was? That albatross on his neck? Don't you know what he meant, that Samuel Taylor Coleridge, the man who wrote that poem?"

". . . What are you talking about?"

"He was an opium-eater!"

"What's that got to do with Father?"

"The cotton's *his* opium, that's what. *He* thinks, in this half-war–half-peace he imagines, that it's every man for himself, anything goes, devil take the hindmost. That's not true. It's not half-war–half-peace; it's war, as Dan Dorsey's been trying to say, and it's not any the less war that your father doesn't like it and it doesn't like him! All of a sudden, with the guilty conscience he's got, he makes a break to help Taylor, and that's wonderful, isn't it? But the cotton's there all the time, it's the main thing he thinks about, as it has been from the start, and though he was hot to join Taylor, he was dead sure that I, as an honorable man, would cut him in on the tin that we would make when I auctioned to Union buyers after a Union court awarded me! Well, he can guess again; he can't have it both ways! I'll cut him in, now that I have his parole, but I'd never have cut in a Reb who was out there shooting at me—and even that much I don't pretend to like! I told him once, and I tell you again, the cotton stinks—and I only live to see the day when I'll be shut of it forever!"

"*But taking it off* her *doesn't stink?*"

"Her? . . . Her?"

"You know who I'm talking about!"

"Is she all that you've got on your mind?"

"Until that cotton is sold, yes."

"There's a war going on that concerns you."

"What do I care about war?"

"All right. Now we know."

We were atremble, and from the beautiful time we'd had, after breakfast that morning, it was cold, bitter, and ugly.

CHAPTER 24

It was true, all right; we'd had the stuffing kicked out of us and skedasis was complete. We were on our way out and overnight, from being a quiet riverside town, with flowers perfuming the air, Alexandria was a hellhole on earth, with wounded men limping in, horses dying in the streets, splintered boats crashing down the falls, and in place of the perfume a smell of death, rot, and war. Hanging over it all was danger, because maybe we wanted out, but Taylor had different ideas and meant to bag us all. He surrounded the town and kept tightening the noose, his fires out in the woods creeping closer and closer, his skirmishers giving no peace. He cut the river below so no supplies could come up, and suddenly rations were short. Also water was short; with thirty thousand men and five thousand horses penned up in place built for four thousand, with no wells and cisterns not refilled since the rain Taylor arrived in, the

206 / James M. Cain

supply ran out fast. That left Red River water, but it was so foul with corpses, swill, and filth that the boys got desperately sick, and their filth was added to the original filth.

Worst of all was the drought in Texas, which made the river low, so it didn't take a rise as it generally did in spring. It fell, and the Navy got stuck in the mud, ten of its best boats, up above the falls. That's what hung things, because instead of continuing its march the Army had to halt, dig in, and try to get them out. And what it decided to do was put in a dam of sticks and stones and trees just above the town, to bulge the water up for enough depth to float the boats. It was such a weird idea that I hadn't the heart to look. The Red River current, which I'd already clocked with my eye by watching snags float by, was at least nine miles an hour, and trying to hold it with a makeshift pile of brush struck me as pathetic, like trying to hold an elephant by tying him with knitting yarn. Just the same, they started in to do it. Colored troops put in a pontoon bridge from a ramp in front of the courthouse to a spot on the left bank, which they finished in one day, and construction crews streamed over, so work could go forward from both sides of the river at once. Every day boats would go up through the swing draw out in the middle, with barges of stone and rubble, and axes would speak all the time, upriver from Alexandria and from the woods above Pineville.

And all during that we sat, she, Mr. Landry, and I, in their sitting room, for an even queerer three weeks than the other three weeks had been. He made it up with me, coming over after she left the same day as our brawl, to thank me "for the information, which Mignon has just

mentioned to me, about Samuel Taylor Coleridge. I hadn't
known it before, but just verified it in the *Britannica*, and
am truly grateful for it." I said you couldn't prove it by
me, but I did hear it in college, and he repeated that such
things to him were important and he counted himself in
my debt. Then he asked me to supper, and I resumed taking
my meals with them—a good thing, since the hotel ran out
of food and otherwise I'd have been out of luck. We didn't
eat well but we ate, dried stuff from the store, prunes and
apples and apricots, beans and peas and rice, stocked in
barrels and sacks and kegs. He wouldn't allow me below
to help bring anything up, and once when I glimpsed the
kegs I suspected they were the reason, and wondered what
was in them. Every day he'd go out for a stroll, to pick up
such news as he could, and I'd go down to the courthouse,
which had been converted into a hospital and stank of
wounded men, to pester for my pass. In between, the three
of us would talk.

"You've no faith in the dam?" he asked me one day.

"Who wants to know?" I said. "A loyal Reb?"

"No, Mr. Cresap," he assured me, very solemn, "a
loyal Union man. And since you bring it up, I may say that
things have changed since we had our last discussion. War
was *not* over in Louisiana—for a few days, at least. Now,
I'm sorry to say, it is—finally, and for keeps. I said it, didn't
I? That I was the fool, not Taylor, but they've drawn
Taylor's teeth and clipped his claws. He's now a tiger made
of paper, with just a token force of no more than five
thousand men, banging away with artillery, lighting fires
at night, and cutting off forage parties—ever since Kirby
Smith, the military genius at Shreveport, took the bulk
of his army away, to meet another 'invasion,' coming down

from the north—if it's coming, *if*. So instead of the bird in hand, this Union army in Alexandria, we're chasing a will-o'-the-wisp, and my allegiance is settled, in heart as well as mouth. Taylor's doing a wonderful job, but it still remains true *there's not one Reb soldier between this place and Shreveport*."

"What's that got to do with the dam?"

"Mr. Cresap, suppose it fails?"

". . . Well? We lose ten boats, I suppose."

"You just walk off and leave them?"

"Not I—this army. What else can we do?"

"I may be crazy, but as a loyal Union man I say—and don't contradict me—no Union army dare pull out of this place and leave ten boats sitting. It would not obey the order; *the men would mutiny first!* The one thing it can do is march on up to Shreveport—and that'll cook Taylor, Kirby Smith, the will-o'-the-wisp chasers, and everything Reb in this section! Because what Richmond is to the East, Shreveport is to the West—a base, a source of food, of munitions, of what's needed to fight. That's what this army can do, and that's what it's *going* to do, once the river tears that dam apart."

"What's the rest of it, sir?"

". . . In Springfield, everything's marking time."

"Springfield? I thought we were talking of Shreveport."

"Both are important to us—to you, to me, to Mignon. Nothing can litigate until the Navy gets out of this river and brings its witnesses into court. So if you don't get there right away, nothing's lost, is there? You'll still have time for Shreveport."

"Yes. Shreveport?"

"The Army takes it, doesn't it?"

"So you say, Mr. Landry. What then?"

"And the Navy doesn't take it?"

"Well the Navy's prevented, sort of."

He said the Navy was prevented, not only by being stuck, but by being blocked off, from a hulk sunk in the river, the *New Falls City*, "at the mouth of Loggy Bayou, which is why they turned back in the first place, not from hearing the Army was whipped, as they've been giving out. They can't get out of the mud, and even if they could, they can't get past the hulk. That means Shreveport's an Army thing—doesn't it?"

"All right, what then?"

"These people have confidence in the Army."

"What people, sir?"

"In Shreveport. No cotton's going to be burned."

". . . More about cotton, and I'm going to upchuck."

"For a million dollars you'd upchuck?"

"*Did you upchuck with* her?"

She'd been sitting with me on the sofa, he facing us in a chair, his eyes roving the river. Now she blazed her eyes at me, then got up and went over to him. In her red-checked gingham dress she kneeled beside him, took his hand in hers, and said: "Go on, lambie—explain us, how do we get the million dollars—oh my, that would be heaven on this earth."

"So?" I said. "The cotton's not burned, and—"

"I acquire it. I have friends in Shreveport."

"You mean, you buy it?"

"I mean I take title, on shares. Once they know it's the Army, once I assure them of that, those people will trust me, I know. But two things I have to have."

"All right. What are they?"

"The first is time."

"I thought we had plenty of time."

"You have time—I haven't. I have to know where I stand, so I can get on the spot and write papers—bills of sale, partnership articles with the different people involved, receipts for the Army to sign. With all the thousands of bales waiting for me up there, I can't do it in an hour; I have to get there ahead of time, I must be there ready and waiting whenever the Army comes."

"Quite a trudge you've picked out for yourself."

"Trudge? I'll go by boat."

"Boat? What boat, Mr. Landry?"

"Reb boats are running again—*Doubloon*, *Grand Duke*, all kinds of different ones. When the Union pulled out, traffic resumed as usual. I can be in Shreveport tomorrow—call it day after."

". . . What else must you have?"

"Godpappy, Mr. Cresap."

"I thought that was it. Meaning me?"

"You'll have it all to yourself—*a monopoly!*"

He said that now the other traders had all been sent back to New Orleans I'd be the only one, "and they'll have to deal with you." Then he started in again on the mess being made of the dam. "The idea," he said, "is to set out the trees in pairs—brackets they're called, I believe—with boards nailed to the trunks. When they're hauled into the stream, the current's supposed to help, by pressing down on the boards and holding them tight to the bottom—and it did, so long as the work was close to the bank, where the water's shallow. But now that they're moving out where it's deep, the current's no help any more. It lifts those trees like Hallowe'en apples and sends them spinning downriver, past the bridge and out. The whole thing's just pitiful."

I said: "You know how you sound to me?"

". . . All right, Mr. Cresap—tell me."

"Like a man working three sides of the street—Reb side, Union side, and Cotton side, all at the same time."

"I'm not running this war. What I propose is lawful."

"And you realize I must report what you've said."

She started, but he smiled, waited, and said: "I would expect you to; in fact I want you to, and realize that until you do you'll not cooperate. So please—you go to your friend Captain Dorsey, tell him what I've told you—*every-thing I've said, especially about Kirby Smith.* When you come back, I think you'll be ready to talk."

She came over to me, not blazing her eyes any more, but mumbling her mouth to mine and whispering: "You're going to, aren't you? See Captain Dorsey? Hear what he has to say? And then line it up? So we make the million dollars? And have our house? And our carriage? And——"

"At any rate, I'll see him."

The *Black Hawk*, the headquarters *Black Hawk* that is, was tied up at Biossat's again, all battered from shelling upriver, and the guard on her plank called Dan. I'd seen him since he got back, but only to say hello, and we spent a minute or two on the usual dumb questions, getting caught up with each other. Then he started to take me up-stairs, but I suggested some place where we'd be alone, and he led on back to the fantail, where we had it with our elbows on the rail. He listened, and then filled me in on the fighting the Army had seen, and how it bore on what Mr. Landry had told me. "The thing to keep straight," he said, "is that two battles were fought—one up in the woods, at what's known as Sabine Crossroads, just this side of Mansfield. That battle we lost—I was there, and it was a shambles, with everything going wrong that possibly could go wrong. You'd think, after Caesar wrote up the folly of trying to fight with wagons up in your van, that we'd have heard about it, two thousand years later. But no—there the wagons were when the Rebs came piling at us, with the horses screaming and breaking, and the wagoners no great help. And there were the girls too, the colored ones that were brought by the boys to do their washing—whipping their mules to the rear and yelling: 'Run! Run! Here come Old Massa—he gwine massacree everyone!' Don't let anyone tell you different, it was a rout! You know what they're singing, don't you?"

He leaned close, and buzzed into my ear:

> "In eighteen hundred and sixty one,
>   Hurrah, Hurrah!
> We all skedaddled to Washington,
>   Hurrah, Hurrah!
> In eighteen hundred and sixty four,
>   We all skedaddled to Grand Ecore—
> And all got stone blind,
>   Johnny fill up the bowl!"

"But," he went on, "next day, at Pleasant Hill, when they tried to finish us up, we cut them to pieces, Bill. Don't let anyone tell you different on *that*! And there's the tragedy of it! This army's not licked—how could it be when it won that Pleasant Hill fight? This headquarters *is!* Of backbiting, disloyalty, undercutting, and bickering you can take just so much. And that's why we're getting out.

Not from defeat, from *disunity!* So, in regard to your friend Landry and what he thinks we'll do next, he could be right. We *could* be going to Shreveport, in case this dam's a bust, we could be doing just that—and we know all about it, Kirby Smith's dispersal of Richard Taylor's army. He sent Price with six thousand men to stop Steele, who's supposed to be working with us, and that army is way the hell and gone up in Arkansas someplace, so it couldn't be a factor. It's quite true, I imagine, that there's no effective force under the Reb command between this place and Shreveport."

"All right, but what do *I* do?"

"Bill, I've told you: the goddam cotton is hooded. It's the cause of all our trouble, the cause of the headquarters bickering, of the Navy's being stuck. If they hadn't gone upriver for this cotton Landry wants, they wouldn't be where they are now. Stay out of it! Don't touch it with a ten-foot pole."

"I can't stay out of it. I'm already in."

I told him about Sandy, the Navy receipt, and the rest. He whistled. "Well!" he said. "You certainly *are* in, all the way, with both feet. . . . Then—a little more can't make much difference. In for a penny, in for a pound."

"You mean let Mr. Landry go ahead?"

"What harm is it going to do?"

"That's it! If we don't go to Shreveport, Dan . . . ?"

"Then we didn't and he did. That's all."

"You're sure I wouldn't be disloyal, doing this?"

"Well? Lincoln wants it, doesn't he?"

CHAPTER 25

$\mathbf{B}$ACK IN THE FLAT I didn't quite say yes, but they smelled
I was going to, and she made herself so sweet butter
wouldn't have melted in her mouth. Next morning she came
early, snuggling close to me, and whispering little jokes in
between the kisses. She got my promise at last, and I went
on down to see Hager and cancel my pass application,
since if I was going to Shreveport it would head off all kinds
of mix-ups if I reapplied up there to the new Provost
Marshal, without still another request dangling in Alexandria. But he waved as soon as he saw me, there in the courthouse door, and left his desk to come over, stepping past
doctors, orderlies, and wounded lying on stretchers. "Surprise for you, Cresap!" he roared as soon as he'd shaken
hands. "You're on your way out, you're leaving! The
Warner's going tomorrow, and I've arranged to get you on
board. And the style you'll be going in! Two gunboats are
taking her down—you'll be like Mason and Slidell!"

"Fine!" I said. "Love to feel important!"

Because of course this couldn't be turned down, just at the drop of a hat, without my making sure how Mr. Landry felt. On his own favorite principle of grabbing the bird in hand, he might want me to go. And even if outvoted, I could decline the honor later in the day. So I talked along, got the various details, like the leaving time of the boat, which was eight o'clock in the morning, and the probable space I'd have, which was half a stateroom. "*But*," he warned, "this is for Cresap alone. It does *not* include a lady, or the lady's courtly father."

"That's understood," I told him.

"You board *tonight*. Get there first."

"I'll be there with bells, Captain."

"I *think* they'll be stopping at Cairo, and you can go to Springfield from there. But if they take you to Cincinnati, that's not so far either."

"Cincinnati's perfect with me."

And it was perfect with Mr. Landry, as I learned when I came charging in with my news—and not only with him but with her. Shreveport was entirely forgotten as both of them got all excited over definite action at last. "It's the difference," she said, "between a million up in the sky and one-twenty thousand there in the bank—sixty thousand for Father and sixty thousand for us. Who wouldn't take what's sure?" He told her: "Nothing's sure, Daughter, especially in this war—but short of having the money, this is as sure as anything can be." We talked of getting married, of going to Dr. Dow, the Episcopal rector there, and having it done at once, that same day, before I left. But she didn't want to be married in Alexandria. "I was once," she said, "and it didn't turn out very well." And also, I think, she was shy of marrying a bluebelly here, where everyone knew her, and starting a lot of talk. We checked their end of it over, and he said: "Don't worry about us, Mr. Cresap—if, as I assume, the Union goes through to Shreveport, that'll end the war in the West, and we'll stay right where we are until navigation resumes and then join you in Springfield, if you care to have us come. If, on the other hand, they're captured or manage to cut their way out, this place will be under the Rebs—but we've nothing to fear from them. We'll leave as soon as we can, and be seeing you before very long." Communication would be a problem, but we left it that they would write me in care of General Delivery at Springfield, and I would write them whichever way I could, in the light of the news as it broke. I asked: "Isn't somebody sorry I'm going?"

"Of course," she yipped. "We both are!"

"I'd like to be missed, a *little!*"

She kissed me, right in front of him, said: "You're going to be missed a lot—morning, noon, and night, but specially in the morning. Now come on, I'll help you pack."

I was sitting there with him, the packed bag beside me, my overcoat, oilskin, and hat piled on top, and she was in the kitchen putting me up some lunch, in case food was scarce on the boat, when a knock came on the door. He answered and then came back with Sandy, who was looking pretty glum, not to say seedy, and whom I hadn't seen since that day on the falls. He shook hands, and seemed surprised when I asked if his boat was one of those stuck. "Why, yes," he said, "in a way. She kind of got permanently stuck and we had to scuttle her."

"Oh? When did that happen?"

"Last week."

"And what boat are you on now?"

"We all got distributed around, pending reassignment, and I got taken on board the *Neosho*—monitor aground on the upper falls. I'm subject to duty as ordered, meaning at-large mud-turtle to this dam they're trying to build."

"Which is not going well, I hear."

"It's not going at all."

She came in about that time, with her packages wrapped in newspaper, and after shaking hands, excused herself while she stuffed them into my bag. He had been eyeing it, and now asked: "You going somewhere, Bill?"

I told him about the *Warner*, and he said: "Well, in that case I'll forget what I came about." I pressed him, of course, and he said: "No, if you have a chance to get out, and especially to go to Springfield, I can't stand in your way. That's important—it's the one way to get the money we're going to need, so let's forget the dam, which can't be built anyhow. It's a completely ridiculous idea." It came out, little by little, that what he had wanted of me was to walk across the bridge and pass out a couple of pointers to the boys on the left bank about how to do their work. "On this side," he said, "it makes sense—not much, but a little. They're building cribs out of logs, hauling them into the stream, and filling them with stone. How much water they hold I wouldn't like to say, but at least they stay there, they don't go floating off. But on the other side it's a madhouse." He explained about the brackets, corroborating what Mr. Landry had said, and went on: "They wash out, they break apart, and it's not only the river. It's the troops, a bunch of Maine woodsmen, who can cut trees down but can't hook 'em together. I've tried to tell 'em, but they won't listen to me, and besides I don't really know. But

you do, and to you I thought they might pay some attention
—that's all. But, you'd have to stay with 'em, of course, see
it through to the end; so let's forget it."

"How long is this thing going to take?"

"It's win or lose in a week."

"You mean, win or starve in a week?"

"Yes, that's *just* what I mean!"

"There's talk going around that in the event the dam
doesn't hold the march will be resumed up the river to
Shreveport."

"Not by the Navy. It doesn't have the water."

"I'm talking about the Army."

"I can't speak for them."

I thought over what he had said, and told him: "You
catch me by surprise, as I hadn't known until now there
was anything I could do—an army does not, as a rule, need
help to run. So I don't know what answer to give you."

"Answer? You haven't been asked, yet."

"Thing like this, I shouldn't wait to be asked."

"You mean, you'd even *go?*"

That was Mignon, and when I said yes, she exploded
in my face. "Well, all I can say, Willie Cresap," she blazed,
switching her skirt around, "is I wish you'd make up your
mind. First you come up here, to condole with me, so you
said—if *that* be something to do. Then, with my help and
Father's help and Sandy's help, you turn around and decide
to trade in cotton—and we sign the papers for you. *Now*
you think you may build a dam! What next, pray tell—if
you know? Picking daisies, maybe, and starting a flower
shop? Or buying a sword-cane and rake and going in business with *her*, running a gambling dive? Is that what it's
been all along? Is that what you're up to, is that what you
really want?"

"She talks like a wife," said Sandy, "and she might even be right. Wife, I've noticed, generally is."

"I wonder," I said. "Maybe."

Mr. Landry got in it then, repeating Sandy's arguments, and not repeating hers, but adding some stuff of his own. And on top of everything else was my own feeling about it, that the dam was just plain silly. And what I might have decided I can't exactly say, but while we were arguing about it there came a knock down the hall. Mr. Landry answered, but came back with word that no one was there. Mignon glanced at him sharply, and I thought he looked very strange. Then the knock was repeated, and he gave her a long stare. That's when I woke up. I scooted down the hall, but didn't turn into the crosshall that led to the outside entrance. I kept on to the trapdoor in the pantry. I flung it up, drawing my gun, and calling: "Come up, whoever you are—you're covered, so keep your hands high!" Then a ragged, filthy, bony thing clambered out, wearing a thick gray beard and squinting with watery eyes. I had slapped it up for guns and taken the Navy Colt before the jackboots told me who it was that I had.

It was Burke.

"I think you know everybody," I told him very coolly, as I marched him into the sitting room. "Don't stand on ceremony. Have a chair, take the load off your feet. Make yourself at home."

"It's my home," snapped Mr. Landry, furiously.

"Then you invite him, why don't you?"

"Frank," he said, "is that you? I hardly know you."

"Aye," Burke groaned in a hollow voice, " 'tis I—but the ghost of the man you knew. I never reached the Sabine at all. I was taken direct to Shreveport as soon as I crossed their lines, and escaped by the barest chance—I'd hate to say what it cost me in bright, yellow gold." He said he'd arrived in the night, but not wanting to be seen, had come in the back way, using his key as before, as soon as he'd had some sleep. Then: "What brought me, Adolphe, is the news I picked up in Shreveport—'tis tremenjous."

"Later, Frank—it'll keep."

"Just now, I could use a bit of food."

"I'll get you some," she chirped.

"Not so fast," I said, blocking her from the door.

They'd been playing it as though they hadn't seen Burke before, but there'd been that exchange of looks, and I took it for an act. If that seems slightly unbalanced, there were things setting me off, like the prickles I felt all over me at her friendly concern for his hunger, and what it was going to be like with me out of the way and him under foot all the time. I stood there waving the gun, trying to calm myself down, but feeling my gorge rising. I said, licking my lips, swallowing now and then, and spacing my words kind of queerly: "Mr. Landry—it's all quite clear to me now—why nobody seemed to mind—that I was shoving off. With someone to take my place—with another godpappy to claim the Shreveport cotton—to pick up that million bucks—why should anyone mind?"

"You talking about me?" she asked. "Well I don't!"

"I'm not talking—about any particular one."

"Then who *are* you talking about?"

"All," I said. "Everyone."

"Not me," said Burke. "Do I care what you do?"

"Oh yes, you," I told him, feeling for some reason humorous. "Take it easy. Stick around—I'll explain where you come in."

"And certainly not me?"

That was Sandy. I said: "Especially you."

Then to Burke, pushing the gun at him: "What's your tremenjous news?" And when he didn't answer: "Come on, talk, *spit it out!*"

"The Rebs—" he began.

"Now we're coming," I said. "The Rebs?"

"Have overplayed it! They're trying to bag two armies, instead of going for one! They've divided their forces, they've left their fortress unguarded! . . . 'Tis all I know, me boy! I thought Adolphe might like to hear it!"

"Why should he like it?"

"Well—he lives here, after all!"

"You've heard the Union's going to march up there?"

"Aye, if this dam goes out they'll have to!"

"And then there'll be the cotton?"

" *'Twas the whole reason for this fiasco!*"

"That's all I wanted to know."

I waited, no doubt with a grin on my face such as Samson may have had before he pulled down the temple. I said, mainly to Burke, but including them all: "There'll be no march on Shreveport, no million made by claiming the Shreveport cotton. *That dam is going to be built!* It can't be done, but I'll build it! So calm down, one and all— Burke's tremenjous news has been superseded by Cresap's tremenjouser news!"

"But Bill," said Sandy, *"you're leaving!"*

"Oh no I'm not," I said. "Nobody's leaving! And so no one is tempted to, so there's not any reason to leave, we're doing away with this cotton, this devil's bait we all sold our souls to grab—we're burning it, right now!"

"No!" she screamed. *"No!"*

"Not me own cotton?" wailed Burke.

"The same old stuff!" I said. "*Surprise!*"

"Bill, you can't!" yelled Sandy.

"Oh yes I can—hand me my bag."

Nobody handed it to me, but I grabbed it up and piled on back to the kitchen. They were all on top of me, but a maniac waving a pistol doesn't get interfered with. It was a chorus of despair as I opened the bag and dug into it, coming up with the same swatch of papers, done up in the same Navy oilskin, I had tucked away there six long weeks before. I lifted the lid on the stove, jammed everything in, and poked it down with the gunpoint while Sandy yelled warnings. I banged the lid on again, and waited while the flames licked up. In five minutes I opened the stove up, and nothing was there but red, black, and gray fluff, curling around. I holstered the gun, picked up the bag, told Sandy, "Come on, let's go." But I didn't get out of there before Mr. Landry told me, a venomous look in his eye: "Maybe you build that dam, but it's not going to stand, I promise you."

"It'll stand till the fleet gets down."

"We'll see about that, Mr. Cresap."

With Sandy, who was so furious he couldn't talk, I clumped around to my own flat and flung the bag inside. When I got down to the street again, she was there talking to him, her eyes squinched up mean, her mouth twisting around. When I saw she was making spit, I fetched her a clout on the cheek that sent her staggering back to the front of the Schmidt store. Then, grabbing Sandy's arm, I marched on down to the courthouse and turned in my pass. Then, still with him to take me through, I headed for the bridge.

CHAPTER 26

I DROVE THEM LIKE ANIMALS; but driving was what they wanted, I have to say that for them all—the 29th Maine, which was hewing the trees, and the colored infantry outfits, known as the Corps D'Afrique, which were detailed as labor. I worked under a Captain Seymour whom Sandy took me to, in the woods on the Pineville side, which smelled of cut wood, where various squads were at work, chopping and sawing and hewing. But he wasn't at all pleased, in spite of what Sandy had said, about my experience, my previous rank of lieutenant, and my willingness to help, at having a boy wonder, as he called me, "standing around in the shade, with his hands stuck in his pockets, telling me what to do." He had a Down East way of talking that annoyed me more or less, and I said: "I wouldn't dream of doing it—how the hell do you tell someone that sounds like a goddam quahog sucking water up with his foot and squirting it out of his eyeballs?" That kind of slowed him down, and he asked: "What's your idea about it?" "What do you think?" I fired back. "I figured to sign up."

". . . You mean, join? My outfit?"

"Now you got it, stupid."

"What about that leg?"

"Leg's been there before."

He called to his supply sergeant: "Pair of pants for this recruit—extra longs! Blouse, if you got one!"

"Shirt'll help," I said.

"And a shirt!" he bellowed.

And then as we stood there, I in my balbriggans, Sandy helping me into the blues, Seymour asked in a quiet way: "All right, Cresap, what am I doing wrong?"

"Everything," I said. "As well as everything else."

"Hell, I know that! But *what?*"

"To begin with, I'd say you have compression, tension, and function all stewed in one fearful and wonderful pot, so each fouls up the other."

"Never mind the Trautwine stuff. Say something."

"I will, don't worry. Those brackets you're putting together—trying to put together—are done wrong from the start. Positioning the trees as they fall, then nailing the boards on, then hauling them down to the water, is just asking for trouble. Before it even gets wet, that set, pretty weak to start with, is so rickety from the trip through the woods that it won't hold up in the water, can't take the strain when you try to work it with lines—and *that's* why it goes floating off. Haul your trees to the water's edge *first! Then* put together your bracket! *Brace* it with proper *struts!* Saw planks into four-foot lengths, notch 'em, and shove 'em between. That'll take care of compression. Then lash on line, and tighten with clubs used as turnbuckles! That'll take care of tension!"

"Where the hell do we get this line?"

"Navy," said Sandy. "We got it."

"Go on," the captain told me.

"Then nail on your boards. They're function."

"I got it now. All right, then we—"

"Goddam it, who's supposed to be talking?"

"I'm sorry, Cresap. What else?"

"When that's all done, when the thing's ready to go, notch the butts of those trees and lash a shackle on. Something a hawser can bend to, so the boats can give you help. Something that's going to hold, so you're running the set and the set's not running you!"

"... Anything else?"

"Split your men into gangs, each with a job assigned that it rightly understands. Then, 'stead of laying around all the time, asleep under the trees, they'll know what to do and do it. If the gang doesn't speak English, pick out one man who does. Get some system into it!"

"You can work a gang?"

"Anyone that has sense can."

"We haven't been having much luck."

"That's because, instead of letting them know what you want, you're making speeches at them about Lincoln, telling 'em how much he loves 'em. They don't care about Lincoln—all they want is their grub and to be told what to do."

"Then you'll tell 'em?"

"I think first I have to tell you."

We fixed it up, since I had to sign on as a private, that

I'd tell and he'd beller, as he called it, but actually, by the time I'd been there an hour, I had it all to myself, doing the telling, bellering, and cussing all at the same time— but with some slight success. I don't say I built the Red River dam. Colonel Joseph Bailey, of a Wisconsin outfit, thought the idea up and was in complete command. I do say that before I got there, things were in a mess, but that after I got on the spot, they began to go right.

By sundown, we had six sets in place which I anchored by floating crosslogs down, then letting them wash up on the brackets and lashing them in place, somewhat out of water to give a bit more weight and offset the tendency to float, which the whole thing suffered from. The Navy helped in grim earnest, and Sandy was there all the time, first on one boat, then on another, taking charge of lines, capstans, or barges, as they came up with stone for the cribs—or with bricks, or busted-up sugar mills, or whatever they could find for ballast. The third night, after I'd eaten the handful of beans my squad had cooked for mess and was stretched out beside the fire, Sandy suddenly appeared, squatting down beside me with a very different look from the one he had been wearing, which hadn't been too friendly toward me. When I'd told him hello, he drew a deep breath and said: "Bill, I want to apologize."

"Oh?" I asked him. "What for?"

"Various things. You heard about the *Warner?*"

"The boat I was to take? No. What about her?"

"She got sunk."

"Ouch. You mean the Rebs got her?"

"Not only her but the *Covington*. And not only *her* but the *Signal*. And not only *her* but the *City Belle*, a boat that was coming up with a bunch of replacement troops. Scores of men were killed, and it's just one more thing. But what gets me is this: Suppose *you* had been killed? I'd never forgive myself. And I'd like to come out and say it: I glory in you, Bill. You burned those papers first, *before* the *Warner* left. And told everyone why—including me. Including her."

"Leave her out, if you don't mind."

"All right. She has her troubles, though."

". . . What troubles?"

"Death. She was in a funeral procession."

"When was this, Sandy?"

"Today. The *Forest Rose* had to heave to and idle in the current while this hearse went over the draw, a little bunch of people following along behind. It was kind of pathetic, at that. No horses now, you know—at least available to the Rebs. Pulling the hearse was Mr. Landry on one side of the tongue, with a rope harness hooked to one single-tree, that fellow Burke to the other. She kind of brought up the rear, in that black dress she wears, looking damned cute, with the wind whipping her bottom."

"I said leave her out! *And* her bottom!"

"Bill, you're still stuck on that girl."

"I'm not. I hope never to see her again. But—"

"You are. If you weren't, you'd be the first to tell me that bottom is all mine, if I can manage to get it. Well, I'd love to, I own, if it weren't—"

"You want a puck on the jaw?"

". . . Who died, do you have any idea?"

"What do I care who died?"

"I'm just curious, that's all."

Two days later it was done, and we'd succeeded only too well. We'd got a rise all right, five feet of it at least, reaching back to the head of the falls, and enough, you'd have thought, for the *Great Eastern* to turn around in. Still the Navy wanted more depth, and as no bracket could possibly hold out there near the middle, we put six cribs in, like the ones on the other side, and the Navy filled them with stone. But even that wasn't enough, and the Navy drove pilings, in threes braced with planks, and hauled four barges up that they moored to the pilings with hawsers. The water rose still more, until you stood there holding your breath, watching the whole thing shake from the pressure backed up behind it and its own will to float, knowing as you did that something had to give. The whole Army started to yell that now was the time, or never, that the Navy had to come down. They built a fire, a great thing of pine logs that blazed to the sky from the burning resin, so it looked like a scene from hell. The idea was to give light for the boats to come down by, but still nothing happened, and word came through the woods that the Navy didn't have steam. That was the last straw, and the yells began to sound ugly.

Still, I was done, and the captain was, and we were stretched out by his fire, sipping some coffee he had, when suddenly Sandy was there. By then, the Navy or anything like it had kind of a rat-poison look, so the welcome he got from the captain was not of a rousing kind. But when he came up with the news, and made it pretty curt, that the reason no boats could come down was "this insane fire you've built, that has blinded all our pilots," it kind of quenched the discussion, and I could feel Sandy out, as I thought he had stuff on his mind. "Bill," he said when the captain subsided, "this may be nothing at all—a mare's nest pure and simple. But I keep thinking about it."

"Go on," I said. "Shoot."

"My boat," he began, "the *Neosho*, is moored to the right bank up there—and of course we don't keep a lookout posted. Just the same, a seaman was there, in the pilothouse polishing brass, when he saw a skiff upstream—a joeboat, they call it. Square-ended thing that seemed to be drifting down. Then he didn't see it, that's all."

"You mean it disappeared?"

"That's it. It was there, and then it wasn't there."

"Could have grounded. Maybe bushes hid it."

"Maybe. Maybe."

"What did your skipper say?"

"Told the boy thanks."

"Well, that's not much of a help."

"Bill, I can't shake it out of my head, the threats that man made, your friend Mr. Landry, as we left that day—and he wasn't just talking to talk; *he meant something.* And he has some motive, I gathered, for wanting this dam to go out?"

"Just a million dollars is all."

"That's in cotton, up at Shreveport?"

"That he can grab with Burke as godpappy."

"Providing, Bill, that the Navy doesn't get out, and the Army, to save its face, marches upriver again, 'stead of down?"

"Which *I* say we should do," said the captain.

"Now you've got it," I said.

"Then Mr. Landry," said Sandy, "if he had a skiff, if he brought one down on a tether, if he hauled it into the bushes and had it there tonight, he could fill it with powder, couldn't he? And start it drifting down? To explode it against our dam?"

"That danger," said the Captain, "occurred to *me*."

"At least he could try," I said.

"Still," said Sandy, "where would he get powder?"

"*Out of his store!*" I yelped, jumping up.

And as they both stared, I told them: "Out of stock that he kept on hand to sell for blasting stumps! Now we know who died! It was as many kegs of powder as would fit in a nailed-up coffin. Captain, have I your permission to scout these woods with Sandy?"

"I'll scout them with you, Cresap."

CHAPTER 27

H<small>E BELTED HIMSELF</small> for duty with a Colt sidearm he had, a .44 six in a holster. Then, so I needn't carry a musket, he called a lieutenant and borrowed a sidearm for me, another Colt in a holster. Then he called the supply sergeant and had a lantern brought, the regular Army bull's-eye, but didn't light it yet. All that took a half-hour or so, and it was half past eight at least, when he, Sandy, and I started out to look for our skiff. By that time, we each knew the woods like the back of our hand, yet it was suddenly strange, especially in the light of the fire, which made everything a glare of dancing light or else a dancing shadow. But what got Sandy was the few sentries we met. "It makes my blood run cold," he said one time; "bivouacs everywhere, thousands of men around putting this dam in, and hardly one on duty to guard it from destruction." But the captain wasn't impressed. "You know what a sentry means?"

he asked Sandy sourly. "He's not like a fencepost or mail-box that you put there and then forget about. He's a man, who does a two and six, and it takes a guard to post him, four men and a corporal, a special place to sleep him, and a mess squad to feed him. Who has that many men, and who takes that much trouble?"

They both had a case, I thought, but it was too dark and the going much too rough for me to get into the dis-cussion. We pressed on to the place where the skiff had been seen, a spot across from the *Neosho*, which was lit, with banjos banging on deck, to the wreck of the steamer *Woodford*. We saw nothing, not even the ghost of a skiff, and had to start on back. We went several hundred yards and then had to cross a bridge over a little stream called, I believe, Rock Creek, that ran down to the river from the high ground known as Spanish Hill. And as we started over, my nose caught something I couldn't mistake. It was the sweetish, heavy smell of perique smoking tobacco, and I knew of course who used that. I whispered to Captain Seymour to stay where he was but to get his lantern lit. Then I told Sandy to take one side of the stream while I took the other, and comb it down to the river. But the captain, being armed, reversed me, taking one bank of the stream while Sandy handled the light. We crept along, having perhaps two hundred feet to cover from the bridge to the river. Up in the trees it was light, as the glare from the fire flickered, but down in the stream bed, in under the bank, it was dark as pitch. And then all of a sudden, sound-ing almost in my ear, he said very quietly: "Skiff's here. I can hear the water slapping her."

"River's right there," I said.

"Gregg! Bring your lantern! *Now!*"

"Aye, sir!" called Sandy. "Coming, lit."

He must have already lit it, because now he shot its beam, and there was the skiff on a sandbank, her painter made fast to a bush. But there too, staring at me, were two tremendous eyes in a pale, beautiful face. In a thicket nearby Mr. Landry and Burke were crouching, but what froze the blood in my veins was the realization that here with this fatal evidence was Mignon.

"Well there it is, a floating torpedo."

The captain almost whispered it, at the same time covering the prisoners; then, as Sandy held the light, we all three crept closer to look. It was the usual square-end joe-boat, with four kegs up near one end, held with wire two-and-two. Each had a cork in the bung, with a copper cap in the cork. Leading out over the end, set in a screwed-on oar-lock, was an outrigger thing made of fishing pole, and wired to that were four prongs, thin rods made of iron, that led to the copper caps. Controlling the pole was a spring, also bound on with wire, of the kind used in store scales. In the other end of the boat was a pile of chain attached by a heavy staple, apparently meant as a drag once the craft was started down, to hold it on its course, and especially to keep the business end pointed to the dam. "Quite a contrivance," said the captain. "No wonder they took all night getting it wired up." And then: "Lieutenant Gregg, I'm not organized to guard this bunch tonight—and besides it could happen that if something goes wrong at the dam I'll need every man I have. Could you take them up to your boat?"

"I can hail and ask for orders," said Sandy.

And then, as he still stared at the skiff: "But it does seem to me that before we talk about *them*, we ought to dismantle this mine. It's dangerous, even sitting here."

"*We* ought to? They *have* to, you mean."

He turned to Landry and Burke, who hadn't opened their mouths. "Hey you," he roared, "get in this skiff and uncouple it. Disconnect this outrigger, and especially these prongs that lead to the caps."

"Then—stand back," said Mr. Landry.

"Don't worry, we will."

Then the captain noticed that Burke hadn't moved. "You too," he bellowed, waving the gun. "Get in there and help."

"Me man, I'm not a mechanic," said Burke.

"No? Then you're learning, right now!"

"Disarm him first," I warned.

"That's right. I should have done it before."

He slapped Landry for weapons, didn't find any, made a half-hearted slap at her. Then he turned to Burke. If Burke made a swipe at his gun I can't rightly say. It seemed to me that he did, and I opened my mouth to yell. It must have seemed so to the captain, and he fired, and Burke pitched into the stream, lying there in a heap, water rippling over his head. She screamed and started to whisper. "Speak louder!" I snarled. "He can't hear you!" Then I could have cut my tongue out; she was praying, in French.

"That's not so good," growled the captain.

No one said anything, and for some moments the chill settled down, with her still whispering, the river lapping the boat, the stream purling at Burke. And then, in a half-hysterical way, the captain turned on Mr. Landry, yelling: "Didn't you hear me? Start dismantling, I said!"

"I'm sorry, it can't be done."

"You're telling *me* what can be done?"

"You want to be blown sky-high?"

Mr. Landry wasn't fazed at the gun the Captain was

waving, and seemed scientifically interested in explaining
what must be done: The torpedo couldn't be touched; it
would have to be exploded. "I'll be glad to show you why,"
he said, wading into the stream. But he didn't point to the
kegs, or approach the outrigger end of the skiff. Instead,
he picked up the chain, and with a tremendous kick, sent
the skiff into Red River. I saw the flash, I heard the report,
I suppose I glimpsed Mr. Landry falling over beside Burke.
But all I could really think of was that dreadful, destruc-
tive thing that was plunging down on our dam, her kegs
connected up, her drag chain keeping her headed. I didn't
wait to know who was killed, but went splashing into the
river, fighting my way waist-deep, trying to catch up, to
grab the chain, to do anything to head off what was coming. Then, to my horror, in the glare of the fire ahead, I
saw one end of the skiff rise on a sunken rock, and then I
had my hands on the gunnel. Then I was wrestling it, trying to tip it over, to spill those kegs into the water before
that outrigger hit something. At last I got a capsize and
the danger was over. Then I was spinning, as the current
swept me along, and then I broke into ten thousand pieces
as my game leg hit a rock that was sticking up. I heard
screams coming out of my mouth, and then heard nothing
but a ringing in my ears. Then bushes touched my face,
and the lantern was shining on me. A cutter was there by
the bank, so close I could almost touch it, and seamen were
standing around. Then I caught the smell of Russian
Leather, and she pulled my head against her. "Speak to me,
Willie!" she whispered. "Say something!"

"Yes," I said. "I'm all right."

"Kiss me. *Kiss me!*"

". . . Kind of public for that, don't you think?"

"Willie! Theyre fixing to do something to me, for what we tried with that boat! You may not see me again! Kiss me, tell me you love me!"

"You know I do, don't you?"

Then we both kissed, sweet, long, and holy.

All during that, the captain held the lantern; he was soaking wet, so I knew who had got me out. When the seamen had put her in the cutter and shoved off for the other side, he half-carried me back to the bivouac and began bellowing for an ambulance to take me to the courthouse, "where you'll be under a surgeon, who'll put you in for discharge, unless I miss my guess, as I seriously doubt if you'll be fit for duty any more." But no ambulance came, and he stripped off my clothes, did the same for his own, and hung all our things on a line that he stretched between trees, where they'd get the heat of the fire. Then he wrapped me in a blanket, pulled one over himself, and sat there a while thinking. Then: "That girl," he said, "what is she to you?"

"In all but name, my wife."

"She's in damned serious trouble."

"She damned well knows it."

". . . Or she would be, except for you."

"What have I got to do with it?"

"You destroyed the evidence against her."

"Oh—you mean the skiff?"

"And powder and wiring and outrigger."

"Well, what did you want me to do—let it go sailing downstream to blow the dam up so they'd have a case to hang her? What's more important to the Navy, their boats or one poor girl's neck?"

"Hey! I'm trying to cheer you up!"

"I'm sorry. I'm off my usual."

"I'd say she deserves to be hung, but may not be."

"It wasn't her, it was her father, and—"

"Calm down, take it easy."

So the horrible night wore on, but at least I did have a ray of hope, and it wasn't so bad as it had been. Once, we all but jumped out of our skins and thought the skiff had made it, in spite of my turning it over, when two barges went out with a noise like cannon shot, when their hawsers parted and they slammed down on the rocks two hundred feet downstream. He cursed and raved and wept, assuming it all would spill out, the depth we'd worked so hard to get. It was my turn to cheer *him* up. I assured him things were improved, that the pressure would now be eased, "so back-up and outflow will be equalized, without the whole dam going out." He shook my hand, felt our clothes, and got us dressed. When daylight came, an ambulance pulled in, but he had it wait while he helped me out, crawling along the catwalk, to the second of the two remaining barges, so I could see the show of the boats coming out. "After all you've done, you're certainly entitled to that much," he said.

We sat on the upstream end, holding on to a cleat, and as far as you could see, on both banks of the river, was blue, because, except for men on duty, the whole army was there to see how the thing came out—no one believing in it. You could see men moving around, but as though in a dumb show; you couldn't hear a thing from the roar of the torrent beside us, plunging down through the chute between the barge we were on and the cribs on the other side like a young Niagara. Then, along toward seven o'clock, we made out smoke on the falls. Then we could see a hull, with foam under the forefoot. That meant power, and the captain began to scream: "No, *no! Cut those engines, man, cut 'em!*" Not that the pilot heard him, but once more I cheered him up. "He has to have power!" I yelled in his ear. "*He must have steering way!*" I don't know if he even heard me, but the boat came right on, at express-train speed, her own fifteen miles an hour plus at least twelve from the current. That brought her down on us fast, and then here she was, up over our heads, coming into the chute. Then she was roaring by, so close we felt her breeze. Then she was down, and then she crashed into the nearest barge, where it hung below on the rocks. It seemed she must come apart, but then she was caroming off, then spinning around, right in front of the hotel. And then, so help me, she tooted.

The cheer that went up was deafening—I think the most inspiring thing I ever heard in my life. In spite of the strain I was under, I cheered. The captain cheered, hugged me, and—I think—kissed me. Once the joy got started, nothing could stop it, and not even a Niagara could drown it out. Another boat came down, and the men went on dancing, laughing, screaming, and patting each other on the back. And then, all of a sudden, more smoke showed, and another boat came on, low in the water this time, so it had to be the monitor. I strained my eyes, and my heart gave a thump, as something flapped on deck, and I made out a black skirt. I waved like something demented, and it seemed to me she waved back. The boat came close enough for me to make out her face, as she stood by the gun turret, taking everything in. And then suddenly the thing happened. The admiral, so I've heard, blamed the pilot for it, as a deliberate act of treachery, but I myself don't believe it. A monitor's pilothouse is just aft of the stack, and I would imagine he never saw the chute, to know what it actually looked like, until he was almost on top of it. Then, I think, he just lost his nerve and grabbed his bell-pull in panic. He cut his power just at the crucial moment, and then there the ship was in a yaw. It was swinging broadside onto the current, but that left the water picking up speed, him *not* picking up speed—in other words, it began going faster than he was. Then the stern wave rose and swept right over her deck, as the cheers turned to a yell of horror. And then, as the boat swept down all under, with everything out of control, there was my love, my life, my beautiful little Mignon, shooting by in the muddy water, gasping for breath, and staring up at me.

I grabbed the gunnel to dive, but something rapped on my neck, pulling me back in the barge. "You can't!" the captain screamed. "You're damned near dead already!"

"Let me go, I got to save her!" I yelled.

"Who do you think you are? Jonah?"

The boat crashed into the barge, caromed, came up, and let go with her whistle, the way the others had done, but all I could do was howl, trying to be heard above the torrent, that it should "forget your damned tooting and start looking for her." He tried to calm me, saying, "Don't worry, they'll put out a boat—they'll get her, this is the *Navy*." But I couldn't be calmed, and he all but had to fight me to get me ashore again, where the ambulance was, and push me in by main force. Another boat came down, but I never even saw it. I was stretched out in the ambulance bed, where I collapsed at last, so wracked with sobs it seemed I would come apart.

CHAPTER 28

NEVER MIND MY TWO DAYS at the courthouse, with my leg swelled twice its size and turning black and blue, while they put the wing dams in to bring down the other boats. Never mind the burning of Alexandria, the Bummers' grand contribution, or the dreadful trip downriver. I batted from boat to boat, out of my head all the time, partly from the pain and partly from the uncertainty of not being able to find out if Mignon was living or dead. And never mind the trip in an ambulance, to some barracks below New Orleans, or the week I spent there, threshing around in a cot. When I opened my eyes once, Olsen was standing there, to get names of Maine wounded, he said, to send his papers up north. He asked me quite a few questions, but I asked him just one, to find out if he could if Mignon had been saved, and if so, where she was. He said if he found out anything he'd surely let me know, and that was the last I saw of him. And then one day a second lieutenant came, my discharge in his hand, and a St. Charles bellboy was there, helping me dress. He had with him my same old bag, the one I'd checked with the hotel before I left, and helped me into clean shirt, fresh balbriggans, and my regular dark suit. When I asked him how come, he said he didn't know, and it made no sense at all, but I didn't argue about it. I got in the cab with him and rode with him up to the hotel. And then there I was, back in my same old suite, with no more idea than the Man in the Moon what I was doing there or who I had to thank.

I still had some money, as in all my slamming around I'd clung to my pocketbook, but when I'd send down for my bill no bill would come up. Someone was paying for me, that much was clear, but who I didn't know. I supposed for a time it was Dan, as he came every day for a visit— the General, by now, was back on headquarters duty, though relieved in the field. But when, in between plaguing for news of Mignon, which he said he hadn't been able to get, I offered to square things up, he looked perfectly blank and knew no more than I did what I was talking about. Then I began to have my suspicions, but couldn't do much about them, pending surgery on my leg. It would puff up, be lanced, and then puff up again, until the doctor said to me: "I have to lay it open if it's ever going to heal. Trouble is, you were stabbed only halfway through, so the wound acts as a pocket to trap the corruption *in*. We have to drain it out, especially that bruised corruption that the crack in the river caused. I must open your leg from behind, to let the wound drain *down*, so gravity works for us, 'stead of being our worst enemy."

I told him do what he had to, and he did, bringing

another doctor to help, spreading oilcloth on the bed, and in all ways doing a job. The pain wasn't so bad, but the laudanum almost finished me. It affected my lungs, somehow, so they seemed to be paralyzed, and wouldn't draw any air. I lay for hours stifled, fighting for my breath, and when at last the paralysis went, I was completely gone. My leg, I thought, would get well, but all I could do was sleep. And then, one day when I woke up, Sandy was sitting there, in his Vicksburg blues but neatly brushed and clean. He started in, pretty nervous, talking about his transfer to headquarters duty in New Orleans: "The fighting's pretty much over, here on Western waters."

"What about Mignon?" I asked him.

"You mean Dan hasn't told you?"

"He couldn't find out anything—he said."

"He probably wanted to spare you."

"You mean, they never got her?"

"That's right—we grappled all morning, not only for her, but for a seaman that was lost, boy by the name of Cassidy, who never came up after the cutter capsized when they took her down separate. No bodies were found."

He came over, patted my shoulder, stood around, and said all the dumb things one friend says to another who's been hit in the head with an axe. At last I said: "Well, the end of our little adventure."

"In New Orleans, you're talking about?"

"Yes, Sandy, of course."

"You feel you can't go on?"

"What do we go on with? Whiff?"

". . . I'm sorry I got you into it."

"Takes two to get into a thing like that, and I don't blame you for it. Just the same, Sandy, I stick around New

Orleans and I'm on the town. Well, I don't want to be."
And then, as I began to shift from what was to what was
going to be, I went on: "I'd like you to do something for
me. I have the fare home—not much more, but enough to
get me there. Not enough, however, to settle my hotel bill,
doctor, and so on. They've been paid for me, in a somewhat
mysterious way, and what I want you to do is see a woman
for me; I think she is responsible." I told him the little he
needed to know about Marie and said: "What I want you
to do is see her, find out how much she's spent, and assure
her I'll remit when I get to Annapolis. I want you to talk
to her nice as you can, but if she has any idea of starting
up with me again, get it out of her head. That would be the
last straw—she's a sweet, wonderful person, who'd be perfectly capable of paying for me here out of the goodness
of her heart. But I must mourn my dead, and my dead
wouldn't like it if I got outside help. Will you take care
of it for me?"

"I'll do my best, Bill."

I didn't see him for several days, and in that time I
gained enough strength to sit up. I'd taken my first staggering stroll, to the sofa in the sitting room, and was reading
the *Times* there when a tap came at the door. "It's open,
come in!" I called, expecting the maid. But who opened the
door was Marie. She had on a white summer dress, with
floppy straw hat, and carried a bouquet of flowers tied
with a white ribbon. I jumped up to greet her, but she
pushed me back on the sofa, then sat down, laying her
flowers aside, and took me in her arms. "Guillaume," she
said, "are you better?"

"I'm fine," I said. "I'm going to be all right—thanks to you, I think. And that's what we're talking about."

"No, please," she whispered. "First, about me."

"Then—what about you?"

"You may *félicite* me. I am *mariée*."

"That means—married?"

"Yes, Guillaume. Are you angry at me?"

"Angry? I'm so happy I want to cry."

"*Alors. Alors. Alors.*"

She got up, as though to go to the door, but I grabbed her, pulled her down again, kissed her, and kissed her again. I said: "It's the most wonderful news, Marie—especially to me, after the lousy way I treated you—"

"There shall be no talk of louses! You were in love, with a fine, wonderful girl, half *poupée*, half *tigre*, so where is the louse, for example? But you ask not, *petit*, who my husband is."

"All right, who is this lucky hombre?"

She got up, went to the door and beckoned. I expected her guard to come in, or Dumont, or someone who had been in her life before she met me, but Sandy stepped through the door, a self-conscious grin on his face, his Lavadeau suit glittering like a Christmas tree. I said: "*You?*"

"That's right, Bill. I'm the one."

"Pardon me, I think I'm going to faint."

He took a seat in a chair, quite pleased with himself, while she sat by me again, no longer afraid of what I might say, but friendly, cuddly, and ramping to tell me about it. She said: "Alexandre came to me, with messages of you, who I heard about of m'sieu Olsen, but it seemed discussions were required. So—we walked, in Jackson Square. We had coffee, in the French Market, perhaps—

gras, greezee but droll. *Ainsi,* next day, more discussion appeared to devolve, so we lunched at Antoine's, some hours. Then, it was time for dinner, and then we attended the theater. Then, we walked more in Jackson Square, and next day we resumed our discussions. *Ainsi, ainsi, ainsi* —today, we go to the City Hall, and—pardon if I draw breath."

"You mean—there's more?"

"Little bit, Bill," said Sandy. "She'll tell you."

"Cresap *et* Gregg," she said.

"Gregg and Cresap," he corrected.

"*Cresap et Gregg!*" she repeated, jumping up and stamping her foot. "Who tames one river may perhaps tame another, and we know who this tamer was!"

"Then—Cresap and Gregg, *all right!*"

"What are you talking about?" I asked them.

"The twenty-five thousand bocks," she said.

"Bill," he told me very solemnly, "you don't *have* to go home if you don't want to. I didn't bring this up, and in fact knew nothing about it, except that crack I heard that Mignon made one time—but it didn't really connect. And *she* didn't bring it up, until after the knot was tied in City Hall just now. But then she *did* bring it up—and that's what brought us here. One of the things."

"Marie," I said, "now I *am* going to cry."

So, in the mornings I read the papers, for the U.S. marshal's auction sales of stuff we're going to need, and sometimes go out to bid, having the gear delivered to a waterfront shed we rented over on the Algiers side. In the afternoons I write, on a stack of foolscap I got, of the hours I spent with her, to explain how everything was, so

I'll have it to read later on, and so perhaps it'll ease the pain. Because at night is when my life gets bad. I turn out the light, I go to bed, I make myself sleep somehow. Then I open my eyes and she comes—through the walls, floating in, her hair wet, her cheek cold, her hands pressing mine, telling me how she escaped; how she swam ashore at Biossat's, at the bridge, at the Catholic church below town, and was hidden by kind friends, so the Navy couldn't find her; and how, if I'll give her a little time, we'll be together soon when the war is over at last. Then I moan and try to tell her I would have dived in to save her, but I was forcibly stopped. Then I get more and more worked up, and then she goes—through the wall, waving as she did from the monitor's deck.

So, the hoodoo passed me by at Red River but didn't forget me, at all. He sleeps in the other bed.